———————— ★ ————————

"MR. STRODE, THAT'S *DIABOLICAL!* MEPHISTOPHELIAN!"

Strode laughed. "Thank you! By god, Castleberry, I haven't felt this good since we started business. Those three are going to learn the hard way they can't threaten *me* and get away with it!"

"Where will they be meeting?"

"Here. In this house."

"You can't mean that! You're going to meet those three right *here* where they can—"

"No, no—I'm not going to be here at all! They'll only *think* I'm going to be here."

"But still, bringing those three murderous people together under your roof—"

"They have to think they have a chance of getting me, don't you see? I'm the bait."

———————— ★ ————————

"**A delightfully diabolic whodunit. Readers will savor this caper!**"
—*Publishers Weekly*

"**This is the sort of book that one inhales in one long, delicious draught.**"
—*Hartford Courant*

"**A decidedly devious mystery . . . recommended to all mystery lovers.**"
—*Nashville Banner*

A Forthcoming Worldwide Mystery by
BARBARA PAUL

IN-LAWS AND OUTLAWS

Barbara Paul
He Huffed and He Puffed

WORLDWIDE.®

TORONTO • NEW YORK • LONDON
AMSTERDAM • PARIS • SYDNEY • HAMBURG
STOCKHOLM • ATHENS • TOKYO • MILAN
MADRID • WARSAW • BUDAPEST • AUCKLAND

HE HUFFED AND HE PUFFED

A Worldwide Mystery/February 1992

This edition is reprinted by arrangement with Charles Scribner's Sons; an imprint of Macmillan Publishing Company.

ISBN 0-373-26089-X

Printed in U.S.A.

PART 1

The Victim

ONE

"ONE OF THESE PEOPLE," A. J. Strode said, spreading out the file folders on his desk. "Only one of these three people caves in, and I'm home." He scowled. "But which one?"

"Go for the violinist," Myron Castleberry suggested. "She's the weakest."

Strode raised an eyebrow at his assistant. "You think? Seems to me any babe who can ice her own parents won't fold easy." He opened one of the folders. "Where is she now?"

"Pittsburgh. Concert tonight—she's the guest artist with the Pittsburgh Symphony. Next she goes home to Boston for a while and then on to a couple of European engagements."

Strode was reading from the folder. "Did you believe the mercenary?"

Castleberry considered. "Yes, on the whole I did. He embroidered a little to make himself look good. He claimed he was the one who pulled out of the deal, but I'm sure he was lying about that. She was having second thoughts— which means her conscience was bothering her, and that makes her vulnerable."

Strode grunted. "It could also mean she just decided he wasn't the right man for the job. Where'd they meet—New Orleans? Why New Orleans? He lives in Texas."

"Neutral ground. She didn't give him her right name, and he didn't have any idea who she was until I showed him one of her publicity photos. He had trouble believing me at first when I told him the two people she wanted killed were her mother and father. To him, she was just a confused lady who'd answered his ad in a gun magazine. He doesn't admit to being a killer for hire, of course."

Strode closed the folder and opened another one. "What about the missing helicopter pilot? Any line on him?"

"Pierce says he has a soft lead—he'll get back to us in a day or two." Castleberry looked at his employer quizzically. "You think McKinstry's the one to tackle?"

Strode smiled tightly. "He's been leading such a pure and virtuous life lately, he won't want to see himself back in the headlines again. Besides, don't tell me it was coincidence that pilot dropped out of sight the minute I made my offer. McKinstry paid him to get lost, you can make book on it."

"I wouldn't be surprised."

"But I can't do anything about McKinstry until we find the damned pilot. And I sure as hell don't want to go after that other guy in L.A. if I don't have to." He closed the folder and lined it up neatly with the other two. "So it looks like the violinist by default. Call the airport and tell them I'll want the jet in an hour, and book me into the same hotel where she's staying."

"Yes, sir." His assistant turned to go.

"And Castleberry—call my wife and let her know. Wait until after I'm gone."

Castleberry nodded and left to make the arrangements.

Strode stood at the window with his hands clasped behind his back and stared at the building on the other side of Forty-seventh Street. In the office directly opposite his a woman bent over her work, unaware she was being scrutinized. But Strode wasn't interested in her; she was a dog. It was the woman in the next office he was looking for... and there she was.

Even from this distance it was clear she was a real dish, and *she* knew when she was being looked at. She was sitting behind an open-front desk when she became aware of Strode's gaze; she looked up, smiled, and slowly crossed her legs for him. Oh, yes—she was used to attention, that one was. A man came into her office and started talking; Strode turned away from the window.

He didn't have a whole lot of time. House of Glass would soon be out of reach.

Strode coveted House of Glass, pretentious name and all. He'd been buying stock wherever he could find it—quietly, without fuss, not at all like his usual juggernaut takeover techniques. And now he was so close—*so* close. All he needed was one more block of stock, just one. One of the three whose folders lay on his desk.

He'd made a straightforward offer to buy and all three had turned him down flat. That was the problem with House of Glass: relatively few outstanding stockholders. When one of them said no and made it stick, there weren't many others to turn to. So he'd raised his offer, and all three said no again.

House of Glass had started out at the beginning of the century as a maker and purveyor of expensive items for those who could afford them—crystalware, stained glass, chandeliers, fancy mirrors. From one small shop in London it had grown into a multibranched specialty chain. Ownership had changed hands several times, with corporate headquarters ending up in New York. Then a California vintner had commissioned House of Glass to design and manufacture a wine bottle with a unique silhouette easily identifiable as the vintner's own. House of Glass expanded its facilities to accommodate the necessities of large-scale bottle-making, and it had been expanding ever since.

The move into the industrial market had been made at exactly the right time; almost everything the company tried ended up making money. Now if you bought an overpriced condominium, the chances were good that the plate-glass windows had been supplied by House of Glass. Almost a third of the American cars on the road had House of Glass windshields. There wasn't a laboratory in the country that hadn't been equipped with at least some test tubes or beakers or pipettes made by House of Glass. House of Glass fiberglass wool provided thermal and sound insulation for everything from factories and airplanes to home refrigerators and furnaces. House of Glass did a lot of work for airports, hotels, shopping malls. House of Glass was trouble.

The first company A. J. Strode had owned was a construction firm, and that's where he'd originally come into contact with House of Glass. He'd been impressed by the low-keyed elegance that enabled the outfit to ask outrageous prices for its wares—and get them. Only twenty-nine years old at the time, Strode had inquired and found that all the stock was privately owned. He let it be known he was interested and since then had picked up a few small blocks of shares when they became available. House of Glass had not been the driving interest in his life; anything that could make money was sufficient to capture his attention.

Money still made money. Over the years Strode bought or traded or tricked or bullied his way into control of a power-tool manufacturer, a grocery chain, a newspaper, a heating-and-cooling outfit, a string of radio and TV stations, a football team (recently and profitably disposed of), five small software companies that he'd merged into one moderate-sized one. Two years earlier he'd acquired the controlling interest in LesterWorks, one of the biggest suppliers of industrial glass in the country.

One reason he'd been able to buy in so easily was that for the last few years House of Glass had been steadily eating into LesterWorks' profits. But when House of Glass took a government contract away from Lester, Strode decided it was time to act. Once he'd gained control, he planned to divert all industrial jobs to his own company. If Lester could make use of House of Glass's facilities, so much the better; if not, he'd shut them down. He'd let House of Glass go on making its pretty crystal decanters and such, as long as they showed a profit. But Strode had made up his mind that House of Glass would steal no more industrial work from him; he'd shut down the whole goddam operation before he'd let that happen.

The phone whirred. "Mrs. Strode's on line two," his secretary's voice said.

"I'm not here."

"She's very insistent."

"I'm still not here." Strode hung up and went back to the window for another look at the dishy babe in the building across the street. Her office was empty.

He was going to have to do something about Katie; she was getting to be a nuisance. He'd meant to wait until later in the year to tell her, but now he thought he might as well give her the bad news as soon as he got back from Pittsburgh. She knew it was coming anyway. He'd be sixty next year; time for a new wife.

Katie was wife number four. Number one had been Janie, his school sweetheart, whom he'd married on his twentieth birthday. But mousy little Janie hadn't been able to make the transition to the high style of living Strode adopted once he began building his fortune. Strode had pleaded, bullied, cajoled; he'd even hired someone to redo her appearance for her. But he'd never been able to make her understand how important it was for a man to have a classy-looking woman on his arm. Janie was afraid of the world he was moving in now; she was too hesitant, too easily intimidated. Strode had given up and divorced her. To make sure she understood the extent of his displeasure, he'd married his second wife on his thirtieth birthday.

Her name was Mollie, and Mollie had been an indefatigable sex machine. That should have warned him, but he'd been so delighted with their life in bed that it was over a year before he began to suspect he'd married a nympho. There was something abnormal about a woman who enjoyed sex that much. Strode grew suspicious and had special bolts installed in every door in the house, so he could lock Mollie in whatever room she happened to be occupying whenever he left. Even the bathrooms could be locked from the outside. And when the private detective he'd hired had brought in evidence that she was managing to cheat on him in spite of his precautions, he'd been able to get rid of her without having to pay one cent of alimony. Nobody cheated A. J. Strode.

He'd celebrated his fortieth birthday by marrying Suzie. Suzie had been the perfect wife... for a while. She had the face of a movie star, the style sense of a fashion model, the body of a porno queen, and the IQ of a philodendron. Perfect. She asked no questions and she made no demands. But then Suzie had started drinking—in secret at first, then more and more openly, as if wanting to parade her discontent before the world. It didn't help a man's image to have a lush for a wife, and once she'd embarrassed him by showing up drunk at a public function. Once. He'd kicked her out the next day.

To mark the anniversary of his half century on earth, he'd married a sophisticated woman well skilled in the art of hostessing. By then it was a running joke about how A. J. Strode took a new wife every ten years, but Katie had just laughed and said all that was over now. On the whole, she'd done her job well. But as the end of her tenure approached, that polished façade she showed to the world began to slip;

behind it, Katie turned out to be almost as insecure as his first wife had been. She'd started pestering him and asking questions, checking up on him and phoning him at the office. He couldn't have that.

Besides, she was starting to get fat.

Janie, Mollie, Suzie, Katie. Strode liked women's names that ended in that *ee* sound. Cute names.

Myron Castleberry came in to say the company jet would be ready by the time Strode got to the airport. "Sure you don't want me to come with you?"

"Not this time. I don't want her to feel she's being descended upon. If she still won't sell, I'll want you and one of the lawyers to pay her a visit." Strode rarely traveled alone, taking at least a secretary with him so as not to waste time en route. But this time a personal, private touch was called for. "What's a concert violinist doing with House of Glass stock? She can take the money and invest it in something else."

"She probably just doesn't want to be bothered," Castleberry suggested. "She leads a pretty busy life."

"Yes, we're all busy," Strode said, unimpressed. "Call me when the stock market closes."

"Right." Castleberry didn't have to be told which companies to watch. "Shall I tell Mrs. Strode you'll be back tomorrow?"

"Tell her I'll try."

THERE'D BEEN A TIME when A. J. Strode knew Pittsburgh as well as he knew New York. But the town had changed so in the last few years. Strode was no longer sure he could find his way around. It didn't matter; he wasn't planning to stray far from the hotel.

When he checked in at the Hilton, he'd asked the desk clerk for Joanna Gillespie's room number. The clerk replied that Ms Gillespie had requested that she not be disturbed before her concert and suggested he leave a message. Strode wrote a note inviting her to lunch the next day.

In his room he'd tipped the bellboy a hundred to get him a ticket to the concert. The bellboy politely but firmly refused the other hundred Strode offered to find him a woman for the night. Strode took a call from Castleberry and ordered a light meal in his room. Then he left for the concert, his last-minute ticket in his billfold.

Heinz Hall was only four or five blocks from the Hilton, on Penn Avenue, but Strode took a taxi. In the overdecorated interior of the concert hall, he was mildly surprised by the buzz of excitement running through the gathering audience. He knew Joanna Gillespie was considered hot stuff with a fiddle, but he didn't know people got worked up over things like that. He'd been to symphony concerts perhaps a dozen times in his life; on each occasion the audience had been composed and politely attentive. What made the Gillespie woman so special? Strode couldn't tell one violinist from another, or even one piano player from another. He did a little better with singers; he could tell the tenors from the sopranos.

He settled into his red plush seat and looked at the program. That evening Joanna Gillespie was playing a concerto by someone named Bruch. Strode had never heard of Bruch; he'd been hoping for Tchaikovsky. But first he had to sit through something modern and ear-jarring from the orchestra. Then Gillespie walked out on the stage.

Strode watched the audience around him. They were all leaning forward in their seats as they applauded, eyes gleaming and mouths open; that was some reputation she had, to get that kind of response before she'd even played a note. But that couldn't be all of it; these people must have heard her play before. And they *loved* her. No wonder the woman was so damned indifferent to what A. J. Strode wanted.

Joanna Gillespie was dark and intense; very East Coast. It was no secret that the violinist suffered from diabetes, a disability that didn't seem to be hindering her career. She was wearing a sparkly blue straight-up-and-down formal gown, held up by the thinnest of straps over her shoulders and leaving her bare arms free; it was a dress made to allow unimpeded physical movement. Gillespie had that special kind of lean body so many diabetics had, and she looked comfortable with it. Her posture wasn't too great, but the woman clearly felt at home on the stage; Strode couldn't detect so much as a glimmer of self-consciousness.

The concerto began. Gillespie did not caress the violin tucked under her chin, she *attacked* it; Strode had never before seen a musical instrument handled so roughly. And all the time she played, Gillespie's mouth kept working. What was she doing—talking to herself, singing along with the music? Wincing? Her whole body was in motion, a far cry from the sedate image of concert violinists Strode had in his mind. She'd thrown herself into her playing one hundred percent; at that moment nothing else in the world existed for Joanna Gillespie except the music she was making.

What crazy things people get excited about, Strode thought. The audience was clearly enchanted; he'd had no idea there were so many fiddle-enthusiasts in the world. He tried to assess what it meant. If Gillespie lived for music, that ought to mean she was a babe in the woods when it came to monetary matters. But Strode seldom took anything for granted; besides, getting her to sell House of Glass stock wasn't so much a matter of exploiting her financial naïveté as it was a matter of personality, of will.

The concerto at long last drew to a close, and the audience erupted into applause. Most of them rose to their feet, a few were cheering. On the stage, Joanna Gillespie beamed confidently at the audience, sweating slightly from her exertions. She was good; she knew she was good; she knew other people knew she was good. Strode was unhappily aware that the kind of adulation she was getting was bound to have an effect on her, especially if it was the standard response to her performances.

Strode scowled. He'd have preferred a more insecure adversary.

He slipped out before the orchestra started its next piece, whatever it was. If he remembered correctly, there was a corned beef place nearby—and there it was, right across the street. He ordered extra-lean and sat watching the front window until the street began to fill with well-dressed people. Strode paid his bill and left, heading back toward Heinz Hall.

He went in through the front lobby and found his way to the backstage area. Some twenty-five or thirty people were crowding around the door to Joanna Gillespie's dressing room, over half of them quite young—music students, Strode decided. A thin young man with a beard that successfully hid his face was saying that Ms Gillespie was changing now and would be out in a few minutes and please don't push. Then he caught sight of two men and a woman approaching and called out a greeting. He opened the dressing-room door and let them in.

There was some under-the-breath muttering among the students that The Beard pretended not to hear. Strode stayed at the back of the crowd; obviously this was not a good time to catch Joanna Gillespie, but he'd only halfway had that in mind anyway. Mostly he wanted a close-up look at her natural habitat and the woman herself when she was not performing. The presence of The Beard told him she felt the need for a buffer between herself and her admirers.

The dressing-room door opened and Joanna Gillespie came out, dressed in party clothes and followed by the two men and the woman The Beard had just admitted. The smallish crowd surged forward, everyone talking at once. Strode listened to her accepting their compliments in a somewhat lackadaisical manner; but when a boy of twelve or thirteen wanted to know why she'd played a certain passage the way she did, she held up her party long enough to give him an answer.

The Beard laid a hand on her arm. "Don't stay too late, Jo. And for heaven's sake, *eat* something!"

"I will, I will," she assured him. "Don't fuss so, Harvey."

"You *pay* me to fuss."

She grinned at him and left with her friends. Once the star attraction was gone, the others started drifting out through the nearest street door. A woman in her forties came out of the dressing room carrying a garment bag and a small suitcase. Strode held the street door open for her and followed her outside.

Three cabs were lined up along the curb. The maid, Strode supposed she was, got into the first one and rode away. Strode went to the second, handed the driver a fifty, and said, "Get lost." The cab took off.

Strode climbed into the third cab and told the driver to wait. The street door opened and The Beard came out, a violin case in his hand. He headed straight for the one cab in sight, but his face fell when he saw it was occupied. "Oh, *why* is it so hard to get a cab in this town?" he complained. He asked the driver to come back for him.

Strode rolled down the window and said, "Can I give you a lift? I'd be happy to."

The young man hesitated. "I'm only going as far as the Hilton."

"Then there's no problem," Strode smiled. "That's where I'm going too. Please—get in."

The Beard got in next to Strode, hugging the violin case to his chest. "It's only a few blocks, but I do hate to walk on the streets at night when I have this." He patted the case. "Thank you for giving me a ride."

"My pleasure." The cab driver had been listening and knew where to take them. "That wouldn't happen to be Joanna Gillespie's violin, would it?" Strode asked.

"Yes, it is. It's a Guarnerius, so you can see why I have to be careful."

Strode had never heard the word; but from the way The Beard said it, *Guarnerius* obviously meant *valuable*. Strode made several extravagantly complimentary remarks about the concert. The young man was pleased, and by the time the cab pulled up to the Hilton he'd agreed to have a drink with Strode. First he had to see that the violin was put safely in the hotel vault, and then the two men went into the bar.

His name was Harvey Rudd, the bearded young man said, and he was Joanna Gillespie's personal assistant. *Dogsbody*, Strode translated. He ordered bourbon while Harvey asked for an Australian lager Strode had never heard of. "I don't like this town," Harvey confessed after tasting the lager. "I'm never comfortable here. Jo likes it. She knows people here, and they're always making a fuss over her. But I feel at loose ends in Pittsburgh."

Strode mentioned having seen the maid leave. "Are there just the three of you?"

"At the moment, yes. Jo's manager will be joining us later in Boston. And when she gives a recital, we have her accompanist and his valet. We're at half strength just now." Politely he inquired why Strode was in Pittsburgh.

A business deal he anticipated closing tomorrow, Strode told him, and turned the conversation back to Joanna Gillespie. "I was delighted to find she was playing here tonight—a real stroke of luck. Have you been with her long?"

"Three years. You know, I've just realized I'm hungry. Do you want something to eat?"

Since Strode was still digesting the corned beef he'd had only a short time earlier, he declined. When Harvey Rudd had some food and a few more lagers inside him, he relaxed and began to chat easily. He seemed happy to have found someone to talk to, in a town he considered less friendly than New York.

"I just hope Jo remembers to eat," he worried, pushing back his empty plate. "She doesn't always. When she's practicing or sometimes just out having a good time, like tonight, she doesn't always remember. Did you know she's diabetic?"

"Yes, I'd heard," Strode said. "Amazing how she manages to do so much."

"Well, everything doesn't always get done. Diabetics are supposed to eat on a regular schedule, and when she forgets—she's going along just fine and then *bang!* It hits her. The shakes, cold sweats, dizziness. Really knocks her out. It takes her a couple of days to get back in stride again. And that makes it hard on everybody."

Meaning yourself, Strode thought. "Does she ever have to cancel a performance?"

"Very rarely. But it shouldn't happen at all. Then I have to notify her manager if he's not with us and change all the transportation arrangements and hotel reservations and the like. And it's all preventable. I dearly love Jo Gillespie— she's a terrific person and the greatest violinist in the world and if she'd just remember to eat when she's supposed to, she'd be *perfect*."

Strode laughed. "I wonder why she's so careless about something as important as that?"

"I have a theory. Her mother insisted on treating her like an invalid when she was a child, and I think Jo is still proving Mama was wrong. Even though the poor woman's been dead nearly two years."

"Did you know her? The mother?"

"Unfortunately. Mustn't speak ill of the dead and all that, but I swear that woman enjoyed playing the invalid herself. She was diabetic too, you know. And Jo's father as well. Both her parents were diabetic."

"That seems odd—two diabetics marrying? Or is that something the blood tests don't test for?"

"According to Jo, they had two different kinds of diabetes. Her father didn't develop his until he was well into middle age. He was one of those sluggish, overweight people who sometimes get it late in life. But Jo's mother had juvenile diabetes, and Jo inherited it from her. It was just a nasty coincidence that Papa became diabetic too, later on."

Strode shook his head. "What an unlucky family. That's a lot to overcome."

Harvey nodded vigorously. "You bet it is. But Jo's kinda sick of hearing about it. Nobody seems able to write up an interview without mentioning that she's the diabetic offspring of diabetic parents. It makes Jo sound as if she's pitching for sympathy, you know?"

So Joanna Gillespie wants to play down her diabetes, Strode thought. *Interesting.*

"But the really dumb thing is," Harvey Rudd went on, "it wasn't *that* that made the most trouble for her. I'm not telling tales out of school, everybody knows about it. I mean her parents. *They* were her biggest obstacle."

"Mmm . . . I think I read somewhere they didn't want her to play the violin?" Where he'd read it was in the file Castleberry had prepared.

"They didn't want her to play *in public*. It was Papa, mostly. He was adamantly opposed to her 'displaying herself'—as he so charmingly put it. Papa thought music was a perfectly acceptable hobby to pursue in the privacy of one's home, but that's all. Just a little skill that one develops for one's own amusement." Harvey uttered the last sentence with all the disgust such philistinism warranted. "Even when she emerged as the premier violinist playing today, he never really understood what a special person his daughter was."

"Unfortunate. Parental obtuseness...well."

Harvey played with his empty glass. "She is special, you know. There's nobody else quite like her. She can do things with a violin the rest of us can't even think of, much less do. People like that shouldn't have to put up with stupid obstacles in their paths. They should have things made easy for them." He laughed self-deprecatingly. "That's my job. I try to make things easy for her."

Strode was capable of the occasional generous gesture. "I think she's lucky to have you," he said, and meant it. His companion grinned with pleasure. Harvey Rudd was an intense young man whose entire life was wrapped up in Joanna Gillespie's career; what hurt her, hurt him. "Where do you go next?" Strode asked.

"Home to Boston, then London and Berlin. And then six glorious weeks with nothing to do at all! I think it's called vacation. For Jo, of course, that just means more time to practice."

They talked a few minutes longer and then left the hotel bar. The two men parted company at the elevators, each heartily glad to have made the other's acquaintance. On his way to his room Strode was thinking young Harvey had provided him with a perspective he'd lacked. Joanna Gillespie was a rich woman; she could give free concerts for the rest of her life and still die rich. By the same token, she could live quite well on what she made playing the fiddle and never need the money she'd inherited. There was, however, a considerable difference between being able to live *quite well* and being out-and-out *rich*.

But it wasn't just the money. The Gillespie family relationships had evidently been more strained than Strode knew. If parents and daughter had been on good terms, the violinist would never have thought of killing them, money or no money. But she'd been deprived of a normal childhood by being told she was an invalid; there was bound to be some resentment left over from that. Papa had opposed her pursuit of a career; he'd never understood or cared that music was the *raison d'être* of her life. And Mama—well, Mama had made her sick.

Strode unlocked the door to his room and went in. He was fidgety, not ready to sleep yet. One used to be able to count on bellboys to provide certain services, he mused, but no longer. Strode knew he'd want a woman tonight; he always did, when he was moving in for the kill. He should have brought Tracy with him.

No, that would have been a mistake. Tracy was beginning to think of herself as Mrs. A. J. Strode number five, and that was bound to mean trouble. Strode had no intention of marrying her. Tracy was a great-looking babe, and she was funny; he got a kick out of listening to her chatter. But she was also willful—she'd probably say *independent*. A kept woman, independent!

The truth was, Tracy just liked getting her own way. Still, he would have been glad of her company right then. He decided to call her number in New York. He got the answering machine; she was out.

Strode frowned. That was something else that needed looking into.

A RINGING TELEPHONE woke Strode at eight the next morning.

It was Joanne Gillespie herself. After apologizing for calling so early, she explained she already had a luncheon engagement. "I'm still not going to sell, Mr. Strode," she said pleasantly. "I hope you didn't come to Pittsburgh on my account."

"Ah, but I did," he said smoothly. "At least let's talk—don't make my trip a complete waste. It won't hurt to talk about it, will it?"

"No, so long as you aren't expecting anything," she agreed. "I tell you what. I was about to order breakfast—why don't I order for two? We can talk while we eat."

"Sounds good. I'll need half an hour."

Thirty minutes later Joanna Gillespie opened her door and greeted him with an automatic smile. She wore a bulky top of the kind Strode hated because it so successfully hid a woman's figure. Last night she'd worn a floor-length skirt and today she had on gray slacks. *Must have bad legs*, Strode thought. Her face was bare of make-up; she certainly hadn't put herself out any on his account. But she seemed relaxed and at ease, quite a contrast to the intense ball of fire he'd seen in action at Heinz Hall the night before. He complimented her on her performance.

"Thank you. It did go well, didn't it?" she said, taking it for granted that he would have gone to hear her play. "It was a good audience. Very *up*."

"They were ready to applaud before you'd played a note," Strode remarked with amusement.

"Some audiences are like that. Others come in with *Show me!* written all over their faces."

"Which kind do you work harder for?"

She shrugged. "Once I start playing, I forget there is an audience. It doesn't really matter."

They were in a comfortable-looking suite; Strode could see one bedroom and a small kitchen. When breakfast arrived, Strode insisted on signing for it and they sat down to eat. He spotted a couple of sweet pastries on the cart and knew they were for him. Joanna Gillespie put a jar of diabetic honey beside her plate for herself.

She slouched at the table and ate slowly, chewing each bite thoroughly before swallowing. Her movements were deliberate and unhurried, and she looked Strode straight in the eye when she spoke. She was courteous and pleasant to him, but it was obvious she was not at all impressed by having someone like A. J. Strode seeking her out.

Well, that would change.

"Where's your, er, retinue?" Strode asked innocently. "You don't travel alone, do you?"

"No, but I don't sleep with them. They'll be here at ten. And I told the desk to hold my calls. So you can say what you've come to say without fear of interruption."

But Strode waited until they were almost finished eating. "How'd you come to buy House of Glass stock in the first place?" he asked her.

"It was my financial manager's advice. He handles all my investments."

"And he's the one telling you not to sell?"

"Not exactly. I called him after your second offer, and he said I was right to hold on to the stock. I watch my investments, Mr. Strode, and House of Glass has sent me some nice dividends."

"Call me A.J."

"Glad to. And I'm Jo."

"You know, Jo, there are other companies I could put you on to that'll return even bigger investments. I made you a generous offer. You could make a nice profit on those shares right now and reinvest the entire amount."

She shot him a quizzical look. "But the fact that A. J. Strode wants those shares so badly tells me they must be pretty valuable. Why? What's going to happen with House of Glass?"

"What's going to happen," he said softly, "is that I'm going to close it down."

Her eyebrows shot up. "Close it down?"

"About ninety percent of it. And when I do, how much do you think your shares will be worth then?" He let her think that over for a minute. "I am going to take over, you know. If not with your shares, then with someone else's. So you either make a profit now or take a big loss later. Up to you."

She stared at him a moment and said, "God, how I hate being bullied! Why do you want to shut down a profitable business like House of Glass?"

"Business," he answered shortly.

"Business." She thought a moment. "House of Glass must be hurting you somehow. Are you a competitor? And you're out to smash the competition? Is that it?"

"Very good, Jo." He gave her the lupine smile that had intimidated stronger adversaries than Jo Gillespie. "I'm doing you a favor, coming to you first. I go to the next guy, I buy his shares, he makes a profit, you take a bath. So what's it going to be?"

She didn't answer immediately. Then: "What if the next guy says no, too? And the next one? And the one after him? You wouldn't have raised your first offer to me if you had a string of stockholders lined up eager to sell their shares. I'm sorry, A.J., but something doesn't ring true here. I'm going to have to talk this over with my financial manager."

Strode shook his head. "Jo, Jo...you know you're forcing me to do something I didn't want to do. I was hoping to keep this friendly. I come all the way here from New York—''

"A fifty-minute flight."

"—and I show you how to keep from losing money on your House of Glass shares, and you still won't sell." He paused. "Do you remember a man named Ozzie Rogers?"

Her face tightened. "Who?"

Strode repeated the name. "An old-style Texan. A familiar type—all muscles and bullets and shoot first and ask no questions at all. Ozzie's one of those mercenaries who advertise their services in gun magazines. They're really something, those ads are. Some of them are nothing more than thinly disguised offers to commit murder for a fee. Ozzie's ad is one of the thinnest."

"Why are you telling me this?" she asked with a show of casualness.

Strode smiled. "Ozzie tells an interesting story. He says a lady sent him a plane ticket to New Orleans for what he calls a 'meet'—and meet they did. She was looking for someone to kill two people, an older man and his wife. But then she changed her mind and backed out." He leaned over the table. "You were that lady, Jo. Ozzie identified you from a picture we showed him. And I have his signature on an affidavit saying so."

She was silent a moment and then muttered, "How much did you pay him for that?"

"Five thousand," Strode answered blandly. "Ozzie's not the brightest chap in the world—he had no idea how much his identification was really worth. But that's neither here nor there. What's significant is the fact that you consulted him about committing two murders for you. You wanted him to kill your parents."

"What are you talking about? My father had a coronary and my mother died of insulin overdose!"

"That's what their death certificates say, yes. But you and I both know they were helped along. What was the matter, Jo? Just couldn't wait for a natural death?"

"I didn't hire Ozzie! You know that!"

"But I don't know why. Afraid the killings could be traced to you? Or did you just decide Ozzie didn't have the brains to do the job the way you wanted it done? It sure as hell wasn't conscience, because you went ahead and did it yourself. You killed your father, and then you waited a year and you killed your mother."

"You're crazy as a loon." Jo stood up abruptly, jarring the table.

"How'd you kill your father, Jo?" Strode asked. "An air bubble in the blood stream? That would look like a coronary, and it seems to me a needle would be a diabetic's natural weapon. It's what you used on your mother a year later. Oh, I know the coroner's report said she'd been drinking and forgot she'd already taken her daily injection—at a time when she was alone in the house and there was no one to help her. Supposedly. But you were there, weren't you? *You* gave her that overdose. What did you do then, Jo? Did you wait long enough to see the sweating, the confusion, the coma? Or did you leave her to die alone?"

"Get out of here!" she shouted. "Get out right now!"

"It was a pretty nice setup," Strode went on unheeding. "On top of their diabetes, your folks had other problems, didn't they? Your father had developed emphysema. He smoked too much, he ate too much, he drank too much. The man was a walking coronary waiting to happen. And your mother was in even worse shape. Nephritis, wasn't it? They were two mighty sick people. So if you were caught playing your needle games, you could always claim they were mercy killings and hope to get a jury that went for that sort of thing."

Her mouth was working but no sound was coming out. Strode took her speechlessness as a favorable sign.

He bore down even harder. "You became a wealthy woman when your father died, Jo. Half his money went to you and the other half to your mother. But you wanted it all, didn't you? Money you never earned. That must have been quite a year for you, right after you killed your father— waiting to find out if you'd got away with it and cranking yourself up to do it again. Or did you enjoy doing it?"

"You're sick, Strode," she hissed. "You're sick and twisted and perverted. How dare you accuse me of killing my parents? How *dare* you!"

"I dare because I've got Ozzie Rogers in my pocket," he said bluntly. "I own a newspaper, in case you didn't know. They'll run the story as long as I want them to. And that's exactly what's going to happen unless you get down off your high horse and let go of those House of Glass shares. Is that what you want? All that bad publicity, the police reopening the case?"

She whirled and ran into the bedroom before he'd finished his last sentence. Strode smiled and got up from the table to follow her. Hysterics were good. Hysterics meant he was winning.

But he'd taken only a few steps when she was back—and now she had a gun in her hand. She pointed the gun directly at his face. "Now you get out of here, you piece of slime," she said furiously, "or by god I will shoot you! Just give me the excuse!"

Strode believed her. He left as fast as his legs could carry him.

Back in his own room, he sank to the side of the bed and willed himself to calm down. She'd pointed a gun at him. Joanna Gillespie had pointed a *gun*...at *him*! He looked at his hands; they were trembling. He'd been doing business for forty years and no one had ever pulled a gun on him before. Jesus, Jo Gillespie was supposed to be the *easy* one! God damn the woman. There'd be blizzards in hell before he'd let her get away with that.

He went into the bathroom and washed his face with cold water. Then he leaned over the sink for a few moments, bracing himself with his arms. Joanna Gillespie would regret this day. Strode's first impulse was to go ahead right then and there and do what he'd threatened: publish the Ozzie Rogers story. But Strode hadn't gotten to be a fat cat by yielding to impulse. He'd work on the other two stockholders first; and as soon as one of them sold, he'd lower the boom on that Gillespie bitch.

But he couldn't risk exposing her until he was sure House of Glass was his. There was always the chance she'd change her mind and sell to protect herself; she couldn't be feeling any less upset right now than he was. Just wait a bit, let her cool off. If she thought it over and decided she had no choice, he'd buy her shares—and *then* he'd publish the story. The bitch.

When some measure of calm had returned, Strode called the desk clerk and told him he was checking out.

MYRON CASTLEBERRY was impervious to Katie Strode's tears. The silly cow must have known what was going to happen, but she'd made no preparations for her future. *I don't have anyplace to go*, she wailed. What nonsense. There were lots of places she could go. Mr. Strode would give her a generous settlement; he always did, with all his wives, all except that whore Mollie. Katie wouldn't be hurting for money.

Castleberry had finally gotten Katie Strode into a taxi to the airport. He'd suggested she go someplace warm and take it easy for a while before she made any decisions. Evidently he'd sounded just the right note of concern because she'd nodded agreement, shoulders slumping in defeat. But she was out of Mr. Strode's house now. Castleberry didn't feel sorry for her; she'd had a good nine years. But he did feel Mr. Strode had been unnecessarily harsh with her. Castleberry knew his boss; if Joanna Gillespie had agreed to sell, Mr. Strode wouldn't have been so rough on Katie.

Castleberry got into one of the company limousines. On the way back to the office, he wondered who would be next to inhabit the mansion just off Park. He didn't think it would be Tracy. Twice Mr. Strode had married his current mistress, but that wasn't likely to happen this time. Castleberry didn't know what had gone wrong, but it was plain that Tracy wasn't playing her cards right; Mr. Strode had on several occasions shown displeasure at something she'd said or done. She'd probably be following Katie to the airport before long. Too bad; Castleberry rather liked Tracy.

He wondered what his own wife would think if she knew some of the things he did for Mr. Strode. She'd probably be shocked, but then she'd pretend not to know anything. Alice was on the whole a placid woman, accepting what came her way without fuss; it had been years since she'd last complained about his devoting all his time to work to the neglect of herself and the children. She was resigned to the fact that she was married to a company man—a man who was totally absorbed in his work, who had an infinite capacity for handling detail and for adjusting his ethical standards as needed, and who had not one spark of originality or creativity in him. Myron Castleberry had found his niche in life, and he gave himself to it heart and soul. He'd never been unfaithful to Alice; he'd never had time.

Women were the one indulgence Mr. Strode allowed himself. He drank in moderation and didn't smoke at all. He tended to wolf his food down, but he never overate. He was orderly in his habits, both work and personal. Life was created for the conducting of business, from A. J. Strode's point of view, and that suited Myron Castleberry just fine. If Mr. Strode needed women as a pressure valve, his assistant would be the last to criticize. Mr. Strode controlled his personal life as stringently as he controlled everything else; he never allowed sex to interfere with business. The women served a legitimate function.

But one woman was giving them trouble. Castleberry had been appalled when Mr. Strode told him Joanna Gillespie had threatened him with a gun. What a primitive creature she must be. Castleberry was forced to revise his original assessment of the violinist; unlike his employer, he'd never been convinced that Gillespie's murder of her parents had been anything other than two mercy killings spaced a year apart. Mr. Strode had been sure from the first that she'd killed them for her inheritance. There was no doubt in either man's mind that she *had* killed them; one doesn't consult hired assassins when one's intentions are benign.

Maybe she did kill them for the money after all. Joanna Gillespie was a patricide and then a matricide. Was there a word for someone who killed both parents? Other than *orphan*. What was she doing with a gun in her hotel room anyway?

Well, now, wait a moment, Castleberry thought; she might have a legitimate reason for carrying a gun. A woman who traveled as much as she did, a celebrity besides—she might have need for protection. Transporting firearms on an airplane was simple enough; all she had to do was pack the gun in a suitcase going into the baggage compartment and then declare it at the check-in counter. She probably took it with her on all her out-of-town engagements. Then when Mr. Strode had moved in for the kill, she'd become frightened and confused and turned to the only form of defense immediately available to her. Though from the way Mr. Strode told it, she'd been more angry than frightened.

The limousine stopped and let him out. He'd barely walked into the office before his secretary said, "Mr. Pierce has been trying to reach you all morning, Mr. Castleberry. He says it's urgent."

"Get him back, please."

Castleberry felt a stir of excitement. Pierce was the private detective Mr. Strode kept on permanent retainer; he wouldn't have said *urgent* unless he had something. When the call came through, Castleberry lifted the receiver and said, "Yes, Mr. Pierce?"

"I found him. I didn't approach him, like you said. But he's here, living in a fleabag."

"A fleabag? He doesn't have money?"

"Not now, he doesn't. I found out he was trying to negotiate a coke buy with some Cubans, but he's flat now. It's my guess the Cubans burned him." Pierce filled in details of what he'd learned.

"Give me the address." Castleberry wrote it down. "Stay where you are until I talk to Mr. Strode—I'll get back to you. That was good work, Mr. Pierce."

On his way out he told his secretary to book him on an afternoon flight to Miami. In Strode's outer office, he looked a question at the efficient-appearing woman guarding the fort. She nodded; he was in. Castleberry opened the door and stepped inside.

Strode didn't ask if he'd gotten Katie out of the house; that was taken for granted. "Something?"

"Pierce has found McKinstry's helicopter pilot. He's in Florida, and down on his luck." He explained about the failed attempt at a drug deal.

"So he had a stake and he blew it," Strode mused. "He must be scraping bottom about now. Better strike while the iron is hot."

"I'm flying down this afternoon. Any inducement other than money?"

"Offer him a job if that's what he wants. But try cash first."

Castleberry nodded and left. Strode took out the file folder marked *McKinstry* and smiled as he looked through it. He had him now.

The phone whirred. "Joanna Gillespie on one," his secretary's voice said.

"I'm not here," Strode said.

Let her stew.

TWO

NORMALLY A. J. STRODE avoided California during the warm months, and he tried to avoid the Los Angeles area all year round. But the McKinstry family business was in Southern California, so to Southern California A. J. Strode had come. He'd sent Myron Castleberry earlier with his second offer to buy Jack McKinstry's House of Glass shares; but since the answer had been no, Strode felt compelled to make this trip himself.

The third House of Glass stockholder also lived in Los Angeles. Strode wanted nothing to do with him.

Jack McKinstry had seemed affable and open on the telephone; he and Strode were quickly on a first-name basis. McKinstry had said he'd be happy to sell his House of Glass shares if he could; unfortunately, he'd used them as security for a loan and couldn't touch them until the loan had been paid. Strode offered to pay off the loan in exchange for the shares. McKinstry had said, *Well, now, A.J., I don't know—let me think about it.*

So it had to be a face-to-face. McKinstry was stalling; he'd want to consult someone in the family more knowledgeable about the buying and selling of stock than he was. He'd inherited his House of Glass shares, just as he'd inherited everything else he owned. Jack McKinstry was not known for his business acumen.

What Jack McKinstry *was* known for was his ability to have a good time wherever he was, whatever the circumstances. For most of his adult life he'd been labeled with that quaint term *playboy*. Jack's only discernible talent was for making himself liked; he was always welcome in the posher playgrounds of the world. He did not supply drugs or try to invent new variations on *la dolce vita*; he was just a pleasant fellow that everyone liked. A good host, a good guest. Good company. He'd been married once, briefly; both bride and groom had quickly decided a workable marriage required more effort than they were willing to put into it. There'd been no hard feelings on either side; it was a friendly divorce. Jack was a friendly man—friendly, self-confident, easy to get along with, and utterly superficial.

But four years ago something had happened to change some of that. The McKinstry family fortune had been built on the manufacture and sale of light aircraft, a fortune that had grown dramatically when one of the more astute McKinstrys had decided that helicopters were where the big money was coming from in the future. Now McKinstry Helicopters, Inc., supplied police and the armed forces of several countries as well as a sizable chunk of private industry. Four years ago the company had announced a new model, a technological marvel that, it was rumored, would revolutionize helicopter design. Jack McKinstry, then playing in France, had taken four of his friends to the branch of McKinstry Helicopters that was located near Marseilles to try out the new model. Jack had recruited one of the company's pilots, and they'd taken off.

The six of them had headed east over the Mediterranean, following the coastline in the direction of the Riviera. But they'd barely passed Toulon when they ran into trouble. Witnesses on the island where the accident took place said they'd heard no engine sounds to indicate anything was amiss; they'd watched in disbelief as the helicopter sailed serenely into the side of a high cliff that ran straight down to the sea. There'd been no explosion, no burst of flames; the helicopter had wavered there a moment like some giant insect burrowing into the cliff face, its tail bobbing gently in the air. Then the craft had begun a slow-motion slide downward, breaking into pieces as it fell into the sea.

Only Jack and the pilot had survived.

They were the only two who'd been able to jump into the water before the helicopter hit the cliff. At the subsequent inquiry the pilot had testified they'd been cruising along on autopilot when he spotted the cliff ahead. But when he tried to return the helicopter to manual control, the autopilot lock had refused to yield. In spite of his best efforts, he could do nothing to increase the craft's elevation or change its direction. An investigation of the recovered parts confirmed the pilot's testimony; the helicopter had indeed been on autopilot when it crashed.

The crash had made headlines not only because the new model was the latest thing in helicopter technology but also because its passengers had belonged to the beautiful-people set. At the time A. J. Strode had thought there was a fishy smell to the story; but it was something he had noted only in passing as a matter of idle curiosity. It wasn't until Jack McKinstry emerged as one of the obstacles on his road to the ownership of House of Glass that Strode became actively inquisitive about the accident. Strode's detective, Pierce, pretending to be an old friend of McKinstry's, had talked casually to a number of his real friends. While every one of them was sympathetic, they all shared a suspicion that it had been Jack who was flying the helicopter when it crashed.

The reason was simple: Jack loved helicopters. He couldn't resist the big noisy toys that lifted him up off the ground and then put him back down again. He'd been licensed to fly since he was nineteen, but he'd taken a pilot with him on the ill-fated jaunt along the Mediterranean coast because the new model had instruments and controls he wouldn't have been familiar with. But his friends were all agreed that Jack could no more ride in a brand-new helicopter without trying his hand at the controls than he could learn Sanskrit overnight.

One friend speculated that the pilot had been teaching Jack how things worked, and they'd both gotten so engrossed in what they were doing that they hadn't looked up and spotted the cliff until it was too late. Pierce didn't explain that the helicopter had an audible proximity warning system that made such an eventuality virtually impossible. None of Jack's friends saw anything wrong with his jumping to save himself. They quite reasonably pointed out that his dying wouldn't have saved the others.

So did he pay off the pilot to take the blame? Strode had wondered. It was certainly consistent with the image of Jack-the-playboy. And it went a long way toward explaining the change that took place in Jack after the accident. For the first time in his life, Jack was putting his talent for making friends to work for the family business. Atoning? More likely the family had just laid down the law; after all, he'd cost the business a small fortune by his spectacular demonstration that the new model still needed work. Whichever way it was, Jack became a PR man for the company; his years of socializing with the rich of two continents had given him an enviable list of contacts. The McKinstry sales department quickly learned to schedule Jack for a softening-up visit before sending in their hard-sell specialists to clinch the deal.

Jack took his job seriously. He was as amiable as ever, but he no longer wanted to spend his life playing. A whiff of his own mortality had made him look back over the life he'd led and left him dissatisfied? That was the view taken by those who knew him well.

But A. J. Strode, who didn't know him at all, wasn't buying it. Look further, he'd told Pierce. Check on those four who died in the crash.

The detective did just that—and came up with something interesting. Three of the dead passengers had been Jack McKinstry's playmates for years; but the fourth was a man relatively new on the playground. His name was Tony Dwyer, and he was as nouveau riche as they came. He tried very hard to fit in with those who'd always taken it for granted that life was one big catered party. But Dwyer just didn't have the knack; no matter what he did, he remained instantly identifiable as The Outsider.

He didn't look right, for one thing. He was short and stocky and he wheezed whenever he exerted himself. His clothes were always brand-new and he never seemed at home in them. He talked incessantly, as if afraid the others would forget his existence if he ever stopped making noise. He laughed too loud and too often. He was rude to waiters. His feelings were easily hurt. And whenever he felt particularly left out, he'd throw it up to the others that it was his own money he was spending, not Daddy's or Grandpa's or Aunt Helen's.

Jack's crowd tolerated his presence for two reasons. First, it was fun having someone around to laugh at; and second, Tony Dwyer picked up the tab more frequently than anyone else. He could also be counted on to come up with a quick loan in time of need. But Dwyer didn't have the same casual attitude toward borrowing and lending money as the others. He expected to be repaid, and within a reasonable length of time. Jack McKinstry had borrowed from him on many occasions.

From what Pierce had been able to dig up, it looked as if Jack had been deeply in debt to Dwyer at the time of the accident. Jack lived on the dividends paid by the various stocks he'd inherited; and while the family did not exactly look upon him as a black sheep, the work ethic ran strong in the McKinstry clan. The family had long since made it clear it would not bail him out if he lived beyond his means. Jack's elder brother, who now ran the business, was less tolerant than the others. He'd disapproved openly of Jack's unproductive life and threatened to take his younger brother to court on a charge of fiscal irresponsibility, with the purpose of having the control of Jack's money put into the hands of a court-appointed banker or lawyer. Only his deep-seated distaste for airing family troubles in public had restrained him thus far.

So Jack had borrowed from Tony Dwyer whenever he ran a little short. But the day inevitably arrived when he was unable to pay him back. One of Jack's friends told Pierce she'd heard Dwyer threatening to collect from Jack's brother if he didn't make good immediately. How much was the loan, Pierce had asked. No idea, she'd said.

Strode thought it must have been a sizable amount. In debt and threatened with the loss of control of his own money, Jack McKinstry might have been driven to desperate measures. He could have planned the crash ahead of time, taking the controls himself and pretending something was wrong with the autopilot. It would have been tricky, leaping to safety just before the helicopter plowed into the cliff, but McKinstry was experienced in the ways of helicopters; he would have known how to time it. The one thing he hadn't counted on was the pilot's getting out too.

If all that was true, it meant that Jack McKinstry had deliberately killed three of his friends to rid himself of one enemy.

Strode was a steely man, but McKinstry's callousness appalled him. Pierce had been unable to turn up any hard evidence that McKinstry had been paying off the pilot, but good-sized hunks of his income remained unaccounted for ever since the helicopter crash. Perhaps that was the real reason the former playboy had gone to work: to keep up the blackmail payments. The significant question was whether the seemingly good-natured Jack McKinstry was in fact cold-blooded enough to sacrifice the lives of three people he liked to get himself out of a financial hole. Strode didn't spend much time puzzling over that; no one was ever exactly what he seemed.

The clincher, as far as Strode was concerned, was the pilot. The man had been living in Redondo Beach ever since the so-called accident. But when Strode had sent Castleberry with his second offer for McKinstry's House of Glass shares, McKinstry had let it slip that he knew Strode was making inquiries about the helicopter crash. That was about the same time the pilot had suddenly dropped out of sight. What a coincidence.

But now Pierce had found him, and the man turned out to be just as corruptible today as he was four years earlier. The pilot was a lot shrewder than Ozzie Rogers; he hadn't come cheap. He'd wanted to be set up in his own business running a helicopter charter service in Florida. Strode had agreed.

Myron Castleberry and the pilot worked out a statement in which the latter attested that Jack McKinstry had deliberately rammed the helicopter into the face of the cliff. The pilot stated that McKinstry was at the controls and that he himself had tried to take back the controls when he saw they were in danger of hitting the cliff, but the other man had fought him off. When McKinstry jumped, the pilot had followed suit; he was sorry about those other people, but there was nothing he could have done to save them. No mention was made of any hush money the pilot had been collecting from Jack McKinstry ever since. Castleberry had to draw up three drafts before the pilot read one he liked, but in the end he even agreed to testify in court if it ever came to that. No one thought it would.

Strode was feeling confident. The hold he had over Jack McKinstry was even stronger than the one he had over Joanna Gillespie. And since they were to meet at the well-populated McKinstry family beach house, it wasn't likely that Jack would pull a gun on him.

Strode rented a limo to take him to the McKinstry place. The various members of the McKinstry clan had their own homes scattered all through the Los Angeles area and Orange County, but the beach house at Malibu was the family gathering place—fully staffed year round, available without notice to anyone named McKinstry in need of a little R & R. Jack McKinstry had said that was where he'd be on Saturday afternoon. The uniformed driver who came with the limo headed north through Santa Monica and then west on the Pacific Coast Highway toward Malibu.

When they got there, Strode was not surprised to find a wall around the place. The gate was electronically controlled; the limo driver pressed the speaker button and pronounced Strode's name, which proved to be the only open-sesame needed. Inside the walls, Strode saw that the house was large enough to do service as a medium-sized hotel. The maid who answered the door said they were all out back and led the way. Strode had a quick glimpse of exquisite tile flooring and expensive-looking furnishings in such a variety of styles that he suspected every McKinstry in the clan had taken a hand in the decorating. On a rear deck that ran the width of the big house, the maid pointed to a stairway leading down to the beach.

Strode sighed and started down. Below, a spirited volley-ball game was in progress on the beach; very California. The players ranged in age from about ten to over sixty; they were yelling and whooping and giving it their all. Strode recognized the man about to serve; he was Philip McKinstry, Jack's older brother and the present head of the family business. Philip didn't serve open-handed; he jumped into the air and punched the ball with his fist as hard as he could toward a girl of fourteen or fifteen. She managed to keep the ball in the air and someone else took over. Strode noticed quite a few scraped elbows and knees; these people played for keeps.

Jack McKinstry was standing on the sideline wiping his face with a towel. He was wearing a burgundy-colored tank top with white shorts and sneakers. Strode was amused. The man was thirty-nine years old and he still dressed like a teenager. Lean and tan, flashing white teeth. Only the dark brown hair spoiled the California-surfer image. But Strode thought wryly that he himself was the one who looked out of place, in his business suit and shoes not made for walking on beaches.

Jack saw him coming and hurried over, hand outstretched. "Hello, A.J.! Welcome to Jocksville. You ever play this insane game?" Without waiting for an answer he went on, "Sometimes I think it's just a socially sanctioned outlet for sadomasochistic tendencies, with which the McKinstry family seems to be embarrassingly well endowed. You have to love punishment to be any good at the game."

"Giving or getting?" Strode asked with a smile.

"Both, alas. But when the getting starts to outweigh the giving, you can always take a discretionary breather. Which is precisely what I am doing now. Want a beer?"

Chatting away, he steered Strode over to a cooler and fished out two bottles; Strode was surprised to see they were the same Australian lager Harvey Rudd had ordered in Pittsburgh. Jack took a long swallow and looked back at the game. "Now I ask you, A.J.—isn't that a sight to warm the cockles of your heart?" he asked in a bantering tone. "Assuming your heart has cockles, whatever they are. But just look at them. Restores your faith in the American family institution, doesn't it? Six days a week we're sweet as pie. Then on Saturdays we all get together and *kill* each other. It's our weekly catharsis."

"It looks a bit strenuous to me," Strode said easily. "I play a different kind of game myself."

"Aha! I suspect that was a subtle introduction of the subject of my House of Glass shares. Frankly, A.J., that game is a little out of my line. I don't know the rules."

"Have you thought over my offer?"

"I asked my brother Phil for advice, and you know what he told me? He said to beware of the big bad wolf!" He laughed so infectiously that Strode smiled back, even though he didn't find it funny at all. "That's a hell of a reputation you got yourself there, A.J. Why do you want House of Glass?"

It was the same old story. The minute A. J. Strode showed interest in a company, suddenly everyone else was interested too; even Jo Gillespie had reacted that way. He told Jack McKinstry the same thing he'd told her: "I'm going to shut it down. Sell your shares to me now and you won't take a licking."

Jack raised an eyebrow. "Shut it down? My, my—what did House of Glass ever do to warrant such harsh and inhumane treatment? A nice company that works hard and pays its taxes and builds a better world in which to live and all that." He rolled his eyes in mock horror. "And why, pray tell, is A. J. Strode so eager to save me money? Not that I doubt the purity of your motives, A.J.—never think that! I can see the altruism written all over your face. But as

Shakespeare so elegantly put it, what the fuck are you up to?'' He grinned.

Just then a young voice piped up, ''Uncle Jack! *Uncle Jack!*''

''Whoops, I'm up. Back in a few minutes.'' Jack trotted over to join the game, and an exhausted twelve-year-old boy sank heavily to the sand on the sideline.

Strode finished his lager and sat down on a beach chair. He and big brother Phil McKinstry caught each other's eye and exchanged nods; each knew the other by reputation. Strode sat watching and listening to the players yell *I got it*. One of the players was a particularly long-limbed young thing who didn't seem to be wearing any panties under her bright red short-shorts. He was going to have to get Jack away from the game to someplace they could talk free of distractions. A pier jutted out from the beach with two motorboats tied to it. The yacht—and Strode was sure there was a yacht—would be in a nearby marina. Out on the pier someone was working on the engine of one of the boats, leaving the other free; but Strode had no intention of getting into a smallish boat alone with Jack McKinstry. He looked along the beach toward an impressive outcropping of rock; that looked isolated enough to be private.

After a few more minutes of bone-jarring play, it was Jack's turn to serve but he flipped the ball to a teammate instead. ''Oh, Martha!'' he called out. ''Aunt-ie Mar-tha! Wouldn't this be a good time to give your poor aching bod a rest?''

''It would be a perfect time,'' panted an older woman on the opposing team. She left the game the same time as Jack; the two sides were still balanced.

''Let's walk,'' Strode said, and headed away from the volleyball game toward the rocks farther along the beach. Five steps and he had sand in his shoes. He felt sweat running down his back and took off his jacket. Strode was reminded of a certain photograph of Richard Nixon, taken as a part of the desperate last-ditch attempt to generate sympathy during the man's final days in office. The photo showed a preoccupied President walking on a California beach with a dog (later revealed to have been borrowed for the occasion); Nixon was wearing a dark business suit and tie and didn't seem to notice the seawater soaking his expensive city shoes. Strode felt as phony as Nixon looked in that staged photograph; god, how he wanted to be back in New York. He loosened his tie and wiped his face with his sleeve. When they got to the big outcropping of rock, Strode saw two rough paths leading through.

"The one on the left," Jack's bantering voice directed. "That path was hacked out of solid rock, at the expense of strained muscles, blistered hands, and several cases of terminal stoop—all to accommodate city softies such as yourself. You have to be a mountain goat to manage the other one."

Strode took the left path and once among the rocks began to think that hadn't been such a good idea. The footing was uneven and the path was so narrow they had to walk single file; it was hard to talk that way. "Does it get any wider?"

"Not much, but there's a place to sit down up ahead."

A minute later they came to a flat area. Strode lowered himself gingerly on to a bed-sized rock that was warm from the sun. Strode sat there uncomfortably, squinting at the sea and listening to the water slapping at the rocks below. Well, he'd done business in stranger places than this. He looked at the man sitting near him—so open, so friendly. Such a good actor.

He said, "All right, Jack, what's it going to be? I pay off the loan, you reclaim the shares you used as security and pass them on to me. I'll even see to it that you make a profit. So what do you say? A nice friendly sale we agree on right now?"

Jack laughed. "Oh me—I can almost hear you thinking *or else*. What are you going to threaten me with, A.J.?"

"I think you know. The minute you heard I was asking questions about your helicopter accident four years back, your pilot buddy dropped out of sight. Is that what you needed the loan for, Jack? To pay him to get lost?"

"You mean Billy? He's still living in Redondo Beach as far as I know. Haven't seen him for a while, though. All that business about the helicopter crash—that was a long time ago, in a galaxy far far away. It's over, man." Still smiling.

Strode grew impatient. "Enough of this, Jack. You were the one who set the time and place for this meeting. So I come here, I see the picture of family unity you want me to see, I get the message that the McKinstry clan is solidly behind you now. But do you know something? It doesn't make one damned bit of difference. I want your House of Glass shares, and you're going to let me have them. You're going to do it for the simple reason that you don't want brother Phil to find out you murdered four people because you owed one of them money."

The smile disappeared. "Hey hey, A.J.—that's not funny. Not funny at all!"

"It's not meant to be. You intended to kill all five of them when you flew that copter into the cliff, but one of them got away. Why didn't you just kill the pilot later, Jack? One more death shouldn't have bothered you."

Jack stood up slowly, his eyes boring holes in Strode's face. "You're out of your fuckin' mind, do you know that? Billy was flying that bird."

"Bullshit. Tony Dwyer was putting the screws on you for the money you owed him, and you sent three of your oldest and dearest to their deaths rather than pay up. When it came down to it, greed outweighed friendship. You call *me* a wolf? I'm a lamb compared to you.''

Jack looked as if he were entertaining thoughts of strangling Strode. The younger man said, slowly and carefully, ''I don't know what makes you think you can accuse me of a thing like that and get away with it. You try spreading that story and I'll have your balls on toast for breakfast.''

Strode snorted in derision and reached into his jacket pocket for an envelope which he handed to Jack. The envelope held a photocopy of the affidavit the pilot had signed.

A tic appeared under Jack's right eye as he read the paper through. ''It's his word against mine.''

''Yes, you can argue that if you think it'll do you any good. But don't you imagine the French police can find what my detective found—once they know there's a reason to look? The debt to Dwyer, the payoffs to Billy the pilot.''

''You didn't find any record of a payoff. You couldn't have.''

''Does it matter? All I have to do is make that paper public and the case will be reopened.'' Strode gave him his lupine smile. ''What do you suppose brother Phil will do when that happens, hmm?''

Jack growled low in his throat and tore the affidavit into pieces that he hurled angrily toward the sea. A breeze carried the pieces back and scattered them across the rocks. ''Don't bother telling me that was just a copy. I could see that!'' Abruptly Jack charged off deeper into the rocks; he scrambled over a boulder and was out of sight.

Strode used the time to empty the sand out of his shoes. His buttocks had grown numb from sitting on the rock; he stood up and gave his backside a brisk rub. Let Jack have his little tantrum; in the end he would do business. Then Strode

remembered something: Joanna Gillespie had charged off
into her bedroom in just that same way, and *she* had come
back with a gun in her hand. What if Jack was looking for
a hunk of rock just the right size to make a good head-
bashing weapon?

He was seriously considering leaving when Jack came
back—empty-handed, Strode was relieved to see. "I'm not
going to let you do this," Jack announced. "One thing you
don't know is that my brother and I are on better terms now
than we've ever been before in our lives. Phil already knows
I was at the controls when the autopilot locked. I told him
so, four years ago. *He's* the one who paid Billy to say he'd
been piloting. And he'll believe me when I tell him you've
bribed Billy to accuse me of murder—just to force me to sell
my House of Glass shares. Well, forget it, Strode. You're
not taking on just me but the whole McKinstry organiza-
tion. You're *never* going to get your hands on those shares."

Strode shook his head in disbelief. "You're not very
quick, are you, Jack? You don't have the sense to know
when you're over a barrel. Do you think I'm bluffing?"

"No, and neither am I. Don't try to bully me, Strode. I
won't let you."

"You're willing to risk a murder investigation rather than
give in to me, is that it? What do you think's going on here,
some boys' game?"

"I think you like making people crawl. Well, not this
time, old buddy. You'll have to get your kicks somewhere
else."

"You think that's all this is? Muscle flexing?"

"What else? I told you before, I'm not going to let you do
this to me." Jack paused. "Now we're going back. And
you're going to smile and act as if we're two good buddies
returning from a friendly little chat. Do it, Strode." He
started back along the way they'd come.

Strode had no choice but to follow. He was angry; the asshole was letting his pride get in the way of his own best interests. Strode wondered if Phil McKinstry really did know his younger brother had been at the helicopter controls instead of Billy. Jack was such a glib liar that nothing he said could be taken at face value.

The volleyball game was over. Two children were splashing in the water. Most of the players had gone into the house to shower or collapse, but a few remained on the beach. One of them, Strode was pleased to see, was the long-legged woman in the red shorts. He stopped by her and said, "That's a vigorous game of volleyball you play."

She grinned at him confidently. "Good for getting the kinks out. It's kind of hard on the younger kids, though."

Strode waited for Jack to introduce them, but his host remained pointedly mute. "You looked as if you were having more fun than any of the others," Strode said to the woman. "Were you?"

"Probably. I usually have fun."

"I thought so. I could tell by the way you moved. I couldn't help but notice the way you moved."

She laughed the same easy laugh as Jack's and said, "I saw you talking to Jack, Mr. . . . ?"

"Strode. Call me A.J."

"All right, A.J. I'm Wendy."

Strode smiled slowly. Wend-*ee*.

He was complimenting her on her service form when he felt Jack's hand come down on his shoulder like a vise. "Hey there, A.J., my man—you're not hittin' on my baby sister now, are you? Won't do you any good. She's already spoken for."

"That doesn't surprise me in the least," Strode murmured toward Wendy and was rewarded with a wink.

"Maybe we'll meet again," he called over his shoulder as Jack firmly steered him away.

Jack walked him up the stairway from the beach and around the house to where the limo was waiting. "If you ever so much as speak to her again," Jack said between his teeth, big grin fixed firmly in place, "I personally am going to cut off all your toes. Do you understand?"

Strode didn't answer. He climbed into the back of the limo and told the driver to get going. Only when they were well away did he relax.

For a moment there he'd been afraid. Afraid of Jack McKinstry! Who would have thought it? Strode didn't expect people on the wrong end of a squeeze play to be accommodatingly pliant; he'd even anticipated counterthreats. But this was the second time within a week that he'd been made to feel afraid—and he didn't like the feeling at all.

The more he thought about it, the angrier he got.

"THIS ISN'T GOING THE WAY it's supposed to," Strode muttered to Castleberry back in his office in New York. "One of them waves a gun at me and the other threatens me with dismemberment. Do the fools think I'm playing a game?"

"Joanna Gillespie has been trying to get you on the phone for the last three days," his assistant pointed out. "Maybe she's had time to see reason. She wants an appointment."

"If she thinks I'm going to put myself within firing distance of *her* again, she's got another think coming. Did anyone ever point a loaded gun at your face, Castleberry?"

"No, sir."

"It's a sobering experience, let me tell you. She's in New York now? Well, let's get her on the phone and hear what she has to say."

Whatever Jo Gillespie had to say, she wasn't willing to say it over the phone. Strode agreed to a meeting and hung up.

Castleberry was aghast. "You're not really going to meet her, are you?"

"No. You are. Take one of the security men with you, and make sure she understands he's armed. You won't need him, you know—it's not you she's mad at. But I'd like her to see that two can play that game. And Castleberry—if she demands the original affidavit her would-be hit man signed, tell her she'll get it when the stock ownership transfer papers are signed."

Castleberry smiled. "Will she?"

"Of course not."

When Castleberry had left, Strode walked over to the window and looked out. The dishy babe directly across the street was no longer there; the office was now occupied by a man. Strode watched for a few minutes as the man grew visibly more frustrated and agitated—until he ended up spanking his PC. Strode went back to his desk.

He took out a file folder and dropped it unopened on the desktop. He sat down and rested his clenched fists on the folder. He didn't want to have to deal with the third owner of House of Glass shares.

Strode was not a physically brave man. He kept more security than was absolutely necessary at both his home and his various businesses. Other than the usual boyhood scuffles, he'd never been in a fistfight in his life. He looked upon physical violence as a sign of ineptitude, as evidence of failure in the more sophisticated forms of persuasion. Now he was in the position of having to deal with three people who had killed for money; and of the three, the other man in Los Angeles was the most dangerous.

Strode had full confidence in his ability to outmaneuver the three who'd had to resort to violence to get what they wanted. But people who'd killed once would find it easier the next time. Look at Jo Gillespie; she'd let a year elapse between her first murder and her second, but she hadn't lost her nerve in the interim. He'd slipped when he'd gone to see her and McKinstry alone; he'd at least have had a witness to their threats if he'd taken Castleberry or another member of his staff along. Well, that was a mistake he wouldn't repeat. Even if Jack McKinstry calmed down enough to realize he had no choice and came crawling on his hands and knees, there'd be no more little tête-à-têtes on the beach.

Jack had threatened to go to his brother Phil with the story that Strode had fabricated evidence to make him look guilty. Strode was hoping that was exactly what he would do. Phil might believe Jack's story, might not; Strode didn't much care. But Phil McKinstry was a businessman; he'd know when it was time to deal. Strode was counting on him to knock some sense into Jack's head. If he didn't hear from somebody named McKinstry in the next couple of days, he'd send a copy of the affidavit to Phil.

What would Phil do then? He'd have several options. He could force Jack to sell his shares to Strode. He could refuse to clean up his brother's messes any longer and kick him out. He could be so horrified by what Jack had done that he'd turn him over to the police. Or, he could hire detectives to investigate the authenticity of the affidavit; but Strode had made sure Billy the pilot was well hidden away until this matter was settled. Billy was just a little too willing to take money from anyone who offered it.

All in all, Strode thought it most likely that Phil would simply kick Jack out. The current amity between the brothers had to be tenuous at best; Phil wouldn't risk the family and business name to cover up for a brother he already looked upon as something of a scapegrace. The only real danger was that he might turn his brother over to the police, thus defusing Strode's most potent weapon. But Strode didn't think Phil would go that far. And once Jack found himself on his own, he'd come around. But he might first think of solving this problem the same way he'd solved the Tony Dwyer problem four years ago. Well, he'd find A. J. Strode was no sitting duck.

Strode buzzed his secretary and told her he wanted to see the chief of security immediately.

IT WAS A TOSS-UP as to whether Myron Castleberry was more nervous or more curious; he'd never met a murderer before. Mr. Strode dealt with some pretty tough people—but a *killer*? Castleberry wasn't worried that Joanna Gillespie would whip out her gun and let him have it right between the eyes. Not here, not in a public place. But there was no way he could view her as just another business adversary. Jo Gillespie was different, to say the least.

Castleberry glanced over to the next table where the security guard was seated. She'd said Fiorello's at four; he and his guard had arrived early and taken two of the sidewalk tables. The inside of the restaurant was a little claustrophobic for a meeting such as this one. Not one to waste a gastronomic opportunity, the security guard had ordered a hot sausage sandwich and was making short work of it.

There she was. Castleberry watched her approach; Joanna Gillespie had an unattractive slouch and a don't-give-a-damn walk. She made her way through the crowd of strangers on the sidewalk, both fists thrust into the pockets of her jacket and a shoulder bag bouncing off one hip in rhythm to her walk. Castleberry stood and said, "Ms Gillespie? Mr. Strode has asked me to meet you. He—"

"He's not here?" she interrupted. "He agreed to come!"

This woman kills people, Castleberry reminded himself. "I'm sure you'll understand when I say Mr. Strode is reluctant to meet with you again in light of what happened last time. We have to take such threats seriously."

"Threats? Oh—you mean the gun?"

"I mean the gun." Castleberry was not prepared for her reaction; she burst out laughing. "It's not funny, Ms Gillespie."

"Yes it is! What about you? Aren't you afraid to meet me alone?" She laughed again.

Silently he gestured toward the next table. The guard moved his jacket just enough to let her see the shoulder holster he was wearing.

She stopped laughing. "Good lord, you are serious, aren't you? You needn't be, you know. It was just that he made me mad, the way he—" She broke off. "There's no way to explain it to someone who wasn't there. And why should I have to? Who are you, by the way?"

"My name is Myron Castleberry." He saw her eyes widen a fraction in recognition and wondered where she'd heard his name. "I'm Mr. Strode's executive assistant. Please sit down."

She sat. "Do you know that man you work for accused me of being a parricide?"

Parricide, Castleberry thought; that was the word he'd been looking for. Interesting that Joanna Gillespie should know it. "Are you sure you want to talk about that here?" In public, he meant.

"I'd just as soon not talk about it at all." She waved a waiter over and ordered antipasto. "I have to eat something during the afternoon," she explained. "Well, what happens now, Mr. Castleberry? Do you want to frisk me before taking me to see Strode?"

"You misunderstand, Ms Gillespie. Mr. Strode doesn't want to meet with you at all. He asks that you tell me whatever it is you have to say. I'm empowered to act on his behalf."

"Meaning you're going to make me another offer for my House of Glass shares. Don't bother. There won't be any deal."

Castleberry studied her face. Was the woman just stupid or did she have something up her sleeve? "Ms Gillespie, I'm sure Mr. Strode made it clear that—"

"Oh yes, he made it clear, all right. He's going to start a smear campaign against me unless I sell. He even got that idiot Ozzie Rogers to sign a paper that makes me look bad. That got me to thinking—how did A. J. Strode know about Ozzie in the first place? I mean, how did he know I'd seen Ozzie's ad and answered it?" She paused. "So I called Ozzie and asked him. He said Strode had wanted to hire him too. Isn't that interesting, Mr. Castleberry? What do you suppose an upright businessman like A. J. Strode would want with a hired gun?"

Castleberry was thinking that Mr. Strode would have found this scene amusing. "Go on."

"I asked Ozzie to put that in a letter and sign it, and he did. And it cost me only *two* thousand. He said my name came up during negotiations and Strode paid him five thousand dollars to sign an affidavit. Only it wasn't Strode himself Ozzie dealt with. He said it was some lackey named Thornberry or something like that."

Castleberry waited, not reacting to the dig.

"So you can tell your boss that if he has any ideas about publishing his little paper that Ozzie signed . . . he'd do well to remember I've got one too. And the newspapers would just *love* the one I've got. I brought a copy, in case you think I'm bluffing." She took a folded paper from her bag and put it on the table.

Amateur, Castleberry thought, ignoring the paper lying on the table. "Ms Gillespie, Mr. Strode has need for a large and highly qualified security force. The men provided by the

Rent-a-Cop agencies aren't quite what we need. So we're always on the lookout for someone sharper, quicker—"

"Like Ozzie Rogers?"

"No, not like Ozzie Rogers. We never made him an offer—we're not looking for Rambo. But we have hired several men whom we learned of through various gun magazines."

"Sure you have."

Castleberry inclined his head toward the guard at the next table. "We found him in *Soldier of Fortune*. And there are others. We can prove it, Ms Gillespie. My interviewing Ozzie Rogers was simply part of our ongoing search for good security men. There was nothing illicit or secret about it."

She stared at him.

"So I'm afraid you've wasted two thousand dollars," he went on. "When I first talked to Ozzie, he said he couldn't start immediately because he thought he'd be doing a job for some lady violinist he'd just met. Why did you tell him you're a violinist?"

She looked disgusted. "Ozzie wanted to shake hands when we met, and I refused—I have to be careful of my hands. Then of course I had to tell him why. *That's* how you traced me?"

"At the time it meant nothing. But when your parents died within a year of each other, I began to wonder if you were the lady violinist Ozzie had meant. Then when your name popped up as a House of Glass stockholder, I thought I'd better find out. It was a simple enough matter to show your photo to Ozzie."

The corners of her mouth turned down. "I hope Strode pays you well."

"Very well indeed." He looked her straight in the eye. "Ms Gillespie, take a word of advice. Don't try to play this game with Mr. Strode. He's too experienced and too ruthless. Sell the shares quickly and be done with it.''

"God, I hate being bullied!''

"Doesn't everybody? But you have no choice. I'm to tell you you'll get Ozzie Roger's affidavit the minute the transfer papers are signed.''

She gave him a disheartened smile. "And of course you won't be keeping any copies.''

"There are no copies. Mr. Strode will have no interest in your personal affairs once the stock is in his name. Incidentally, I'm empowered to make you another offer.''

She picked up the copy of Ozzie Rogers's letter and jammed it carelessly into her shoulder bag. "Put it in writing, will you? I'll have my financial manager look it over.''

"Look it over? Just tell him you want to sell.''

She sighed. "Mr. Castleberry, you got me this time, no question of that. But I know better than to make any decisions when I'm feeling this down. I'll think about it.''

Castleberry pursed his lips. "I'd advise you not to put it off too long. Mr. Strode is not a man of infinite patience.''

"I said I'll think about it.'' She got up from the table and walked away.

Castleberry and the guard exchanged a querying look. Was it a victory or not?

Just then the waiter came up with the antipasto Jo Gillespie had ordered. "Did the lady leave?''

The guard moved over to Castleberry's table. "I'll take it,'' he said, and started in on his third lunch of the day.

THREE

THE COMPANY JET TOUCHED down in Los Angeles around five in the afternoon, too late to do any business that day. Strode had planned it that way; he was not as physically resilient as he used to be, and he wanted a good night's sleep before tackling the man they had come to see. Castleberry never suffered from jet lag, but one of the two bodyguards they'd brought with them was looking a little peaked.

Two days had passed without a call from either Joanna Gillespie or Jack McKinstry. They were both going to lose money when he shut down House of Glass and they were both risking exposure as murderers by not selling to him. But still no word from either of them. There was only one explanation for that. They were both looking for a way to get A. J. Strode.

Regretfully Strode faced up to the fact that he'd run out of time. He had to close a deal for control of House of Glass and he had to do it fast. Then he had to send what he knew about the murderous activities of Gillespie and McKinstry to the appropriate police as well as publish the details in his newspaper. That's the only way he could be safe; he was convinced that neither the violinist nor the former playboy would hesitate to kill him if either ever found a way past his guard.

Unfortunately, there was only one stockholder left. His name was Richard Bruce, and Strode's file on him had been complete long before the other two. But what he'd learned about Bruce made him reluctant to move. Gillespie and McKinstry were small-time; Strode hadn't worried about dealing with them (although perhaps he should have, he now admitted). Richard Bruce, however, was a horse of a different color.

He was the sole owner of Bruce Shipping Lines, which consisted of a fleet of various-sized freighters that regularly sailed between Los Angeles and the Orient. Bruce had started nearly twenty years ago with one ship, the *Burly Girl*, a tramp steam freighter of 12,000 tons with a crew of thirty-seven. The *Burly Girl* was old and barely sea-worthy; the constant maintenance costs and the ever-escalating insurance premiums kept Bruce from being able to get ahead of the game. He was teetering on the edge of bankruptcy.

But an even greater threat to Bruce's solvency came along in the new and radical changes being made in the design and operation of cargo ships that were taking place about that time. The *Burly Girl* was built the way all freighters had been built for over a century—the stackhouse amidships, with three cargo holds forward of the engine and two aft. The cargo was loaded by means of huge derrick-supported nets, a method that had not basically changed since the days of ancient Rome.

The newer ships went about it differently. The engine, the superstructure, and the stack were all moved aft, leaving a long empty hull forward. The hull was then divided by vertical bulkheads into compartments to hold aluminum or steel cargo containers. The containers were loaded with their cargoes while still on the dock and then shifted directly into the hull compartments; the nets were dispensed with entirely. Loading order was determined by a shipboard computer; the introduction of automation cut the usual crew by over half. One of the new container ships could arrive in port with its crew of twelve or fifteen, unload its cargo, load a new one, and be gone in less time than it took the *Burly*

Girl just to unload. There was no way Richard Bruce could keep up with that kind of competition.

Then one August seventeen years earlier the *Burly Girl* sailed from Japan with a cargo primarily of textile machinery, with the remaining space taken up by refrigerators, sewing machines, and motorcycles. It was a full load; the *Burly Girl* was riding low in the water when she left Yokohama harbor. Just off Hawaii she ran into a squall that shouldn't have caused trouble but did. A distress signal was sent out indicating the crew was jettisoning the cargo. But it did no good. Old and tired, the *Burly Girl* just couldn't make it. Before help could arrive, she sank. All hands were lost.

There was much grumbling in the offices of the marine insurers in Los Angeles. The *Burly Girl* had been due for an examination by an insurance inspector upon her return, and everyone who knew the ship agreed she didn't have a chance in hell of passing the inspection. She'd been a serviceable ship in her day, but that day was long past. But the premium payments were up-to-date; the insurers had no choice but to pay.

The insurance check saved Richard Bruce's neck. Instead of replacing the *Burly Girl*, he bought shares in three of the new-style cargo ships. All three prospered; Bruce was on his way.

But then a Honolulu-based salvage company located the wrecked ship. The forward holds were still intact; and to everyone's surprise, the supposedly jettisoned cargo was still there. When the shipping crates were broken open, however, they were found to contain rusted auto parts, twisted scraps of metal, cast-off cast iron. Where the ship's manifest had said textile machinery, there was nothing but junk. What's more, divers uncovered evidence that the *Burly Girl* had been scuttled.

The engine room had been deliberately flooded; the inspection covers had been broken off the main condensers—a big job with two covers per condenser, and with no way it could have happened by accident. The divers looked further; they inspected the bilge suction lines running from each hold. In the aft starboard hold, they found the check valves had been taken out of the lines, causing them to pump seawater back into the hold. The flooding of either the hold or the engine room alone wouldn't have been enough to sink the ship; but the fact that the safeguards in both places had been removed made it clear as day that someone didn't want the *Burly Girl* to make it back to port.

The investigation took over a year. Eventually a shipping broker in Yokohama was found who admitted to arranging a sale of the missing cargo for the captain of the *Burly Girl*. The broker protested that Captain Stone had presented the proper bill of lading, which he himself had had no reason to suspect of being bogus. The cargo had been loaded on another freighter and shipped to San Francisco.

Captain Stone had obviously scuttled the *Burly Girl* to hide his theft of the cargo, and he'd sailed directly into the squall as a cover. But how could one man alone steal an entire ship's cargo? He must have had help. It would have been virtually impossible to hide something like that from the first mate; the mate must have been in on it. And Captain Stone must have had an accomplice standing by in a boat to pick him up. But what of the rest of the crew? There'd been thirty-five other men on board in addition to the captain and the mate. Had Stone just abandoned them?

Something else the salvage company's divers had found: the remains of two bodies in the engine room. There was no way of telling how many, if any had been swept out to sea. Perhaps the men had been evacuated, except for the two unfortunate hands who'd been trapped below. But since none of the crew had reappeared anywhere, it seemed more likely that the captain's rescue plan included only himself and the first mate or whoever it was who'd helped him. But whichever way it had happened, at least two men had died as the result of the commission of a felony. A warrant for murder was issued in Captain Stone's name.

Richard Bruce's insurers had screamed there was no way the ship's owner could not have been in on the plot. What a remarkable coincidence, they proclaimed sarcastically, that all this should happen just before the *Burly Girl* was due for inspection—an inspection everyone knew she couldn't pass. But after months of digging, the investigators were able to turn up no evidence to indicate that the owner had had so much as an inkling of what Captain Stone was planning. Richard Bruce was completely exonerated.

All that had been seventeen years earlier. Captain Stone had never been found, nor any other survivor of the *Burly Girl*'s last voyage. All but the captain were declared legally dead after seven years had passed, even the first mate; there was no proof he had conspired with the captain, only speculation. The three ships in which Richard Bruce had invested the insurance money had done so well that eventually he was able to buy out his partners. Over the years Bruce added to his fleet whenever he could until now Bruce Shipping Lines was one of the dominant names in the overseas freight business.

That's where things stood at present. A. J. Strode had studied all the records of the investigation of the sinking of the *Burly Girl* and said to Castleberry, "Thirty-five dead sailors mean thirty-five grieving women somewhere. Find them. One of them might know something. Check the captain's and the mate's families too."

So Myron Castleberry had sent Pierce to Los Angeles. The New York detective had hired a firm of California detectives to help him. They'd been able to track down twenty-seven of the regular crew's families, but none of them knew any more than what the records showed. Captain Stone's wife had died five years earlier, but a daughter was now living in San Diego. She was of no help, however; she'd been only ten at the time of the incident.

The first mate's widow had been located in Venice. And she knew something.

Pierce reported that the first time he tried to question her she'd grown alarmed and almost panicked. He'd gone back several times, trying to find out what she was so frightened of. The woman's name was Estelle Rankin, and she didn't want to talk about the man she'd been married to. Mrs. Rankin kept saying things like *It was all so long ago* and *Why dredge all that up now?* But eventually it became clear to Pierce that the first mate's widow was afraid of Richard Bruce.

Castleberry flew out to see her. He found a woman down on her luck and depressed. The monthly stipend paid her by the Maritime Widows Pension Fund was not enough to live on; for the past seventeen years she'd been working at a series of petty jobs, each less remunerative than the last as she aged and became less attractive as an employee. Now she was working part-time at a food concession on Venice Fishing Pier and hated it. In other words, she was ripe.

Castleberry quickly caught on that Mrs. Rankin was afraid of losing her pension if her late husband was proved guilty of complicity in the sinking of the *Burly Girl*. Castleberry offered her double her monthly pension payment for the rest of her life if she could come up with some information they could use. Still she hesitated. If she was afraid of someone, Castleberry suggested tactfully, his employer would gladly underwrite her moving expenses if she wished to relocate to another part of the country. She said that for the last few years she'd been thinking of moving to Oregon. He said Oregon was a nice place to live.

Only when Castleberry handed her a contract signed by A. J. Strode himself was she willing to talk. Once she was assured of both her safety and her financial future, she couldn't talk enough. She'd kept it all bottled up for seventeen years, and now it just came pouring out.

Scuttling the *Burly Girl* had been Richard Bruce's idea, Mrs. Rankin said. For his part in the plan, Captain Stone was to receive whatever he could sell the cargo for. But he couldn't manage alone, so he offered to split with his first mate in return for his help. Harry wasn't a bad man, Mrs. Rankin apologized; it was just that things had been going badly for them and they were getting a little desperate for money. She made Castleberry uncomfortable; the woman was pleading with a stranger for understanding, seventeen years after her husband's death.

She'd begged him not to go through with it, she said; but once Captain Stone had approached him, Harry Rankin's fate was sealed. He was afraid to back out; Richard Bruce was a man you didn't cross. So Harry and Captain Stone agreed to divert the real cargo in Yokohama and have crates of junk loaded in its place. They were going to delay sailing until they got the kind of weather they needed to pull it off: bad, but not too bad. Captain Stone showed his mate the place on the charts where Richard Bruce would be waiting with a boat large enough to take aboard the entire thirty-seven-man crew of the *Burly Girl*.

At least that was the plan. But in his last letter to his wife, mailed in Japan, Harry Rankin had expressed doubts that he'd been told the whole story. Over and over he'd asked Captain Stone if he was sure the entire crew would be taken aboard Bruce's boat and not just the two of them. The captain had said, yes, yes, they'll all be safe. But his first mate was suspicious; he'd seen the captain lie too many times before not to recognize the signs.

A letter? Castleberry asked, hoping against hope. She wouldn't still happen to have it, would she?

She would. The ink was faded but the writing was perfectly legible. There it was, the incriminating evidence they'd been looking for. Harry Rankin didn't mind a little stealing in a good cause, but leaving thirty-five men behind to die— he'd balked at that. Harry wrote his wife that he planned to stick to Captain Stone like a leech. It was the only thing he could think to do.

Castleberry folded the letter and put it back in its envelope. "Is that what you think happened? Bruce took off your husband and the captain but left the others?"

She shook her head. "Even if Harry decided to run out on me, he wouldn't have left me dangling all these years. There would have been a postcard, something. No, my husband's dead, I know that. He never got off that ship."

Castleberry watched her pinched face and guessed she must be imagining what it was like, those last moments on the *Burly Girl*. "Then what? The captain, er, overpowered your husband and left him behind with the others?"

"I don't see how. Harry was a big, husky man, Mr. Castleberry. Captain Stone was a shrimp. If there was any overpowering done, it would have gone the other way."

Castleberry understood. "You're saying Richard Bruce left them *all* to drown, Captain Stone included. He didn't show up with the rescue boat."

She frowned. "They wouldn't have scuttled her without first making sure he was out there waiting for them. There had to be a signal of some sort. The ship sank at night, you know. I think he showed up, flashed a light or sent off a flare or whatever they'd agreed on, and then simply pulled away once he saw the *Burly Girl* going down. Richard Bruce deliberately murdered all those men—just to collect an insurance check.''

Castleberry was as appalled as she sounded. ''Does Richard Bruce know about this letter? He'd have paid a lot for it.''

The look she gave him made him wish he hadn't said anything. ''Extort money from the man who killed my husband? What kind of person do you think I am?''

''I'm sorry, Mrs. Rankin. Of course you wouldn't make money off your husband's death. I know that. I just wanted to make sure Richard Bruce doesn't know anything about this letter. He doesn't, does he?''

''No. I thought of taking it to the police. But they'd want me to testify to what Harry told me of the plan…and I was afraid. Any man who'd murder an entire ship's crew wouldn't stop at killing one lone woman. Besides, the pension fund might stop my payments…'' She made a vague gesture with one hand.

Castleberry assured her she wouldn't have to worry about money anymore. Over the next few days he got her to sign a statement, arranged with a moving company to transport her household goods to Oregon, and left her with enough cash for a plane ticket. She seemed relieved at having finally told someone, and Castleberry sincerely wished her well.

Back in New York, A. J. Strode had been every bit as appalled as Castleberry when he learned what Richard Bruce had done. He and his assistant agreed immediately that Harry Rankin's letter to his wife should be turned over to the police just as soon as Strode was finished with it. But the letter stayed in the file folder; at the time Strode still had Joanna Gillespie and Jack McKinstry to try, and he didn't want to do anything about Richard Bruce until he was sure of House of Glass.

The man was too dangerous; he had to be utterly conscienceless. In addition to that, Strode's search for House of Glass stock was costing him an arm and a leg. He totted up his expenses so far and added in what he planned to pay for the stock, assuming someone would sell. He compared the total to a projection provided by his analysts as to his profit over a five-year period if House of Glass were eliminated from the competition. When he saw the takeover would pay for itself in a year, he knew he had to go back to California.

It was standard operating procedure for Strode to dig up something reprehensible or at least disreputable from an adversary's past and use it as a cattle prod. But in nearly forty years of doing business, he had never once had to deal with someone who took human life to get what he wanted. He'd dealt with people who killed indirectly—by ignoring safety precautions for their workers, by putting lethal products on the market. Killing a whole town by shutting down the only source of employment in order to get a tax write-off. But that was business; that went with the territory. But actually planning a murder and then carrying it out with one's own two hands... that was something from another world.

But then he'd set his sights on House of Glass and found himself up against not one killer but three. That made even A. J. Strode pause. Could he have dealt with killers before and not known it? But that wasn't the immediate problem; right now he had to concern himself with Joanna Gillespie, Jack McKinstry, and Richard Bruce. Among them they were responsible for the deaths of forty-three people. Gillespie killed her family and McKinstry killed his friends, but for sheer numbers Richard Bruce was the winner hands down. *Hands down* indeed. *All* hands had gone down, in the stormy Hawaiian waters seventeen years ago. Richard Bruce had seen to that.

This was the man they'd come to Los Angeles to meet.

THEIR APPOINTMENT was for eleven. When Castleberry arranged for a limo to pick them up, he'd asked for a driver familiar with the port area. Los Angeles harbor covered nearly thirty miles of coastline; everything was well marked, but it was still easy to get lost there. The driver took the Harbor Freeway to the West Basin, where Richard Bruce's office was located.

On the way Castleberry was still trying to talk Strode out of it. "You don't know what else he might have done," he argued. "One of his competitors conveniently died in an accident, you know. And Bruce is a widower—maybe he killed his wife. And a harbormaster who was giving him trouble simply disappeared. Disappeared! Mr. Strode, you shouldn't even be in the same *city* with this man!" The two bodyguards were listening with interest.

"Aren't you letting your imagination run away with you?" Strode asked testily, not liking Castleberry's uncharacteristically tactless implication that he was no match for Richard Bruce. "Nobody can go around killing whenever he feels like it and *never* get caught. He's not Superman, for god's sake. I don't want to deal with him, but I'm not going in with my eyes closed. I know what I'm up against."

"Then stay in the car with one of the guards and let me talk to him. Better still, just mail him the envelope. You don't have to see him in person."

"That's where you're wrong. A man like Bruce won't tamely follow instructions that come in the mail. He's going to have to see for himself that I'm not just making noise for the fun of it. And I want to make this as easy for him as I can. Just another business deal.''

Sure it is, Castleberry's face said.

Bruce Shipping Lines occupied a five-story building, with the owner's offices on the top floor. An unsmiling secretary ushered them in.

The inner office gleamed with polished wood, even the floor. Richard Bruce was standing at his desk, his back to a wide window that looked out over the harbor. He was leaning over a set of printouts but stood up straight when Strode and company walked in, showing an almost military bearing. Bruce had a composed, expressionless face and a compact body, carrying no extra weight. Not too tall, in his early fifties, black hair with dramatic gray streaks in it. Bruce was a well-tailored man; he wore his obviously expensive suit with ease. The man was downright elegant. Castleberry thought he could have posed for a chamber of commerce advertisement depicting an idealized version of the successful American businessman.

One of Strode's guards stayed outside and closed the office door behind them. The other positioned himself with his back to the door. Bruce noticed the arrangement but made no comment. He fixed his eyes on Strode and waited; *he* was not the one who'd requested this meeting.

''May I sit down?'' Strode asked, sitting down. ''Thank you.'' He'd deliberately placed himself on an inferior level, having to look up to Bruce when he spoke. The message was clear. He was so sure of his position, he didn't have to play that particular upmanship game—which, of course, was an upmanship game itself. ''I won't beat around the bush, Mr. Bruce. I want your House of Glass shares.''

Bruce let a beat pass before he answered. ''So do I.'' His voice was musical and not as deep as might be expected.

"You've had that stock for less than a year. I understand you accepted it as payment from a shipper whose account had gotten out of hand?"

Bruce's left eyebrow raised a fraction. *None of your damned business*, the eyebrow said.

"You'll make a profit if you sell to me now," Strode went on.

"Yes, I'm aware of that, but I think I'll hold on to the shares."

"Even when I tell you I plan to shut House of Glass down?"

"Even so. You can't shut down without my shares."

It struck Strode that Bruce already knew about his plans; he wasn't surprised to hear of the intended shutdown and he needed no time to think it over before he replied. The shipowner had been doing a little checking of his own; Strode wondered what else the man knew about him. Right there and then he abandoned any further attempt at gentlemanly persuasion. "Castleberry?"

Still standing, Castleberry juggled his briefcase and took out a large manila envelope which he laid on top of the printouts on Bruce's desk. "You'll want to take a look at this, Mr. Bruce."

Bruce kept his eyes on Strode a moment. Then he sat down at his desk and slowly picked up the envelope. Inside was a copy of Estelle Rankin's statement and a copy of her husband's last letter; the latter had been inserted into the original envelope. Bruce read the letter first. When he came to the signature, he lifted his eyes to Strode and asked, "Harry?"

"Harry Rankin," Castleberry answered for Strode. "The first mate on the *Burly Girl*."

Bruce turned over the envelope and looked at the address.

"She's not there anymore," Castleberry said hurriedly. "And she has a new name."

Bruce gave a barely perceptible nod, as if expecting something like that. He read Mrs. Rankin's statement through twice. "She's willing to swear to this in court?"

"Yes, she is," Castleberry answered. "Would you like a notarized letter from her saying so?"

Bruce ignored him and went back to read parts of the statement again; he'd not once looked at Castleberry the whole time. After a few moments Bruce put the papers back in the manila envelope. "So. Because of someone who used to be named Estelle Rankin, I must sell you my shares in House of Glass? Is that it?"

"That's about the size of it," Strode said. "Let's keep it friendly, Bruce. A quick deal and we'll be out of each other's hair."

"Oh no, it's not as simple as that. It also involves making an enemy."

That didn't bother Strode. "I make enemies every day of my life. You're just today's."

Bruce looked amused. "Oh, that's the way it is, is it? I'm merely a minor obstacle to be dealt with, of temporary significance only. I see you have no use for subtlety. Don't bother trying to intimidate me, Strode—that never works in this office. I ask you to think again before proceeding with this."

"Not necessary. I want those shares and I will have them."

"We have nothing to do with each other, Strode—let's keep it that way. It'll be to your benefit as well as mine. I'll buy that letter from you. Fifty thousand."

Strode looked annoyed. "You know damn well House of Glass is worth a lot more to me than that. Why are you so determined to hang on to those shares?"

"I don't give a hoot about House of Glass, other than as a minor investment. But I care even less for the thought that what's mine can be so easily stripped away from me."

"Better get used to the idea, then, because that's exactly what's going to happen. You're no fool, Bruce. You know I'll use that letter against you if you block me. I'm not just blowing smoke. I'll *get* you. I'll send you to the gas chamber and not lose any sleep over it."

Bruce's eyes narrowed. "Yes," he said slowly, drawing it out, "you would do that, wouldn't you?" The words *you bastard* hung unspoken in the air.

Then Bruce stood up and moved over to the window overlooking the West Basin; there was no carpeting on the floor, but still he made no noise when he walked. Castleberry retrieved the envelope Harry Rankin's letter had come in and put it back in his briefcase, leaving the rest of the papers on the desk.

They waited.

At last Bruce turned from the window. The other men could see no change in him; his facial expression told them nothing. He looked straight at Strode and said softly, "It seems you have me."

Castleberry looked relieved; Strode did not. "It's a straightforward business deal," the latter said. "You have something I want, I have something you don't want made public. A swap."

"What guarantee do I have you won't use those papers against me anyway?"

"None, other than my assurances." Strode tried his lupine smile and got no response. "Look, Bruce, I'm not interested in doing the police's work for them. The originals will be yours as soon as you sign the transfer papers."

"And the Rankin woman's new name and address?"

"No. Silence is part of of my deal with *her*."

"I want her name and address," Bruce insisted.

"Sorry, but I can't be party to...whatever you might have in mind. But you don't have anything to fear from Mrs. Rankin. She's kept quiet for seventeen years. If she was going to do anything, she'd have done it by now. When I drop the matter, so will she."

Bruce's eyes narrowed into an icy glaze. "Would you accept a guarantee as thin as that?"

"If I had no choice."

"I see. I'm to take your word for it not only that this woman will keep quiet but you will too, you and however many of your people know about it." He waved an arm in the direction of the bodyguard standing by the door, still ignoring Castleberry. "I wouldn't call that much of a guarantee."

Strode returned his icy stare. "You prefer the alternative?"

Bruce spread his hands on the desk and leaned his weight on them. "No, I do not prefer the alternative." The two men were locked in eye contact, excluding the others in the room from their private battle of wills. Finally Bruce said, "Your terms are abominable, Strode, but I see I have no choice but to accept them. I presume you've already prepared the transfer papers?"

At Strode's nod, Castleberry dipped into his briefcase again and came up with a legal paper.

Bruce gave it a cursory glance and dropped it into a desk drawer. "I'll want my attorney to look it over. If it's a standard form, then we'll arrange another meeting. I will not send you my shares and wait for you to get around to mailing me the originals of that letter and the Rankin woman's statement."

"That is satisfactory." Strode stood up. "I'll expect to hear from you soon." Without another word he turned and walked out of the office. Castleberry and the guard followed, as did the guard who'd stationed himself outside the office door.

Castleberry couldn't contain himself. On the way to the limousine, he kept congratulating Strode. "We should have tried him first! He's not a fool like those other two. He knows when it's time to deal."

Strode didn't share his enthusiasm. "What an icy son of a bitch he is. Did you notice, Castleberry? No protestations of innocence—not one. He didn't lose his temper or complain it wasn't fair or threaten to get me. He assessed the situation and made his decision, period."

"You mean it was too easy? But he saw he didn't have any choice." Castleberry opened the limo door for Strode. "He's not like Joanna Gillespie or Jack McKinstry. Bruce isn't the kind of man to get emotional and have a temper tantrum."

"That's what I mean," Strode said, getting in. "Cold-blooded bastard."

Their route took them past a string of loading docks. Big yellow cranes were at work lifting and moving, and once the limo had to stop to allow one of them to maneuver its way past. "I once owned part of the company that makes those things," Strode mused when the limo started moving again. "About thirty years ago."

"Lawton-Moore," nodded Castleberry, who knew all his boss's investments past and present. "Slow growth."

"I probably wouldn't think so now," Strode smiled. "Nothing moved fast enough for me in those days."

Castleberry was prevented from answering by the heart-stopping *screeeeech* that automobile tires make when a car's brakes are slammed on suddenly. The limo's passengers pitched forward. Before the screech had died there came a thunderous crash from the impact when one of the bodyguards was out of the car, gun in hand. The other guard pushed Strode to the floor and threw himself over him. No one spoke.

After a few moments the first bodyguard came back, dragging a man in coveralls with him. "It was the crane arm," the guard told the others in the limo. "Fell right across the hood—smashed it flat. I've got the crane operator here." He turned to the man in coveralls. "And he's going to show me exactly how this accident happened—*isn't he?*" The man nodded dumbly; he was terrified of the gun the guard was still holding. The guard dragged him away.

The other guard got off of Strode and helped him back to his seat. When Castleberry's heart left his throat and went back to where it belonged, he stepped out of the limo to survey the damage. Seen up close, the crane arm was huge. The engine was indeed smashed flat; but the windshield, which had popped loose at the bottom, didn't have a crack in it. It was that close. Another few feet and the limo driver would be dead. Another few *yards* . . .

Castleberry wrestled the front door open and helped the driver out. The man was white with fear and shaking, but other than a small cut over one eyebrow he was unhurt. "Thank god you've got good reflexes, man," Castleberry said earnestly. "If you hadn't stopped in time, we'd all have been killed. Mr. Strode isn't going to forget this. You'll be taken care of." He wasn't sure the driver even heard him.

About a dozen men had run up to the accident site and were busy saying *Are you all right?* and *Christ, will you look at that?* and other similarly helpful things. Castleberry went over to where the crane operator was showing Strode's bodyguard what had happened. A chain had slipped off its cogwheel, he said, causing him to lose control of the boom. He'd felt it slipping and tried to swivel the boom away from the limo but the controls hadn't responded fast enough. He sure was sorry, Mister, but there wasn't nothin' he coulda done to stop it.

The teeth on the wheel were badly worn; it was easy to see how the chain could have slipped off. "Don't you ever get your equipment inspected?" the bodyguard demanded.

"Sure we do," the operator said, "and on a regular basis, too. There wasn't nothin' wrong the last time it was checked. You can ask my boss."

"Who is your boss?" Castleberry asked. "I don't mean your supervisor—I mean who's your employer?" The name the operator gave was not that of Richard Bruce, Castleberry was relieved to hear. He asked the guard to find a phone and call a cab. Then he went back to speak to the limo driver.

The man had gotten over his shock and was now the picture of gloom and doom. "Not the Rolls," he moaned. "Not the goddamfuckin' *Rolls*. My boss'll kill me!"

"No, he won't," Castleberry said, "not when I finish talking to him. In fact, he'll probably give you a raise. And remember, you'll be getting something from Mr. Strode. I'll make sure he understands you saved his life." The driver actually smiled at that. "I've sent for a cab. Do you want to come with us, or...?"

"I have to stay with the Rolls. You're not going, are you? I have to report this."

Castleberry handed him a business card. "Tell your insurance investigator we'll be happy to talk to him at any time. But right now we must get back to New York. Don't worry—I'll call your boss as soon as we get in."

The cab eventually arrived. Strode was silent all the way to the airport, and Castleberry and the two guards took their cue from him. Even the cab driver picked up on the tension and kept his mouth shut.

Only when they were airborne did Strode finally speak. "He tried to kill me," he muttered. "The son of a bitch actually tried to kill me!"

Castleberry took a deep breath. "Mr. Strode, I don't think he did. It was just what it appeared to be—an accident." He explained about the worn teeth on the cogwheel.

Strode made a derisory sound. "Of course he'd want it to look like an accident. Don't be naïve, Castleberry. That crane was meant to smash *me*."

"But how could he set up something like that in so little time? From the time we left his office to the time the boom fell on the limo...it couldn't have been more than ten minutes."

"He had it set up ahead of time—just in case he needed it. All it took to get it going was a phone call."

"But how did he know which route we'd take?"

"How do you know that crane was the only one waiting for us?"

"But the operator doesn't even work for Richard Bruce!"

"Uh-huh. You're taking his word for that, are you?"

Castleberry had no answer. Anyone would be a little paranoid after what had just happened, but it seemed to him that his boss was assuming too much. "Mr. Strode, why would he try to kill you before he got hold of the evidence you have against him? That wouldn't make any sense. But I could have Pierce investigate the crane operator if you like."

"Do that." Strode turned his head and stared out a window. The subject was closed.

When they got back to New York, Strode's secretary told him that both Jack McKinstry and Joanna Gillespie had called agreeing to sell their shares of House of Glass.

A. J. STRODE was taking the day off.

He sat in the upstairs library of his big house, staring out a window without seeing anything. The place seemed empty with Katie gone. He didn't count the staff or the security guard who sat staring at a bank of television monitors. Or the outside man who checked windows and doors and manned the front gate. They weren't personal; Katie was. She'd left her mark on every room in the house, indulging her decorating skills as well as her acquisitive instincts. Strode had found himself an art collector during Katie's tenure; she'd made some good buys, he'd been told. She'd gradually replaced almost every piece of furniture in the place; the leather lounger he was sitting in had been one of her purchases. She might as well have spray-painted *Katie was here* on the walls.

Thank god she was gone.

The son of a bitch had tried to kill him. The other two had threatened, but Richard Bruce had actually done it, or tried to. He didn't waste time on threats, that one. When Strode had started his pursuit of House of Glass, he'd needed only one stockholder to agree to sell. Now he had all three of them, right where he wanted them. Bruce's attorney had approved the stock ownership transfer papers and the shipowner had requested a meeting, just as if nothing had happened. But with the other two at last giving in, Strode was now in a position to pick and choose.

Not that it would help the seller any. Strode wanted, without exception, to ruin all three of them. He wanted to *hurt* them. These people were killers, for god's sake, and they were all mad at *him*. Not that he'd expected anything less, but he hadn't anticipated how blatant they'd all be about it. But it didn't matter now; he had them all in the palm of his hand.

He'd choose one, make the deal, and then turn them all in; it was the only way he could protect himself. He'd send the file folders with their painstakingly acquired and damning evidence to the police. He'd tell the Los Angeles police what Richard Bruce had done, he'd tell the Boston police what Joanna Gillespie had done, he'd tell the French police—in Toulon, was it?—what Jack McKinstry had done. And he'd make sure the newspapers got the story. All the newspapers, not just his. He'd make sure their pretty lives would never be the same again, what was left of them.

Bruce ought to get the death sentence, in California. But he might not; it depended on the judge. Or wait a minute—the *Burly Girl* had gone down in Hawaiian waters; wouldn't Bruce be tried in Hawaii? As to McKinstry...Strode had no idea what would happen to McKinstry. He knew nothing of the French system of justice. But Gillespie would plead mercy killing and be out again after serving a few years. That's what would happen.

Strode scowled at the picture he'd just conjured up. No. A thousand times no.

It wasn't enough.

He got up from the lounger and stood at the window staring down at one of the servants sweeping the patio. He raised his eyes to the street, oblivious to whatever was there. A small boy holding on to his mother's hand looked up and waved; Strode didn't see him. Ruining those three just wasn't enough. He wanted to get them, really get them, and get them in a way that all three would understand how hopelessly outclassed they were when they tried to play hardball with A. J. Strode. Get them so they would know they had been *got*.

Strode leaned both hands on the windowsill, pressing his forehead against the cool pane of glass. He stood like that for a long time. When at last he'd decided, he called Castleberry at the office and told him to come over.

ONE OF THE DOWNSTAIRS rooms was maintained as a small conference room; it was there Strode met with Castleberry. "I've reached a decision," he informed his assistant. "This House of Glass business is going to be settled this weekend, one way or another."

"You've decided?" Castleberry asked with interest. "Which one?"

"I won't know until the weekend's over."

Castleberry blinked. "How's that? What are you going to do?"

Strode placed the palms of his hands flat on the small conference table, savoring the telling. "I'm going to get all three of them together this weekend. I'm going to give each one a copy of the contents of the file we have on him—and her. I want them to see exactly how much we've dug up."

"They won't love you for that."

"Then I'm going to tell them I need only one block of shares to give me control of House of Glass," Strode went on. He laughed. "And I'm going to leave it up to them to decide which of them sells to me. I set the price, but they choose the seller. *They* decide. And here's the stinger, Castleberry. The two that don't sell get the privilege of seeing their names on the front page of Monday's newspapers. Those two will be made to understand I'm sending the original files to the police. One survives, two do not. And they get to pick the survivor."

Castleberry was awestruck. He swallowed and said, "Mr. Strode, that's...*diabolical!* Mephistophelian!"

Strode laughed. "Thank you! By god, Castleberry, I haven't felt this good since we started this business. Those three are going to learn the hard way they can't threaten *me* and get away with it!"

Still in something of a daze, his assistant got up, walked around the conference table, and sat down again. "Where will they be meeting?"

"Here. In this house."

Castleberry shot back out of his seat. "You can't mean that! You're going to meet those three *right here* where they can—"

"No, no—I'm not going to be here at all! I'll go stay with Tracy. They'll only *think* I'm going to be here."

"But still, bringing those three murderous people together under your roof—"

"Yeah, I don't much like that. I thought of booking them all into the same hotel, but I couldn't be sure they'd come if I did that. They have to think they have a chance of getting at me, don't you see? I'm the bait."

"Well, if you stay with Tracy all the time—"

"I won't budge out of her apartment all weekend. Sit down, Castleberry, and stop worrying. Listen, no one of them will know the other two are coming. I'll send each one an offer to return the incriminating evidence—on condition that the deal is settled here, this weekend. They'll all come thinking they might get a shot at the big bad wolf in his own lair." He grinned at his assistant's expression. "Yeah, I know what they call me behind my back. But those three little pigs will come, Castleberry. They'll come because they want to get me."

"And you won't see any of them? At any time?"

"None of them, ever. And you'll see them only long enough to give them my terms. I think I'll tape it. That way you won't have to hang around. We'll just leave the three of them together and see what happens."

"Good lord." Castleberry took out a handkerchief and blotted the perspiration on his forehead. "I wonder which one of them will win."

Strode grunted. "My money's on Richard Bruce. He makes the other two look like babies."

"Maybe," his assistant said cautiously. "How in the world are they ever going to decide? Mr. Strode, do you know what might happen? Those three people could end up killing one another!"

Strode smiled his lupine smile. "Now wouldn't that be a pity," he said contentedly.

PART 2

The Suspects

FOUR

ONE DECENT THING about Myron Castleberry—he didn't gloat. He even managed to sound sympathetic as he explained that A. J. Strode didn't want to talk just then but would settle accounts with me during the upcoming weekend. At the time I was so dejected it didn't even occur to me that "settle accounts" might have more than one meaning. Then I understood I was expected to spend the weekend in Strode's home; I said I'd stay in a hotel. But Castleberry insisted that Mr. Strode wouldn't hear of it. He was very smooth about it; he managed to make Strode's command that I come to his home off Park Avenue on Friday afternoon sound like a genuine invitation. I protested I couldn't go an entire weekend without practicing, and Castleberry told me to bring my violin with me if I wished. That made me laugh. I had no intention of taking something as clean and pure as the Guarnerius into A. J. Strode's house and risk contaminating it.

Nevertheless, the so-called invitation surprised me. If Strode was as frightened of my pointing a gun at him as he claimed to be, what was he doing bringing me right into his home? It was almost as if he were inviting me to take a shot at him. And why an entire weekend? How long does it take to sign a set of papers? Strode had something up his sleeve, but I couldn't begin to guess what. What else could he do to me? He already had me where he wanted me. But if the only way I could get my hands on the affidavit that that fool Ozzie Rogers had signed was to go for the weekend, then I'd go for the weekend.

I'd seen my lawyer in Boston; the papers Castleberry had forwarded were checked and officially pronounced proper and aboveboard. I didn't tell my financial manager I was selling; it would be easier simply to present him with a *fait accompli*. Similarly, I did not at first inform Harvey Rudd where I'd be over the weekend. I left a message on his answering machine that I wanted to get away for a few days and I'd call him Monday morning. Poor Harvey; he'd be tearing his beard out by Saturday night. Then I had second thoughts. Entrust myself to A. J. Strode for two and a half days without letting anyone know where I was? That wasn't one of my brighter ideas. I called back and left another message telling Harvey exactly where I was going and how to reach me. Then on Friday I'd casually mention to Strode that I was expecting a call from my assistant. A little insurance never hurts.

What was the man up to? I'd be hard put to name someone in the world I detested more than A. J. Strode. That slimy, grasping man actually thought I'd killed my parents for money. There are times when it's simply impossible to *rise above* what other people think of you, as we're always being told we ought to do, and this was one of them. Ozzie Rogers was the biggest mistake I ever made in my life; I knew two minutes after I met him that a Texas mercenary couldn't solve my problems for me. And now Ozzie himself was the problem. To tell the truth, I didn't mind giving up my House of Glass shares all that much; the company meant nothing to me and I could always reinvest the money elsewhere. But I had only Castleberry's word for it that Strode would keep no copies of Ozzie's affidavit. Strode was a vengeful man, and I had made the mistake of failing to kowtow when the Great One had made his wishes known. He could easily ruin me just out of spite.

I *loathe* being coerced.

Perhaps he just wanted to gloat a little; that certainly seemed in character. If a weekend of letting Strode stick needles in me would keep him out of my life from now on, then that was a price I was willing to pay. So I showed up at the big house in Manhattan late Friday afternoon. An armed guard at the gate checked my name on his clipboard and let me in.

Castleberry met me at the door, his mouth full of apologies about how Mr. Strode had been detained but would see me at dinner. The interior was about what one would expect—large rooms with high ceilings, ostentatious furnishings chosen primarily and perhaps solely to show off the owner's wealth. I glanced into the living room, a misnomer if there ever was one; the place looked more like an art gallery than a space to live in. Spotlighted paintings, museum-quality furniture, niches in the walls to show off the modern sculpture. There were even *display cases*. In a room just off the foyer I could see another guard, seated before a bank of television monitors. One of the screens was a regular TV tuned to a game show with the sound turned down. The other screens showed rooms and hallways; a few were dark.

I objected. "I can't be spied on like this—this won't do at all."

Castleberry assured me my privacy would be respected. "Most of the cameras are located on the first floor and outside the house. Upstairs, only the halls and stairways are covered. There are no cameras in any of the bedrooms or bathrooms."

"Oh, that's considerate of you. Is that supposed to make me like it?"

"Nobody likes it," he said regretfully, "but Mr. Strode has to have strict security. Every burglar in the city would like to get into this place. Besides, the insurance company insists upon it."

So there was nothing to do but put up with it. A maid—actually dressed in black uniform and wearing a frilly white apron, heaven help us!—led me upstairs to a guest room that must have been decorated with an eye to getting coverage in *Architectural Digest*; the article would have been titled "How To Achieve Perfect Symmetry When Money Is No Object". Everything in the room focused toward a lovely, wide bay window that led the eye out-of-doors beyond the limitations of the building's walls, like a central vanishing point in an old perspective painting. I rather doubted that A. J. Strode had overseen the decoration of the room. I wondered who had.

I told the maid I preferred to do my own unpacking, and when she'd left I moved one chair a couple of feet out of position just to give myself the feeling of having some small control over my environment. We all have our little superstitions. I looked around for a radio but there was none; a television, but no radio. It hadn't occurred to me I might have to go the entire weekend without music or I could have brought along a transistor. I tried PBS on the TV, but got two kids extolling the virtues of the number *seven*. Arts & Entertainment? Interview of a mystery writer. Boring.

Then I opened my suitcase and took out the .380 Walther automatic pistol that had so successfully intimidated A. J. Strode in Pittsburgh. Once I'd gotten over my initial distaste about coming here, it occurred to me that I didn't have to be without resources simply because we were on Strode's home territory. The man could be frightened; some opportunity might arise where I could make him back off again—perhaps permanently this time. I didn't think it likely, but I was ready to grasp any straw that came floating by. The guard evidently had not been instructed to search my suitcase; I'd half expected that. There were plenty of hiding places in that overdecorated guest room, but I needed something quickly accessible. I finally decided on one of the throw pillows on the seat in the bay window; the pillow cover had a zipper, and the automatic slipped inside quite nicely.

Then I sat down by the pillow and stared out the window. It was probably just as well that Strode had been detained. I'd just finished six straight hours of practicing before catching the shuttle to New York, and I hadn't yet made a complete mental shift from my world to Strode's. Strode was exactly the sort of big bad wolf my father used to warn me about all the time. I could just hear him saying, *See, you know nothing about the world—look at the mess you've landed yourself in.*

He never did understand. That man kept me ignorant as sin until I was nearly grown. He had a lot of help from Mother, though; the first sixteen years of my life she kept telling me I wasn't like other girls and I couldn't do this and I couldn't do that and I had to be *so careful* to take care of myself all the time. Long naps when I wasn't sleepy, or at least quiet periods of resting. No sports, of course. No public functions of any kind. Brief periods of supervised play, so long as they didn't get too strenuous. Father backed her up, bringing in tutors instead of letting me go to school, even a private school. I'd reached high school age before I read a magazine article that said diabetics could lead perfectly normal lives just through exercising common sense and a reasonable amount of caution.

When I confronted them with what I'd learned, they pooh-poohed the whole thing and gave me those looks that meant I was just a sweet, silly, gullible little girl who needed to be led by the hand all the time. I don't know what I would have done without my Uncle Marcus. That dear man died when I was ten, but four years earlier he'd seen something my parents never saw and gave me a child-sized violin for my birthday. I remember that moment as clearly as if it were this morning; I picked up that tiny instrument—which seemed enormous to me at the time—and I played it. I played a scale first, and then I played a tune I'd heard on the radio that had been haunting me. It wasn't until several years later that I learned it was the theme of the largo movement of Beethoven's *Seventh*; but that one sustained, repeated note sent chills down my back the first time I played it for myself. I knew from the moment I tucked that first baby violin under my chin that there was a *rightness* to making music that I'd never find anywhere else.

My mother and father thought it was cute. They both approved of my playing, because it gave me something to do and kept me from crying because I couldn't go out and play baseball or whatever else might happen to catch my attention. They never stinted on lessons or on replacing the scaled-down violins as I outgrew them, and I'm grateful to them for that. It's just that they had such a hidebound view of the way a correct life ought to be conducted that the idea of living for music was something of a joke to them. *One doesn't compete with others in the arts, dear...and you aren't serious about playing for money, are you? Don't be vulgar, Joanna. You don't need money.*

Money. A. J. Strode actually thought I *killed* them for money.

The light outside had changed; the afternoon was almost gone. I showered and changed and went downstairs to see if Strode was back yet. At the bottom of the stairs I could hear a television blasting away, so I followed the sound to a room down the hall from the main living room. The light was dim; at first all I could see was a huge rear-projection screen showing a tennis player arguing a call. Then I could make out a man stretched out on the sofa watching the TV. "Strode?" I asked.

It wasn't Strode. The man who got up from the sofa was lean and good-looking and as surprised to see me as I was him. "Hello!" he said in a friendly manner, "I didn't know anyone else was here—Strode isn't back yet. My name's Jack McKinstry, by the way."

"I'm Joanna Gillespie. I was supposed to meet Strode here—alone, I thought."

"Same here. Did you say Joanna Gillespie? The violinist?"

"One and the same."

"Hey—no stuff! Terrific!" He laughed. "I can't see you... here, let me turn on a light." He switched on a table lamp, and I saw clearly for the first time the smiling face of Jack McKinstry. "You sure as hell are Joanna Gillespie—I'd know you anywhere. At the risk of sounding like a gushing fan, I've got to tell you I have all your tapes. Well, almost all of them. I've just about worn out the Prokofiev! You don't know what a pleasure this is for me."

"Well, thank you, Mr.... I'm sorry, I didn't get your last name."

"McKinstry. But call me Jack—please."

He had a smile so infectious that I found myself grinning back. "I'm Jo." This looked promising, but the timing was all wrong; the getting-to-know-you game would have to wait. "Did I understand you to say you're here to see Strode too? Well, of course you are or you wouldn't be in his house, would you? I meant to say Strode and I have some business to wrap up and I expected to see him alone."

"Oh, I'm sure you'll have him to yourself for a while. He'll probably take care of your business first, before he gets to me. I'll be here for the whole weekend."

I was starting to get a funny feeling. "Isn't that interesting? I was . . . invited for the weekend too."

His friendly smile started to fade. "You hesitated before you said 'invited'."

"Did I? I didn't notice."

There was an awkward pause. Then he said, "Jo, does your being here have anything to do with House of Glass?"

I sat down on the nearest chair, *plop*, and waved an arm at the television. "Could you turn that off?" He did. "Look, Jack, I don't want to be rude, but why I'm here is my business. Just tell me one thing. Did you think you were going to be the only guest this weekend?"

He nodded. "You?"

"The same."

He grinned crookedly. "And I don't think A. J. Strode just wants to bring two fascinating people together, right? He got us both here without telling either the other was coming. He has to have a reason for that—he never does anything without a reason. Any ideas?"

I shook my head. "Not a one. *Damn* that man!"

"Amen," Jack said, looking surprised. "Why, heaven protect us, I do believe the lady is not an admirer of Iron Man Strode. Can this be true? Does this mean I am not the only one in this show-offy house who is not a member of the A. J. Strode fan club?"

"That's what it means," I muttered. "I don't want to be here at all. I want to be in Boston practicing Mozart."

Jack pulled over a chair next to mine and sat down. "Joanna Gillespie, I think you and I ought to talk to each other. We might turn out to be allies, you know. Frankly, I could use an ally. I don't want to be here either, and it looks to me as if our not-so-genial host is planning a little surprise that involves both of us. I don't know about you, but I hate surprises. Especially when A. J. Strode is behind them. So what do you say—shall we pool our resources, whatever they might turn out to be?''

I was thinking it over when Myron Castleberry came into the room. ''Oh, there you are! I see you've met—good, good. I'm afraid—''

''What's going on, Castleberry?'' Jack interrupted him. ''You didn't say a word to me about Jo's being here, and you didn't tell her about me. What's this all about?''

''I didn't mention it?'' Castleberry said smoothly. ''An oversight on my part, I'm afraid. I've come to tell you Mr. Strode was delayed in Atlanta—bad weather of some sort. But his plane has just taken off and he'll be here in a few hours. We're not to wait dinner for him. The cook says half an hour, if that's satisfactory?''

''And if it isn't?'' Jack asked innocently.

Castleberry pretended not to hear. ''You know where the dining room is? Good. If you'd like a cocktail before dinner, just call the kitchen on that telephone over there.'' He left before either of us could say anything.

''That's the only decent suggestion I've heard all day,'' Jack said and headed for the house phone. ''Martinis okay?''

I said yes. ''Do you believe that?'' I asked when he'd finished at the phone. ''That he just forgot to mention there'd be two of us here?''

''Not for one minute. I doubt if Castleberry ever forgets anything, perfect little toady that he is. I don't like this, Jo. I smell a fish.''

''We could leave.''

He was quiet a moment. ''Maybe you can leave, but I can't. I have to get some business settled with Strode, and it has to be settled this weekend. *Has* to be. I don't have any choice."

That was a familiar phrase. Should I tell him?

Just then another black-frocked and frilly-aproned maid appeared, this one carrying a tray with two glasses and a shaker of martinis on it. "*Bless* you, my dear," Jack said, taking the tray, "and our undying gratitude to you for your lifesaving errand of mercy. Doesn't it give you a warm glow to know you've just rescued two desperate souls from a terrible and thirsty death?"

She looked at him uncertainly; evidently such extravagant language wasn't usual in A. J. Strode's house. But she smiled politely and left without saying anything.

Jack poured a martini and handed it to me. "We don't have a whole lot of time. I'll go first, if it'll help." He poured his own martini and lifted the glass. "To better days." We both drank and he said, "Strode is working an extortion game on me. He wants my shares in a company called House of Glass. Does that mean anything to you?"

I finished my martini and held out my glass for more. "It does."

He refilled our glasses and said, "Strode has manufactured some evidence that implicates me in a helicopter crash that took place in France four years ago. The evidence is garbage, but it can still make trouble for me. I can't afford even the appearance of guilt right now. If he can get the police investigation reopened . . . well, I'll just say our family business is the manufacture of helicopters. See? You can imagine the damage all that adverse publicity would do—not just to me but to the rest of the family as well."

"And you're here to . . ."

"I'm here to swap my House of Glass shares for that phony evidence. I've tried everything I can think of, but there's no way around it. I'm going to have to let him have my shares."

I was stunned. I sat there unspeaking for so long that Jack finally joked, "Jo? Hey, Jo, I told you my deepest and darkest secret—play fair, now. Your turn."

I put down my martini and said, "I'm here for the same reason. He's blackmailing me into giving up *my* shares of House of Glass."

Jack looked as if I'd slapped him. "But…but Strode told me he needed only *one* block of shares to give him control."

"That's right. He needs only one block."

We sat staring at each other, slowly figuring out what it meant. What it meant was that Strode was going to deal with only one of us and throw the other to the wolves.

"He's pitting us against each other," Jack finally said, "and he's doing it for fun. We're his weekend entertainment, you and I."

I could think of nothing to say to that. I got up and walked around the room for lack of anything better to do. The walls were lined with shelves holding videocassettes, the largest private collection I've ever seen. The room boasted stereo speakers for the television and the VCR, but that was all. No radio, no turntable, no tape deck, no compact disc player. Evidently A. J. Strode never felt the need for music, never. Somehow that failed to surprise me.

Jack threw me a questioning look. "Jo—what's he got on you? If you don't mind my asking."

I shivered. "It's too ugly to talk about. The 'evidence' in my case isn't manufactured, but it is grossly misinterpreted. In fact, Strode has done such a nifty job of misinterpreting that I have no doubt he could persuade the police to see it his way. It's very difficult to prove innocence, isn't it? I haven't been able to think of a way."

"So we're both stuck. What in the hell are we going to do?"

We were sitting there gloomily saying nothing when the same maid who'd brought our drinks came to tell us dinner was ready. I asked her if Castleberry was dining too and she said yes.

"Good," Jack muttered. "I have a few things I want to say to our Mr. Castleberry."

But before he got his chance, Castleberry had one more surprise for us. "I'd like you to meet Richard Bruce," he said, indicating an immaculately groomed man ten or twelve years older than Jack. Solid-looking; gray streaks in his black hair. "Joanna Gillespie and Jack McKinstry, Mr. Strode's other guests."

"Jesus," Jack breathed. "Another one?"

The other man, Richard Bruce, turned to Castleberry. "I was not told there would be others here."

"How many more, Castleberry?" I asked.

"No more," he replied pleasantly. "Just you three. Shall we be seated?"

"No, we will not be seated," Jack said angrily. "Not until you give us some answers. Why *three* of us?"

"Please—we'll have to eat sometime. I can't tell you anything anyway. Mr. Strode will be here soon, and he'll answer all your questions. Please sit down."

We all stood frozen; then Richard Bruce broke the tableau by pulling out a chair and sitting. The rest of us followed suit. The first course was served, by the drinks maid and one other helping her.

Richard Bruce waited until they'd left the room and then said, "Castleberry, I want to know why I was brought here." His voice was surprisingly musical. "I came here to transfer some stock, not to take part in a social weekend."

Jack McKinstry laughed shortly. "You're here to take part in a game of cat and mouse. And guess what, Richard my friend. You ain't the cat."

"This stock you came to transfer," I said to him, "it's House of Glass stock, isn't it?"

"I do wish you'd wait until Mr. Strode gets here," Castleberry interposed. "Why speculate when it will all be explained to you soon?"

Richard Bruce was looking straight into my eyes. "Yes," he answered me.

I nodded. "That's why Jack and I are here too. You realize he doesn't need all our shares."

After a moment he nodded back; he realized.

Dinner didn't last long; no one was in the mood for eating. Just as we were getting up from the table, Castleberry cleared his throat and made an announcement. "While we were dining, envelopes were placed in each of your rooms that should be of great interest to you. The contents are different in each case, but I'll just say they are related to what each of you came here to get. Perhaps you'd care to go examine them now?"

I just stared at him; Richard Bruce, as well as I could tell, didn't react at all. Jack McKinstry, however, gave a loud, sarcastic laugh. "Envelopes in our rooms! Well, well—isn't that a *fascinating* development? So mysterious! Now whatever could they be? Clues in a scavenger hunt? Autographed pictures of our conveniently delayed host? Is this Strode's idea of fun and games? Envelopes in our rooms! Tacky, Castleberry, tacky."

Without a word Richard Bruce left the room; I wasn't far behind. Upstairs I saw him go into a room down at the end of the hall from mine. I closed my door behind me; a large manila envelope with my name written on it was lying on the bed where I couldn't miss it. I was just opening it when I heard the door directly across the hall close—Jack, no doubt.

The envelope held several papers. The top one was a photocopy of Ozzie Rogers's affidavit, in which he stated unequivocally that I had tried to hire him to kill my father and my mother. That made me both sick and angry. I never once mentioned my parents to Ozzie; he got that from Strode, or Castleberry. And I never "tried to hire" him. Ozzie was attempting to make it look as if he were the one who'd said no, when in fact it was I who withdrew. It galled me no end to think that my entire future was at risk because of a lout like Ozzie Rogers.

Underneath the affidavit was a copy of a report signed by a private investigator named William Pierce. Pierce had found out exactly how much money I inherited. He'd found out I was in Boston when both my parents died. He'd found out an autopsy was not performed in either case. Attached to the report were copies of my parents' death certificates.

The last sheet of paper in the envelope contained only one typed sentence: *Now that you've seen the papers, look in the bottom drawer of the end table on the left side of the bed.*

Scavenger hunt indeed. The drawer was empty except for a microcassette player. I turned it on and heard A. J. Strode's voice. "So, Jo, have you read all the papers? They're what you want, right? Well, I'm going to keep my word. You'll get the originals if it's your shares I buy. But there's a hitch—two hitches, as a matter of fact. I'm sure you've met both of them by now.

"You and Bruce and McKinstry each own a block of House of Glass shares that I need. But I don't need all of them, so I'm going to buy from only one of you. Incidentally, the amount I'll pay has just gone down—you should have accepted one of my earlier offers. But that's neither here nor there. The question is, which one of you do I buy from? That's a meaty little problem, that is. So meaty, in fact, that I have to admit the solution is beyond me. I don't know which of you I'll buy from—I have no idea. So you're going to have to tell me, you and your two peers in crime. Oh yes, I'd better warn you—Bruce and McKinstry have every bit as strong a motive for wanting to deal as you do. But you three are going to decide who sells.

"And in case you haven't guessed the rest of it, I'll spell it out for you. If I end up buying from one of the men, Jo, the originals of those papers in your envelope go straight to the Boston police. Copies of Ozzie Rogers's affidavit will go to the newspapers. I can promise you my own paper will make it a front-page story for at least a week and maybe even longer. And television—don't forget television! You'll gets *lots* of coverage. So you're going to have to be persuasive, Jo. You're going to have to find a way to convince Bruce and McKinstry *they* should go to prison instead of you. And you'll have to do it before nine o'clock Sunday night. That's your deadline. If you haven't settled it by then, I'm turning all three of you in.

"When you've decided on the winner, call this number—555-4109. You'll reach Castleberry—you won't be talking to or seeing me at all. And save yourselves the trouble of trying to find out where I am. Castleberry will be gone by the time you hear this, and the house staff doesn't know. Don't bother the servants or the security guards. They're in the dark as far as this weekend is concerned. All they know is that they are to feed and pick up after and protect three guests while I'm away.

"That number again is 555-4109. You have tonight and two more days to reach a decision.

"Have fun."

Nothing more came from the microcassette; I pressed the off button. Then I went into the bathroom and threw up.

I could hear someone running noisily down the stairs, but I didn't even go out to look. I slumped down on the window seat and stared out at the night. I still felt nauseated in spite of having just emptied my stomach. My skin was cold and clammy and I couldn't get my thoughts in order; everything kept blurring together. I needed help; I needed something orderly and positive, something clean and uncluttered.

Bach.

So I sat there in the window seat and played in my head the *Presto* movement of his *Sonata No. 1*. I concentrated on the tricky fingering and on keeping the volume constant. I worked on lifting my bowing wrist more quickly and on making the arpeggios crisp and clean. By the time I'd finished, I was out of my shock; I was breathing normally and my skin felt like regular skin again.

Strode had set us all up, just for the pleasure of pulling the rug out from under two of us. He didn't have to do this; he already had what he wanted. Jack was right; this whole weekend was Strode's idea of fun, and we were the entertainment. But where was the audience?

There was a knock at the door; I opened it to find Richard Bruce on the other side, not looking the least bit ruffled by what *his* microcassette must have said. It struck me incongruously that he was one of those men who got better-looking as they grew older; this was a hell of a time to be thinking of that. "We better have a meeting," he said.

I stepped out into the hall. "Where's Jack?"

"Downstairs, trying to bully the security guard. He doesn't know anything."

Which he? I wondered. We started down the stairs. "That telephone number Strode gave on the tape..."

"I called it. A recording."

"Castleberry?"

"Yes. He won't pick up until we've had enough time to reach a decision."

"He's already left, then."

"The minute we finished dinner, the guard says."

We found McKinstry and the security guard glaring at each other in the small room with all the television monitors. "This fellow here," Jack said with exaggerated disbelief, "this fellow who is charged with protecting the entire contents of A. J. Strode's house—he claims he doesn't know where his employer is! Isn't that something? Yes indeedy. The question is, do we believe him?"

"I'm not his secretary, Mr. McKinstry," the guard said with controlled anger. "All Mr. Strode said to me was there'd be three guests staying here while he was gone. He told me your names and what rooms you'll be in. That's all I know."

"That has to be the truth, Jack," I said. "Strode isn't going to spread it around where he is. Not now."

"He may not have even told Castleberry," Richard Bruce added.

"Yeah, I suppose you're right," Jack sighed. He turned back to the guard. "Hey, I'm sorry, man. I got a little overexcited there and took it out on you. No hard feelings, okay?"

"Okay, Mr. McKinstry," the guard said stiffly.

How odd; at a time like this Jack was trying to make the guard like him. "These cameras that are all over the place," I asked the guard, "are they sound cameras?"

"No, ma'am, but there's a microphone in the conference room. Mr. Strode sometimes likes to keep a recording of his business meetings."

"So all we have to do is avoid the conference room," Jack muttered and grabbed my elbow. "Come on, Richard."

He led us to the television room where I'd first met him. We all stared at the small camera mounted above the doorway watching our every move. Without a word Richard Bruce took off his suit jacket and tossed it over the camera. His shirt, I now saw, was silk...and it looked good on him. He raised an eyebrow when he noticed the walls covered with shelves of videocassettes.

Jack went over to the phone and punched the kitchen button. "Alcohol," he said into the receiver. "Lots of it, and a lot of different kinds. And ice. And glasses. And soon."

We waited until the maid arrived pushing a cart loaded with liquid sustenance and then left. When we were all fortified, I said, "I might as well tell you both I have no ideas at all. Consider me open to suggestion."

Jack said, "The first thing we've got to do is agree among the three of us not to go along with this little scenario Strode's set up for us. Simply refuse to play. There's no way we can decide one of us goes free while the other two go to prison. It's got to be us against him. *Strode* is my enemy, not you two. What do you say?"

"Agreed," Richard Bruce said shortly. I nodded.

"All right, then. Richard, I know Strode has something on both Jo and me...I gotta think he's got something on you as well."

"Yes, he does. And there's the problem. Strode has some so-called evidence that could hang me, and if it's the same with you none of us can just walk out of here. He'll use what he's got if we do."

"You better believe it. So we've got to get hold of the original evidence, that's priority number one. Anybody got any ideas about how we do that little thing?"

"The evidence wouldn't be here," I said, "not in his home, and not with *us* here. And I rather doubt that he'd leave it conveniently lying out in the open in his office. Richard, where would you hide something like that?''

''I'd lock it in my office vault. Or put it in a safety deposit box in a bank.''

''I assume none of us is an experienced safecracker?'' Jack asked. ''Shit.''

We sat staring gloomily at the floor. I got up and filled my glass with ice and water. I was getting muzzy-headed.

''If we just knew where he was,'' Jack said.

''Then what? Force him to turn over the evidence?'' I asked. ''Beat him, torture him?''

Jack smiled. ''Wouldn't that be fun.''

''If I had one wish in the world,'' I smiled back, ''it would be to do to A. J. Strode what he's doing to us now. *That* would be fun.''

''I wouldn't mind that myself,'' Richard said softly, ''if we ever get out of this thing. I'd like to get that sonuvabitch.''

''Yeah, me too,'' Jack said. ''Maybe we should kill the bastard.''

I exchanged a quick glance with Richard. ''That wouldn't solve anything,'' I said. ''There'd still be the evidence.''

''Hey, I was just talking,'' Jack said carelessly.

Richard leaned forward in his chair. ''What would happen to the evidence if Strode died? Who would have access to it?''

''Castleberry,'' Jack and I said together.

''And Castleberry is a man who can be bought. Maybe there's a way out of this after all.''

''How do you know Castleberry can be bought?'' I asked, curious.

''All the Castleberrys of the world can be bought. Men who spend their entire lives bowing and scraping to stronger men...what does a Castleberry do when his strongman dies?

He doesn't suddenly sprout into a strongman himself. No, he looks around for a new strongman to attach himself to."

"Such as yourself?" Jack asked archly.

"Such as myself. Or you. Or maybe even Jo, although at first glance she doesn't fit the usual image of a strongman."

"Thank you," I said dryly.

"You're welcome. Our host is not infallible. You can generally tell the measure of a man by the kinds of assistants he surrounds himself with. But once Strode is gone, whenever that is, Castleberry is going to be looking out for himself. He knows what all that evidence is worth. Probably the first thing he'd do would be try to sell it to us. And if all he wants is money, well...then there's no problem. But if he wants a job like the one he has with Strode now, I could give him that."

"What kind of business are you in, Richard?" I asked.

"Ocean freight. Bruce Shipping Lines."

"Let me see if I've got this straight," Jack said sarcastically. "Somehow we magically discover Strode's whereabouts, go there, and proceed to bump him off. Then all we have to do is offer Castleberry some spending money and a little job security, and we all live happily ever after? Did I get that right, Richard?"

"Save your sarcasm, Wonder Boy," Richard said sharply. "We need each other on this one. It's an *idea*. A starting place. I'm simply suggesting it would be easier to deal with Castleberry than with Strode."

Jack didn't like being called Wonder Boy. "It's a *dumb* idea. The whole thing's based on the preposterous assumption that we'd be able to get to Strode in the first place. Look around you, man! Cameras, guards, Castleberry skipping out—everything's timed, *controlled*. We're not going to find Strode when he doesn't want to be found."

"Somebody has to know where he is," I said.

"Why? What's to prevent his taking off by himself, registering in a hotel someplace under a false name? Jo, don't tell me you like this nutty idea? Kill Strode...and then take our chances with Castleberry?"

"Of course I don't like it. But it is the only specific suggestion that's been made."

Jack looked from me to Richard and back to me again. "Are you people crazy? You're sitting here calmly discussing *murder*, for the love of heaven! Is that what Strode has on you? Are you murderers?"

"I'm a violinist," I snapped.

Richard looked surprised. "Violinist?"

Jack threw his arms up in disgust. "Oh, for Christ's sake, Bruce! Castleberry told you she was Joanna Gillespie. You didn't recognize the name? She's only the most famous violinist in the world. The world's best! Jesus."

Richard gave me a crooked grin. "Pleased to meet you."

I shrugged. "Jack—come up with a better idea if you don't like that one. Don't just yell."

All the air seemed to go out of him. "Hey, forget all that, will you? I was just running off at the mouth. Look, I don't seem to be handling this as well as you two. I need a little more time to adjust, okay? Richard, I'm sorry. Jo, I'm sorry." He rolled his eyes heavenward. "God, I'm sorry. Did I overlook anyone? But I think we'd better forget about killing Strode." He suddenly grinned. "For one thing, I didn't have the foresight to bring a loaded gun with me."

"I did," I said. The other two stared at me. I explained how I'd been able to stop Strode's bullying in Pittsburgh by waving a gun at him. "I thought I might be able to do it again...and maybe scare him into returning the evidence. I never dreamed he wouldn't even be here."

"Where's the gun now?" Richard asked.

"Hidden in my room."

"When was the last time you saw it? Before dinner or after?"

Now it was my turn to stare. "You think someone may have taken it?"

"I think we'd better find out. Somebody had to go into our rooms to leave those envelopes, remember. The security guard, probably."

Richard recovered his jacket from where he'd tossed it over the television camera and we all hurried up to my room. The minute I picked up the throw pillow on the window seat I knew the automatic was no longer there, but I unzipped the case and checked anyway; I checked the other three pillows as well. "It's not here," I told the men. "That means either our rooms were searched while we were at dinner, or Castleberry lied when he said there were no cameras in the guest rooms. I just took his word for it."

"Somebody else's word we took without question," Jack pointed out. "The security guard's, when he said the cameras weren't sound cameras. He could have been listening to every word we've said."

Richard turned and started out of the room. "Jack, come with me. Jo, you stay here." Without waiting for an answer, he was gone.

Jack gave me a strained smile. "I do believe our Mr. Bruce likes giving orders." He left, not exactly hurrying.

Only a few minutes passed before the phone in my room rang; it was Jack. "We have stormed the citadel and all is secure," he said cheerfully. "The guard was telling the truth, bless his incorruptible little hide. The cameras are video only. The only sound recorder is for the mike in the conference room, like he said. They only watch for burglars in this house, not listen for them." He lowered his voice. "Whatever you do, Jo, don't get Richard Bruce mad at you. Jesus, you should have seen the way he put the fear of God into the guard—whew. He had that man trembling in his boots.''

"Where are they now?"

"Outside in the hallway." His voice went back up to its normal pitch and volume. "Castleberry did indeed fib about there being no cameras in the guest rooms, the naughty boy. I'm looking at you right now. What we want you to do, Jo, is to go into every room along that hall while I check the monitors. We need an unmonitored room if there is one."

I hung up the phone, walked into the room across the hall, and picked up that phone. "I'm in your room."

"I see you. Keep going."

I kept going. There wasn't one unmonitored room on that floor. The cameras were so well concealed I couldn't spot any of them.

"Well, well," Jack's voice said over the phone in the last room. "It seems our congenial host doesn't trust any of his—hold on a sec." I could hear voices in the background. "The security guard took your gun. He says that's what the cameras in the guest rooms are for, to watch for someone bringing a weapon into the house, and doesn't *that* tell you something about our host."

"Where is it? My gun?"

More muttering in the background. "Castleberry took it with him when he left."

"Oh great."

"Yeah. Hang loose, we're coming up."

They brought the security guard up with them and made him show us where the cameras were located in each of our rooms. Mine was concealed behind the ceiling molding directly over my bed. It couldn't swivel like the cameras in the hallway and downstairs, but the way it was angled it had a perfect view of the window seat. It turned out there were cameras in the bathrooms too. That jerk of a guard had watched me take a shower.

"Your job must be voyeur's heaven," Jack said wonderingly. "Is there anyplace in this house you *can't* watch?"

"Mr. Strode's bedroom suite," the guard said, "over in the other wing. And his upstairs library—that's in the other wing too."

"Are you sure there's only one camera in each of the guest rooms?" Richard asked softly.

"Yessir, honest to god, Mr. Bruce, only one." The guard looked scared; what on earth had Richard said to him?

"Cover them up," Richard ordered.

The guard practically ran down the stairs and was soon back with little squares of cardboard that he taped over the various lenses in our rooms. "Is there anything else, Mr. Bruce?"

"No, go back to your post." The guard bumped into Jack in his haste to get out.

We were then in Richard's room. "Since you seem to have him so well housebroken," I said, "why not just order him to turn off the cameras?"

Richard smiled, a little. "Would you trust him not to take a peek now and then? No, that wouldn't work. And we can't throw him out. He'd go straight to the police. Right now the thing he's worrying about most is that Strode will find out how easily intimidated he was. He won't give us any trouble."

We talked until four in the morning. Plan after plan was suggested, examined, discarded. It seemed to me the only way we had of getting Strode off our backs for good was to get something damning on *him*—make it up, if we had to. But the other two kept saying there wasn't enough time for that, and the arguments went on. Jack had the annoying habit of drumming with his fingers when he was trying to think. Once when it got especially irritating I started whis-tling the *Poet and Peasant* overture to match the rhythm of his drumming and he finally stopped. But it didn't help; none of us could come up with a feasible plan. Almost ev-erything anyone suggested hinged in some way on Castle-berry, and Castleberry wasn't answering his phone. We'd called at midnight, at one, at two, at three. We left no mes-sage.

When we'd finally talked ourselves into a state of ex-haustion, we called it quits for the night. I was reeling with fatigue and ate a little packet of cheese crackers I'd brought with me; I should have eaten more dinner. I barely man-aged to get my clothes off before collapsing on the bed.

But I couldn't fall asleep—surprise, surprise. I was in that condition of mixed exhaustion and anxiety that makes sleep impossible. All the images of the day kept running through my head like a piece of looped film. And hovering over it all like a black shadow was the man in whose house I now lay. Who was this A. J. Strode who'd brought me to this state of affairs? *Who'd brought me to my knees.*

Strode was only a year or two older than my father would be if he were still alive; I'd always had trouble with men of that generation. They were so eager to tell me what to do, and they all took it for granted they had the right to do so. I'd fired my first manager when he started taking that damned paternalistic attitude toward me; the last thing in the world I needed was another father. In a way, my real fa-ther handed me to A. J. Strode on a platter. From the time I was a baby, he was unknowingly setting me up for what was happening now.

Even if I'd understood what was going on at the time, I still couldn't have gone to someone and claimed child abuse, not as it was understood at that time. He never beat me in his life. He never touched me where he shouldn't, and he never asked me to touch him. But on my fifth birthday I learned how boys were different from girls. I learned, because he showed me. He'd had an enormous erection, and he solemnly informed me that what men wanted most in the world was to shove that huge thing up inside little girls like me. I was too scared even to cry. He told me I could never trust any man except himself. He was sick, of course, but a five-year-old doesn't know that.

Almost every day he told me I'd never have anybody who loved me as much as he did. The second half of the ritual was for me to tell him how much I loved him, and I found the way to avoid a lecture was to fake an enthusiasm I came to feel less and less. I had to pay for everything I got with a kiss or a hug, good basic training for prostitution. I learned all the nuances of gratitude and when to express which ones. Winning his approval was to be the one and only goal of my life. When I'd go to Mother and try to articulate what was wrong, she'd reply with *Do what your father says, dear* or *You're lucky to have a father who loves you.*

So I was to be Daddy's girl all my life; that was his plan for me. It was the music that saved me, the music I heard other people making and that I eventually learned to make myself. He sometimes grew irritated that I spent so much time practicing, but he never seriously interfered with my "little hobby." My mother never hesitated to interrupt a practice session, though, whenever she felt I needed one of those rest periods she'd long since decided were essential to my health and well-being. Mother was basically a lazy woman, and the role of diabetic invalid suited her. But it wouldn't do to have a daughter suffering from the same ailment seen to be physically active; that would cast some doubt on the authenticity of her performance. I'm sure Mother never thought any of these things consciously; selfish people are quite gifted at self-deception.

But enforced quiescence was the order of the day. How I hated those rest periods! I quickly learned to smuggle sheets of music into bed with me; if I couldn't practice, I could at least memorize. At age ten I started asking them to let me go to the New England Conservatory for advanced instructions. *But you're a sick girl,* said Mother. *They'll eat you alive,* said Father. It took two years of constant nagging to get them to say yes, two years of my life I still consider wasted. Then when at seventeen I announced I intended to go to Juilliard and pursue a career in music, Father had a heart attack.

It was a mild attack, but a genuine one. In the hospital he told me I wouldn't last a month "out there" and, besides, it was my duty to stay home and nurse him now that he was ill. I suggested that was more properly Mother's role, and he told me straight to my face that I would live longer than my mother and thus would be more useful to him. We had words that quickly escalated into a shouting match until a horrified nurse threw me out of the hospital room.

I left; I made my break. I worked like a dog, although it seems sinful to call something that exhilarating *work*. I met people and found I could talk to them. I made mistakes, and recovered from them. I learned there were men in the world who could be trusted in spite of what dear old Dad had told me on my fifth birthday (and repeated endlessly thereafter), and I thoroughly enjoyed that particular learning process. Sometimes I had to wonder whether my father's sex life had ever known the element of just plain fun; what had happened to him to make him so warped?

I made my Carnegie Hall début; and when I went out on my first concert tour, I found myself being treated with respect. I started playing with the great orchestras and making records and appearing on television, and then woke up one morning to find myself a full-blown celebrity. I went from almost total isolation to being surrounded by mobs of people—*and I loved it*.

My parents were puzzlingly kind during all this, until I found out they looked upon my career as some sort of temporary aberration from the norm and were simply being patient until I came to my senses and returned home. *Being patient*. Several times Father tried to talk me into donating all my earnings to one charity or another, not out of any eleemosynary instincts of his own but because he wanted to be the source of all I had in the world. Mother became more passive and helpless every year; she'd even ask someone the time rather than exert the effort of turning her head to look at the clock. Still, there was a kind of peace between us; it would do.

Then everything happened at once. Father developed diabetes, and emphysema on top of it. Mother was diagnosed as nephritic, and her doctor told me she was not a good candidate for a kidney transplant. Mother went to bed and never got up again. Then Father had his second heart attack.

This one was worse than the first. Father had never been one to deny himself; he'd grown quite stout, he reeked of tobacco, and he always had a drink in his hand. When at last he was able to go home from the hospital, he sat me down and told me what was going to happen. The nurses who were taking care of the two of them were all fine girls, but they weren't family. It was time for me to stop flitting around all over the world and settle down and do my duty. I could still play my violin at home if I wanted to, so long as neither of them was sleeping at the time. He pointed out that I wouldn't be playing the violin at all if he hadn't paid for all those expensive lessons out of his own pocket; I should welcome the opportunity to even things out. But the point was, playtime was over. And if I didn't face up to my responsibilities, he'd make sure every newspaper in the country learned that the oh-so-wonderful Joanna Gillespie was leaving her fatally ill parents to die alone in neglect while she was out having a good time.

My mother never asked me to give up my career to stay home and take care of them. She simply took it for granted that that was what I would do.

And A. J. Strode thought I killed them *for money*.

FIVE

I TELL YOU, A. J. Strode is some kind of sweetheart, he is. First he grinds you down so there's not enough of you to get back up again. Then when you gradually begin to accept ground-downness as a tolerable state of affairs after all and even start to feel a kind of relief that it's over, that's when he steps in and *really* pulverizes you. It ain't over 'til it's over, Jack.

Money money money money, it do indeed make the world go round, yes it do. There was no way I was going to talk the other two into letting me be the one to sell to Strode, so I was quick to propose the three-musketeers routine. Joanna Gillespie likes me; I could tell from the once-over she gave me when we met. But not that much. I suspect Jo's not exactly the self-sacrificing-female type. And Richard Bruce obviously likes to think of himself as a take-charge kind of guy; he sort of reminds me of A. J. Strode. Nope, the only way I was going to get out of this was to have those two working to save my hide along with their own. One for all and all for whatever.

About six in the morning I had to get up and pee; I was heading back to bed when I heard voices across the hall. I looked out and saw one of the maids taking a pitcher of orange juice into Jo's room. I'd forgotten Joanna Gillespie was a diabetic, but her body hadn't and she'd had some kind of reaction. The maid was hovering over Jo's bed, not knowing what to do; I went in and shooed her away. Jo wasn't looking too good, so I sat with her and held her hand. She had long, slender fingers with the filed-down nails that all string players have. Jo was a little twitchy at first but eventually calmed enough to fall asleep. Luckily I can sleep anywhere; I spent what was left of the night in a chair by her bed so I'd be the first thing she saw when she woke up. A couple of hours later she was awake and saying she felt fine. I gave her a quick hug and left her alone. Timing is everything.

As a result of that little episode in the wee hours, Jo and I both had circles under our eyes when we met for breakfast. She greeted me by reaching out and gently squeezing my forearm. (Progress!) Then Richard Bruce came striding in, marching as if he were leading a military parade. He looked exactly the same as he'd looked at dinner the night before; only the color of his suit was different. Yep, he wore a suit and tie to Saturday morning breakfast, yes he did. I was willing to bet he posed for pictures with his jacket hooked on a thumb over one shoulder to show what a regular fella he was.

The take-charge guy took charge. "We ought to do a little exploring," he said over coffee. "The security guard said the only parts of this house not covered by cameras are Strode's bedroom suite and a private library. We'd better take a look at them."

I sighed. "You don't think he'd keep all that evidence here, Richard, you know that. So why bother?"

"To look for some indication of where he is. If he owns a weekend house in Connecticut, for instance, that might be a good bet."

"That's not a bad idea," Jo said. "But what do we do if we find him? We still don't have any way to force him to turn the evidence over to us."

During our marathon talk session the night before, Jo's
favorite plan had been to manufacture some evidence of our
own, something to implicate A. J. Strode in dealings so
down and dirty that even he wouldn't be able to claw his way
out. The trouble with that was it'd take too much time;
Strode had given us a 9:00 P.M. Sunday deadline. But still Jo
stuck to the notion that we needed a bigger stick than
Strode's, so run right out and get one, please, Jack.

"One step at a time," Richard said. "Let's see what we
can find out first."

What we found out was that A. J. Strode kept his bedroom and library doors locked. "His private turf," I
shrugged. "We should have anticipated it." *You* should have
anticipated it, Richard Knowitall Bruce. "Now what?"

"We can't break down the door or pick the lock with all
those cameras watching," Jo said.

There was a camera at each end of the hall and one opposite each of two doors; it was only *behind* the doors that
life would be camera-free. "I betcha the doors aren't
breakable or the locks pickable anyway," I said. "Strode is
a real security nut, isn't he? Why don't we take a little stroll
outside? I'd like to get a look at the exterior of this building."

"You're thinking of windows?" Richard asked. "They'd
be hooked up to the alarm system."

"But surely the window alarms are turned off during the
day," Jo said. "The house staff has to open windows now
and then, I'd think. Let's go outside and take a look."

The house had a patio along one side and across the back.
The first thing we noticed was that several of the windows
were open, thus answering the question about the alarm
system. I'd had some image of myself heroically scaling the
outside of the building by Strode's bedroom, but there
weren't any handholds or trellises or anything to climb. It

took us a while to get oriented, to figure out where our rooms were and Strode's locked-up space was. And when we did figure it out, we saw one of *his* windows standing wide open.

"My god," Jo gasped, "you don't suppose he's been here all the time?"

Just then a maid leaned out and closed the window; nope, he hadn't been here all the time. "Wait," I told the others and dashed into the house. I reached the bottom of the stairs in Strode's private wing just as the maid was starting down. She was short and on the plump side and burdened with a wooden tray of cleaning things as well as a dust mop and a carpet sweeper—not a vacuum but one of those things they use for quick pickups.

"Hey, m'dear, you've got too much to carry," I greeted her. "Allow me to remove some of this impedimenta that weighs so heavily on your fragile young bod. I place my strong right arm at your service—or my left, if you like that one better."

Instead of protesting demurely as a well-trained girl-type servant is supposed to do, she said, "If that means you're offering to carry some of this stuff, grab ahold."

I took the tray and the carpet sweeper, leaving her with the dust mop. "You must be new here," I murmured.

She grinned. "Howja know?"

"You're not invisible yet." She laughed at that, and we went down the stairs chatting easily. I followed her toward the back of the house, where we ran into an older woman in a navy blue dress—the housekeeper?—who, when she saw me helping put away the cleaning materials in a storage closet next to the kitchen, gave the maid one of the most disapproving looks I've ever seen pass from one human being to another.

"Whoops, I think you're in trouble," I whispered to the maid.

"Whoops, I'm always in trouble," she whispered back. She took a key ring from her pocket and put it on a hook in a small cabinet on the wall. "Don't worry about it."

"You sure?"

"I'm sure."

I started to say something to the housekeeper but then she turned that disapproving look on me, so I beat the hastiest of hasty retreats. I found Jo and Richard sitting at one of the tables on the patio. "Ah. Consider the problem semi-solved," I told them as I sat down. "I know where the keys to Strode's rooms are kept."

"Where?" they both asked on cue.

"In a wall-mounted cabinet near the kitchen. The cabinet itself has a lock, but it's not locked now."

"So why didn't you take the keys?" Jo asked.

"Two witnesses, one of whom strongly disapproves of my presence in the servants' domain. We'll wait a bit."

We waited half an hour; and then, because it would have looked funny if I showed up in the kitchen area again so soon, Jo casually wandered back in that direction. I'd told her the last hook on the right in the second row; and when she casually wandered back again, she had the key ring gripped tightly in her hand. Richard went off to distract the security guard (a different one this morning); Jo and I counted to a hundred and hurried off to Strode's private wing.

The first door we tried unlocked to reveal Strode's bedroom. We closed the door quickly and leaned against it, hearts pounding. But no alarms went off, no feet came pounding down the hall, no fists hammered on the door. Okay so far. The bedroom was like everything else in the house, oversized and overpriced. The bed was the biggest

I've ever seen; it had to have been custom-made. The bedroom contained nothing you'd not expect to find in a bedroom. We looked, but we couldn't find any concealed maps with bright red arrows pointing to A. J. Strode's secret hiding place.

Two dressing rooms opened off the bedroom, each with its own bathroom. One of the dressing rooms was empty, stripped bare. "He must be between wives at the moment," I said. The other dressing room was definitely Strode's. We went through everything, shamelessly. I was fascinated to find he had an entire chest of drawers that held nothing but silk underwear. Six drawers of drawers.

"Jack, look here." Jo was holding open a door in Strode's dressing room; it led directly into his library.

The library had four bookcases, a TV, a sofa, a lounge chair, a desk. It may have been Strode's private library, but it sure as hell didn't have any of his private papers there. No tax records, no correspondence, not even any household accounts. No file cabinets. He must have handled everything from his office; this place was for relaxing, not working. We did find quarterly reports and similar papers relating to various corporations, probably companies Strode was considering moving in on. Light reading for him. We couldn't even find any incidental clues, such as a matchbook from an out-of-town restaurant.

Jo looked at me disconsolately. "Nothing."

I put an arm around her. "Hey, Jo, it was a long shot at best. We have to try everything we can think of."

"I know, but it's beginning to look hopeless."

I looked for signs that a long, passionate embrace would be welcomed at that point and decided no. Instead I gave her a quick kiss and said lightly, "We still have the better part of two days to come up with something. Right now let's pray that Richard is still standing so as to block the appropriate monitors or whatever the hell it is he's doing." We left the door between the library and the hall unlocked, if for some reason we should want to get back in again. We slipped out into the hall and down the stairway. Safe.

Jo and I let Richard see us standing outside the security guard's room. When he came out, Jo passed him the keys and then *he* was the one to wander casually off in the direction of the kitchen.

When Richard came back, we all drifted toward the television room, avoiding the living room with its exhibition-hall atmosphere. This time Richard didn't bother tossing his coat over the I-spy camera. I told him the search was a bust, which he'd already guessed, and we all sat there avoiding one another's eyes. I couldn't stand that more than a minute so I jumped up and started inspecting the shelves of videotapes that lined the walls. The cassettes were a fair indicator of their owner's interests in life, ranging from golden oldies like *Debbie Does Dallas* to ones I'd never heard of. *Snow White and the Seven Hunks?* Family porn. The morning was just about shot and we hadn't accomplished a thing. I couldn't think of what to do, but I was damned if *I* was going to be the one to suggest we draw straws to decide who came out of this intact.

How long do you have to go on paying for a mistake? The sheer neverendingness of it was getting to me. Christ, everything I'd tried had backfired. I'd correct one mistake, but then the correction would turn out to be a worse mistake. So I'd correct the correction, and the result would be a still bigger mistake. It had to end somewhere. Didn't it? Sure it did. With my neck in a noose.

If only Sandy and Robin and Chris hadn't horned in! They'd still be alive today, if they'd just minded their own business. I *tried* to get them to stay behind, I did everything I could think of to discourage them—but would they listen? They would not. *Oh no, Jack, you're not leaving us behind!* and *You're taking Tony Dwyer and not us?* and *We're coming, Jack old buddy—no arguments now!*

All I wanted was to get Tony Dwyer up in a helicopter alone; the last thing I needed was an audience. Dwyer was such a jerk. He *liked* lending people money; it gave him power over them. He *liked* being able to point his finger and say *he* owes me and *she* owes me and *they* owe me; it was the only way he could make himself important. And oh, how he loved watching me squirm when he threatened to tell Brother Phil how much I owed! But there comes a time when you have to stop the squirming, when you have to stop letting noodniks like Tony Dwyer twist your balls just to amuse themselves. There comes a time when you have to say *Enough.*

But godalmighty, I never planned on Sandy and Robin and Chris being up in that helicopter with us! I *loved* those three; I'd known Sandy and Chris since college and Robin almost as long. *Why* did they have to pick that day of all days to invite themselves along? And then to make matters even worse, when we got to the Marseilles branch they wouldn't let me check out the new helicopter alone. *Too many innovations, Jack,* they said. *Lots of new features you don't know about,* they said. *Take an experienced pilot with you, Jack.* They said.

So instead of being alone in a helicopter with Tony Dwyer, there I was with four extra people. I didn't know what to do; Dwyer was nervous about helicopters and it had taken me forever to talk him into making our little trip along the coast. I finally got him to come by telling him there was a man in St.-Tropez who owed *me* money. Not enough to pay back the entire amount I was in for—that way he'd still have power over me—but enough to keep him from blabbing to Phil. That's the way I put it to him: *enough to keep you from blabbing to Phil.* He bought it.

So it was kind of then or never; I didn't know if I'd ever get him up again. But still, I was pretty much resigned to not doing it, because of Sandy and the others. And I *wouldn't* have done it, if Dwyer had just had enough sense to keep his mouth shut. But he couldn't resist the captive audience he unexpectedly found himself with. We were all wearing headsets so we wouldn't have to shout and Tony Dwyer was having himself a ball, indeed he was, oh yes. He told them how much money I owed and how Phil was going to put me on an allowance like a kid because I was incompetent to handle my own affairs and how Phil might not even give me *that* if he knew about a few other debts I'd managed to keep hidden from him.

Chris told him to shut up but he just went on and on. He named names and amounts and even dates; one or two of those debts were over fifteen years old. It was bad enough for my friends to be hearing all that, but the pilot (whom I'd never seen before in my life) was sitting there soaking it all in like a man who couldn't wait to sell what he knew to the nearest gossip columnist. And still Dwyer kept talking.

He was giving too much away. It wouldn't do; it simply wouldn't do.

I still get a sick feeling in my stomach when I think about Sandy and Robin and Chris. It was just monumentally bad luck that they happened to be on *that* helicopter on *that* day. If they hadn't crashed my carefully planned party or if Dwyer had kept his mouth shut or if the pilot hadn't been there...well. But that was just part of a whole string of things that went wrong. The pilot saw what I was doing and got out, alive, and had been squeezing me ever since. I actually had to go to work for Phil to pay him. A. J. Strode found out and had put a different kind of squeeze on me.

And what did it all come down to? It came down to this weekend and its carefully orchestrated horrors.

I examined my two fellow squeezees and wondered what the hell *they* had done. I'd asked Joanna Gillespie what Strode had on her, but she'd ducked the question by saying it was too ugly to talk about. Somehow I didn't think it could be much. What dreadful thing could a world-class violinist be caught doing? Pushing plastic chopsticks in China? Smuggling trolls out of Norway? Neither of us, I noticed, had asked Richard Bruce what he had done.

"His office," Richard said out of the blue, "that's where we ought to look next."

I stared at him. "Weren't you the one who said something about an office vault?"

"The combination has to be recorded somewhere."

"So we just waltz in and look for it? Jesus, Richard, even if we could get in that'd be a *tremendous* job!"

"Then we'd better get started."

"Oh, let's go give it a try," Jo interjected. "I want to get out of this house anyway."

"Outvoted two to one," I sighed. "Okay, let's do it, troops."

LET'S DO IT, TROOPS—hah. Break into A. J. Strode's office? We couldn't even get into the *building*.

The building was closed on weekends. We could look into the lobby and see two security guards at a bank of monitors much like the one in Strode's home, only much larger. Richard Bruce tapped on the glass door until one of the guards came to see what we wanted. Richard said we had an appointment to meet Castleberry in A. J. Strode's office, but the guard said nobody had told him about it and we'd have to wait until Mr. Strode got there. He said even if he did let us go up, the guard on Mr. Strode's floor wouldn't let us off the elevators. He himself wouldn't even let us wait in the lobby. It didn't take us long to decide this was not a profitable avenue to pursue.

"Any more bright ideas, Richard?" I asked.

"It had to be tried," he said patiently.

So there we were, stranded on Forty-seventh Street following our second straight failure to breach A. J. Strode's defenses, what a *sterling* day this was turning out to be. Joanna Gillespie announced she had to eat something. We found a bar and slid into the first empty booth we came to, Jo and I on one side and Richard on the other. The menu listed nine different sandwiches; we told the waitress to bring one of each. What with our drinks and the food and the ashtray and the salt and pepper shakers and a stand-up card pushing some "specialty" the bar's kitchen was trying to get rid of, there wasn't room to put your elbows on the table. The club sandwich was closest to me and I started off with that; but everything kept slipping out from between those little triangles of toast so I switched to the Reuben.

There'd been a little eye contact going on between Jo and Richard that I didn't much care for, so to break that up, I asked Jo, "Were you a child prodigy?"

"No, thank god." She was slumped down in the booth, halfheartedly picking a piece of cheese out of one of the sandwiches. "Prodigies usually burn out by their early twenties. I intend to play for another fifty years at least."

I don't know what I was thinking of, I must not have been thinking at all, my brain was on vacation dammit, but it just slipped out: "You figure you're going to be the one to sell to Strode?"

Jo looked startled, but it was the way Richard Bruce was looking at me that made my skin crawl. Nothing to do but bluff it out. "C'mon, you've both been thinking of it, you know you have. Fess up."

"Well, it's clear *you* have," Jo said indignantly. "Whatever happened to our agreement not to accept Strode's rules?"

"*I'm* sticking to it," I said as earnestly as I knew how and blotted my hands on my trousers. "But I can't help but wonder whether you guys are having second thoughts. Are you?"

They were both silent for a moment. Then Richard said, "It's a little early to give up yet. We still have some time left."

"That says it for me," Jo added.

I allowed myself to look relieved, and it wasn't entirely show. "Okay, sorry I doubted. It's just that I've got so much riding on this weekend . . . it's not just me that might get hurt, it's the whole family business that could go down the toilet."

"McKinstry Helicopters," Richard said, not asking.

So he knew my company—and was working hard at not looking impressed. "That's it. I'm one of those McKinstrys. Unless they all disown me after this weekend."

"Do you think so?" Jo asked, not really interested.

"They might. My brother's always ready to believe the worst." I told Richard the same story I'd earlier told Jo, that Strode had manufactured evidence to implicate me in a helicopter crash that had taken place in France four years earlier. "People *died* in that crash," I pointed out. "That means I could be charged with murder if Strode convinces the French police I'm responsible."

"But only if they think you caused it deliberately," Jo objected. "The charge might be criminal negligence or something like that, but not murder."

"Oh, that's the cute part," I said. "You see, I was in that helicopter when it crashed, and only one other guy and I got

out alive. The other guy was the pilot, and Strode has bribed
him to say I wrecked that bird on purpose."

"Why?" Wouldn't you know, Richard just had to ask
that.

"Why am I supposed to have wrecked it? Strode's version is that I owed money to one of the passengers and killed
them all to get rid of him. Good god! For one thing, I'm not
in the habit of taking my creditors with me on little jaunts
along the southern coast of France. For another, those four
other people in the helicopter were my friends, I'd known
them all for years . . . I could no more kill them than I could
kill myself. And I'm supposed to have risked my *own* life
just to get out of paying a debt? It's absurd."

"Can you get to the pilot?"

I shook my head. "Strode's got him hidden away somewhere."

Jo evidently saw something in Richard Bruce's face.
"That's what he did to you too, Richard, didn't he? He got
somebody to sign something and then hid the person away."

"That's exactly what he did." Without any prologue he
went into some song and dance about a ship called the *Burly
Girl* that sank with a full crew and an insurance check that
came when it was needed most. Then he turned to me.
"You're in danger of being charged with killing . . . what,
four people, Jack? Strode has accused me of killing thirty-
seven."

Jesus, a mass murderer sitting right across the table from
me! I couldn't think of a damned thing to say. Thirty-seven
people!

Jo was frowning. "But if the entire crew went down on
the ship, who was left to sign something that could implicate you?"

"The first mate's wife," Richard said. "The mate told her
I had sanctioned the plan for scuttling the *Burly Girl*—to

quiet her doubts, I suspect. If the boss himself was behind it...well, that takes the onus off the poor lowly seaman who was sucked into a whirlwind of events he couldn't control, don't you see. And now *I* can go to the gas chamber just because some thieving son of a bitch of a sailor didn't have the nerve to tell his wife the truth.''

"Your word against hers," I suggested.

"Not entirely. He put it all in a letter before he died."

"Ah. And Strode has the letter."

"You guessed it. Something went wrong on the *Burly Girl*—the captain was in on it too, but neither he nor the mate ever got off the ship. So the mate's credibility increases a thousand-fold by virtue of his being dead."

I felt like applauding, he did that so nicely. Just the right touch of bitterness in the voice, the troubled look in the eye, the mouth drawn into a straight line—none of it overdone. I was fascinated. Why oh why do you suppose King Richard the Bruce would suddenly choose to reveal such damaging information about himself? I watched Jo watching Richard. Was it for her benefit? Was Richard hatching some little plot involving her that would leave yours truly out in the cold?

"The first mate's wife," Jo said, "is she the one Strode has hidden away?"

"She's the one. She's even changed her name, according to Castleberry."

"Then you'll never find her," I said. "Not if Strode doesn't want you to. No more than I can find Billy—he's the helicopter pilot Strode bribed. Those two are *gone*. Forget 'em."

"I already did. The answer isn't in looking for a sailor's widow and a helicopter pilot and...?"

Ah, that was it. He wanted to know what Jo had done. She was aware of both of us watching her, waiting for her to complete the sentence. She didn't. She didn't squirm, she didn't look away, she didn't *anything*. Finally I said, "C'mon, Jo, we told you our secrets. Who's Strode got locked up from your dark and undoubtedly disreputable past?" I grinned to show I was kidding.

She slumped down farther in the booth. "In my case, it's a mercenary."

I couldn't believe my ears. "A mercenary... *soldier*?"

She sighed. "Yes."

"You were, er, planning to take over a country? Start your own survivalist camp? What?"

"It was a mistake. I never hired him."

"But you were thinking of hiring him. For what?"

"It doesn't matter for what. What matters is that Strode got him to sign a statement saying I offered to hire him— which I didn't."

It was like pulling teeth. "Hire him to do what? Talk to us, Jo."

"All right, all right," she said irritably. "Strode paid him to accuse me of trying to hire him... to kill my parents."

Pow! Talk about *awesome*. "You mean... mother-and-father-type *parents*? Jesus Christ?" In a way, that was even worse than Richard's thirty-seven victims. Umm, on second thought, no it wasn't. Richard was worse. "Strode must have gone off the deep end. Your parents! Why are you supposed to have wanted them dead?"

"For their money. They both died recently—my mother two years ago and my father a year before that. They left me money—a *lot* of money. So Strode has decided I killed them for it."

"Yeah, everybody knows what a failure you are," I said with disgust and gave her hand a squeeze. "I can't imagine anyone believing that story." Sympathetic Jack, crying shoulder available without prior notice, that's me.

Richard said, "Did you try to buy off the mercenary? Or is he in hiding too?"

"He's not in hiding—he's at his home in Texas. But Strode's got him in his pocket now...and I can't get him out. I tried."

"You know," I said, "of all the rotten stunts Strode has pulled, that one has got to be the worst. I'm sorry, Jo. I wish I could help."

She was in the process of mustering up a smile for me when Richard stacked up a few of the plates of half-eaten sandwiches and reached across the table to take her hand away from me and hold it in his own. "It won't wash, Jo," he said gently. "You did seek out the mercenary, remember. Whether you ultimately hired him or not doesn't matter. You were trying to buy yourself some firepower."

She jerked her hand away. "That's no concern of yours."

"Yes, it is—unfortunately. The same way that what happened to my ship and to Jack's helicopter is *your* concern. We've each got to know what the others are up against if we're going to come up with a workable plan. You can't hold back now. There's more to the story than you're telling us."

I'd never before seen a woman age ten years right before my eyes, but I swear to god that's what happened then. Everything that made Joanna Gillespie vital and special drained right out of her as I watched. It scared the shit out of me. Richard saw it too, and for once I was glad to let him take the lead. He waited a moment or two and then simply said her name.

She roused herself with an effort. "God, I just can't take this anymore. You might as well know—what difference does it make now? It's all coming out anyway. Yes, I killed them. I killed my mother and my father. You two may be pure as the driven snow, but Strode was right about me. I'm a murderer.''

Alarums and excursions! I know the world didn't actually stop rotating at that moment, but that's sure as hell what it felt like. It's not every day of your life that you hear someone say, *I'm a murderer*. She'd really done it, she had actually *done* it—and here she was admitting it! I found I was holding my breath and let it out. "Jesus, Jo, that's a hell of a thing. Why? Do you need money that badly?"

"I don't need money at all!" she snapped with a flash of her old fire. She took a deep breath and said in a low voice, "I killed them because they asked me to."

It belatedly occurred to me that we were in a public place and here was this world-famous violinist admitting she'd killed her parents and who knew who might be listening? I did a quick look around, but all the other customers in that place were so wrapped up in their own confessions that they weren't paying any attention to us. "They asked you to," I prompted.

"They were ill," Richard guessed.

"Terminally," she said. "It was only a matter of time before they both died without any help from me. But they were in pain—such *incredible* pain. My father was suffering from emphysema, and he'd already had two coronaries. Just the simple act of breathing was torture for him. He wasn't allowed much in the way of painkillers because of other drugs he was taking—he got at most a couple of hours' relief a day." Her eyes turned inward, remembering. "Every day I'd go into his room, and he'd beg me to put an end to it. That big, strong man reduced to a lump in a bed—*begging*." Her eyes focused again, and she looked first at Richard and then at me. "Finally I did what he wanted," she finished simply.

Hmm, yes. Ah-ha. It was a touching story, all right, all about a loving daughter risking her own freedom to bring her dying father relief from pain. *Real* touching. I might even believe it if she hadn't inherited a fortune. *I don't need money at all*, she'd said. What bullshit. Everybody always needs money.

"The mercenary?" Richard asked.

"Oh yes—Ozzie. Ozzie Rogers is his name. I contacted him when I'd decided to go ahead with it, but that was a mistake. I couldn't *hire* someone to kill my father for me. I had to do it myself."

Sensitive, too, with a nice sense of propriety. Or maybe she just got cold feet dealing with a hired killer? Naw, it couldn't be something as unwonderful as that; perish the thought. I put an arm around her shoulders. "Don't dwell on it," I said. "It's over now."

"Not completely," Richard said. "Your mother—it was the same with her?"

"Oh...Mother." That inward gaze again. "It was nephritis in her case. Do you know what she said to me? She said, 'You did it for your father—why won't you do it for me?'" Jo looked at us both with pleading eyes. "How did she know I'd killed him? *How did she know?*"

That *How did she know?* got me. I know something about acting, and I was willing to bet every one of my shares of House of Glass that Joanna Gillespie wasn't acting then. She really didn't know how her mother had found out. Dear me, could she be telling the truth about her two-time excursion into homicide and it really was euthanasia after all? More likely she'd just bumped off the old lady because she'd found out. *How did she know.*

"Your father must have told her what you were going to do," Richard suggested.

"I'm pretty sure he didn't," Jo said. "I don't think they were ever alone together toward the end. They were both bedridden and in separate rooms... but aside from that, I don't think he *would* have told her. Not him. Well, it's not important now." She lapsed into silence.

So there we sat, three little killers out on a limb. I was as sure as I was that God made little green apples that Richard Bruce had sent thirty-seven people to their deaths a hell of a lot more easily than I had sent four to theirs. Whether Jo Gillespie's murder of her folks was a family-sized mercy killing or not didn't make a hell of a lot of difference; Strode had her and she knew it. I took my arm from around Jo and used it to lift a nearly-empty glass. "A toast," I said. "To Ozzie, Jo's mercenary, and to Billy, my pilot, and to... what's your finger-pointing widow's first name, Richard?"

He had to think. "Estelle."

"To Ozzie and Billy and Estelle—may they all meet in hell." It rhymed. Only Richard joined me in my toast; Jo sat staring at nothing, a million miles away. She'd given up; she'd told us about killing Mommie and Daddy because she was convinced she was going to be one of the weekend's two losers. Well, I was real sorry about that, but somebody had to lose. The waitress came up and asked if we were happy or did we want to do it again; it was time to leave.

Lo and behold it was starting to turn dark. We'd wasted the entire afternoon eating and drinking and telling lies. Then out of the blue something uncomfortably akin to panic hit me *bam*, like that. The sidewalks were crowded with people hurrying in a vain attempt to beat the rush-hour traffic and I suddenly felt disoriented. Like I didn't know where I *was*—Christ, that's scary. What if the other two hadn't been lying after all? And what if Richard honestly had been caught in the backwash of other men's cupidity?

What if I was trying to convince myself of their guilt so I wouldn't feel so alone?

"Jack?" Jo's voice said from what seemed a great distance away. "What's the matter?"

I bumped into a bag lady who for some reason was holding a big pretzel against her ear. But my mini-anxiety attack passed; I muttered nothing's the matter, I'm all right, it's okay. Richard stepped into the street and flagged down a taxi. All of New York was trying to grab a cab at that hour and Richard got one, wouldn't you know. We piled in and Jo said, "I don't want to go back to that house."

"I do," I said, and gave the driver the address. "I want to go and burn it down."

"Or at least break a few things," Jo agreed with a forced smile. She was looking for things to joke about, coming out of her funk.

"Where would you like to go, Joanna?" That was Richard the Protector, noble solicitousness personified. And dig that *Joanna*.

"Where? Boston. Berlin. Timbuktu, I don't know." She sighed. "There's no place to run to. We might as well go back to Strode's."

Sensible of her. But when the cab pulled up to Strode's place, I felt a stab of the same reluctance to go back inside there; I wanted to split in the worst way. But I fought down the urge and said in my best ringmaster manner, "Well, well, here we are again, lady and gentleman! Step right this way and behold the eighth wonder of the modern world—the house that greed built. Which is not all that wondrous, come to think of it, greed being as it is a class-A requirement for social acceptability nowadays. And what have we here? A guardian at the gate? Abandon hope...good evening to you, sir. Don't tell me—we have to sign in."

The security guard was one of those people who've never smiled in their lives; a real Spanish sense of humor. "No sir, Mr. McKinstry, just go on in."

Inside, we separated immediately; we all wanted a little time away from one another. I checked to make sure the cardboard was still covering the camera in my room and then lay on my bed for a while, seriously considering cutting out. But that wouldn't solve my problem, and it would just make things easier for Jo and Richard. I didn't want to make things easier for Jo and Richard.

After about half an hour I crossed the hall and knocked on Jo's door. When she let me in, I said, "Were you and Richard serious last night? When you were talking about killing Strode?"

She sighed. "I don't know whether we were or not. It doesn't matter, since we don't know where Strode is. We've been through all this."

"And he doesn't have any children we could kidnap or whatever. What if we should start wrecking this expensive home of his?"

"Why do you suppose he hires security guards?"

"But my god, Jo, we're right here where he lives! We ought to be able to do *something* to him! Something to make him back down."

"I'm open to suggestion," she said dryly.

"Are you? I thought you'd given up."

She thought about it. "I guess I haven't—not completely, anyway." She shot me a look I didn't understand. "Of course, if we all do get out of this...I'll still have you two to worry about, won't I?"

"What do you mean?" I stalled.

"You know what I mean. You and Richard. You'll both be in a position to blackmail me."

I was saved from having to answer by a knock on the door; it was Richard, wanting to know if we'd thought of something. "Jo has," I said in a hurt tone of voice. "She thinks you and I are going to blackmail her."

They exchanged a long look. Richard said in that soft voice of his, "How can we, Joanna? We have no more on you than you have on us."

"You have my true confession," she said poker-faced.

"Worth about as much as all the rest of the creative bullshit that's been flying around here lately," he said.

"But my confession was uttered in a dark moment of self-flagellation and soul-wringing despair. I should think that would be worth something."

"I'll give you a dollar for it."

"I'll take it. But I did admit to murder. To two murders. I placed myself at your mercy."

I didn't get it; Richard was laughing. "Thus convincing us that you are the weak member of this trio? The one we don't have to watch because she's no threat. It didn't work, Joanna. I'm more afraid of you now than I was before."

Afraid? Of Jo? Richard Bruce was afraid of Joanna Gillespie? And now she was laughing, too—quietly, as if sharing a joke. What the *hell*? "Hey, remember me?" I said. "How about letting me in on it? Jo, was any of that stuff you told us this afternoon true?"

"Oh yes," she smiled. "Almost all of it."

And it was up to me to guess which part wasn't. I flopped down on Jo's bed, trying (for Richard's benefit) to look as if I'd been there before. "Isn't this jolly?" I said with a big smile. "Here we've known one another for less than twenty-four hours and we've already got a dandy Three Stooges act going. Oh, I'm really enjoying myself. Aren't you enjoying yourselves?"

Richard pulled a chair up to the side of the bed and sat, staring down at me. "Cards on the table, Jack. We're all three killers, and A. J. Strode has found us out. All we've got is one another. We've spent too much time lying and not enough planning."

"*I'm* not a killer!" I sputtered, sitting up. "Speak for yourself! Those people who died in the helicopter were my friends!"

"I'll bet at least one of them wasn't. You caused that crash, Jack, just as surely as I arranged for the *Burly Girl* to be scuttled. Just as surely as Joanna killed her parents."

Jo was slouched in the window seat, disassociating herself. I looked at Richard. "What are you up to? What do you want?"

"I want to survive," he said quietly.

It was a trick; it had to be a trick. They both confess to crimes they didn't commit so I'll be a good old boy and confess too. Then once they're sure I'm a real killer, they just forget about me and work out the Strode thing between them. Well, I didn't care much for that script. "We all want to survive," I said carefully. "But I'm not sure how much chance I've got up against two admitted killers."

"Make it three and join the club."

I glanced over at Jo, who was staring moodily out the window; no help there. "Why is it so important," I asked Richard, "for me to say I'm a killer?"

"Because," he answered slowly, "I have to know how far you are willing to go."

That brought Jo back to life. "You have a plan," she said.

"Just the beginnings," Richard told us. "But I know already it won't work if there are any faint hearts among us. I'm sure of myself, and I'm almost as sure of you, Joanna." He looked at me without saying anything.

I swallowed. "I'll do anything," I assured them both. "Anything anyone can think of to get us out of this, I'll do."

"Even kill?" Jo asked, damn her.

"I've never killed anyone before," I said in my sincerest voice, "but I think I could, if I had to."

Jo made that *tsuh* sound that means both amusement and contempt with the emphasis on the latter. Richard said, "I don't think it'll come to that, but we ought to be prepared to. Before I can figure out details, I'll have to know more about the layout here. I need to know every door and window in this place that's locked—look, you two have been in the private wing and I haven't. Can you draw me a floor plan?"

Jo rummaged through drawers looking for paper. Richard wouldn't explain what he had in mind; he said only that we had to find a way to get back in here once the guards thought we had left. Crack Strode's security system, in other words. A diversion, I suggested. He acknowledged the possibility and bent over the drawing Jo was making of Strode's private quarters. "You said you left one of these doors unlocked?" he asked. "Which one?"

"The door to the library," she answered, pointing to the drawing. "From the library you can go through Strode's dressing room to the bedroom and on to the other dressing room, currently unoccupied."

"Bathroom?"

"One off each dressing room." She sketched them in.

Richard nodded. "All right, let's map the rest of this place.

We split up. I got the exterior of the house. I went around trying every door and window I could find; everything was locked. The security guard at the front gate came up and wanted to know what I was looking for. I told him secret passages. He blinked and went back to the gate. I worked my way around back and found another gate, for deliveries. It was electronically controlled. I wrote it all down and made a little sketch.

The kitchen staff had left a cold buffet for us, so we gathered in the dining room when we were finished. Jo and Richard drank coffee from the big urn on the sideboard, but I wanted something cold. I grabbed a can from the fridge, but it turned out to be one of those artificial lemonylimony things that taste like something dipped up out of a public swimming pool so I had to go back and make sure I got a beer that time. There was no comparing of sketches while we ate, because of the ever-watchful camera making sure we didn't abscond with the silver. But we could talk, and I let Richard know I was getting just a trifle annoyed with his hush-hush approach to problem solving. He said be patient, as if he were talking to a child.

"I found a wine cellar," Jo said. "And it has its own outside door, around at the side of the house. If the key is in that little cabinet near the kitchen, that could be our way in. But I assume there's a camera outside aimed at the door."

"Wait 'til we get upstairs," I said. "I marked all the outside cameras in my sketch of the grounds."

We finished in a hurry and went up to my room. We spread out all our papers on the bed and started piecing them together. Jo located her wine cellar, and I found the corresponding place in my sketch of the grounds. Sure enough, there was a camera pointed at the wine cellar door.

"Damn those things!" Jo exploded. "How can we hope to get anything done with those cameras watching our every move?"

"Yes, we've got to do something about them," Richard muttered. "Jack, a while ago you suggested a diversion.

Could you plan one? To get the security guard away from his station so one of us can get in there and disable the cameras.''

Ah wow, wasn't that mahvelous. The man in charge was delegating authority. Showing his leadership qualities. "If I come up with a diversion, do you know how to disable that bank of cameras?''

He shrugged. "Pull out wires.''

"Uh-huh. And when exactly is this diversion to be pulled off? And how long must it last? And must I do it alone or do I get some help? And last but by no means least, *why* am I doing all this? Come on, Richard, stop playing mystery man." I put on a phony-polite voice. "Some of us are beginning to wonder whether you really do have a plan, Mr. Bruce, sir, yes we are. And if you have a plan, Mr. Bruce, sir, why, pray tell, do you keep it secret? Could it be, shocking though the thought is, could it possibly be, that your secret plan has Jo Gillespie and Jack McKinstry going belly-up while Richard Bruce, Esquire, comes out smelling like a rose?''

His facial expression never changed. "Do you think you could do a better job of disabling the cameras than I could?''

I made a noise of exasperation. "I know I could. I've done my share of wiring on helicopter control panels. Television monitors are child's play.''

"All right, plan it that way then. You—''

Damn him, he was ignoring me. "*Richard*—''

He used his hand as a stop sign. "I'll tell you this much. My plan assumes that the original evidence we want is locked in a vault in Strode's office. If it isn't there, the plan isn't worth spit. Now—do we go with it?''

Jo and I exchanged a look; I rolled my eyes and shrugged. "We go with it," Jo decided for both of us. Oh, why the hell not. Anything was better than sitting around doing nothing.

It was growing late. None of us had gotten much sleep the night before and it was beginning to catch up with us. But on we talked, about doors and keys and cameras and security guards and other equally boring subjects. Jo and Richard between them decided the wine cellar door was the best way back into the house because it would be the least used of the house's various exits and entrances. (Exactly why we wanted to come back into this place, Richard didn't deign to explain.) Finally he announced he had to sleep on it and would tell us in the morning whether he thought the plan had a chance of working or not.

That was fine with me; right then I just wanted him out of my room. I was tired, really beat. When Richard had left, Jo came over and gave me a little hug. "Don't look so glum, Jack," she told me. "It'll be better in the morning."

I held on to her. "He's enjoying himself, you know. Doing all the planning, keeping us in the dark."

She didn't pull away. "I suspect that's the way he does everything. Richard's used to giving orders."

I held on tighter. "Yeah, well, I'm not used to taking them. And neither are you, I imagine. That had better be one hell of a plan."

She still didn't pull away. "We'll know in a few hours. Try to relax, Jack—you're so tense."

Now I ask you, was that an invitation or was that an invitation? I kissed her. But before it could turn serious, she backed off. Not quite yet, it seemed. "I'm going to stand in a hot shower until I'm asleep on my feet," she smiled and went across the hall to her own room. "Good night, Jack."

Sure, good night—I got it. Suddenly I didn't feel so tired anymore. I took a shower and shaved and brushed my teeth twice. I hadn't brought a robe or pajamas (never use 'em) so I pulled on a pair of trousers. Had I given her enough time? Yeah, I'd given her enough time.

But I hesitated. An idea had been teasing at me, something I wanted to take to Richard. And this looked like the only chance I'd get to talk to him alone; ten to one tomorrow we'd be sticking to one another like leeches. A quick trip down the hall first, then Jo.

I knocked on Richard's door. His voice said, "Just a minute!" and I could hear him moving around inside. He was still pulling up his pajama bottoms when he opened the door. "Something wrong?" he asked, casually bracing his arms against the doorjambs and thus effectively blocking my entrance.

"We need to talk, Richard. Let me in."

"In the morning. I was going to bed."

"Not in the morning—now. It won't wait."

His facial expression didn't change but his eyes bore holes in me. He dropped one arm and allowed me to enter the royal chambers, I felt so honored. "What is it, Jack?"

"A proposition." I cleared my throat. "If your great plan doesn't work, there's still a way you and I can improve the odds. It's Jo. Say Strode turns in his evidence to the police—what happens to her? She pleads mercy killing, she gets a light sentence, she's out again in a few years. It's not going to be that easy for you or me."

"What are you saying?"

"You know damn well what I'm saying. If we end up drawing straws, let's make sure it's just you and me doing the drawing. A fifty-fifty chance beats one in three any day. Jo doesn't have as much to lose as we do. What do you say?"

His eyes narrowed. "Just shut her out?"

"Why not? What can she do about it?"

"She can break your bloody head, that's what she can do about it." It was Jo's voice that said that, and Jo herself was standing in the doorway of Richard's bathroom. I wanted to sink through the floor; she'd heard what I said, there was no way of denying it, how was I going to get out of this one, *and what the hell was she doing in Richard's bathroom?* Jo was wearing a clinging robe-thing that made it pretty clear that she didn't have anything on underneath. She charged over to stand directly in front of me, her eyes blazing. "Gee, Jack, you sure are one swell fellow, you are. I feel so lucky, getting to meet you. What a *prince* of a guy."

Brazen it out. "Yeah? What about you? Using your bedroom charms on Richard—to get him to give me the shaft, no doubt. That's okay, I suppose."

She punched me in the nose. She didn't slap, she didn't scratch, she didn't beat on my chest with her fists. She punched. And immediately regretted it, I was delighted to see. "Oh my god—my hand!" she yelled. "What was I thinking of?" I felt the blood trickling down my lip and hoped every bone in her goddamned precious hand was broken.

I had my fist up to hit her back but Richard stopped me. "Let's see," he said to Jo and took her hand. "Wiggle your fingers."

She wiggled them. "Oh, it's all right. I just scared myself, that's all. How foolish—risking my hand because of a piece of filth like Jack McKinstry."

"Tell me," Richard said, pinning me with that icy look of his, "is 'Jack' short for 'Jackass'? Haven't you figured it out yet? Strode isn't going to let any of us go. *None* of us walks away from this. You want to draw straws for who sells his House of Glass shares? Jack, *it doesn't matter who sells.* He's out to get us *all.* Now do you understand?"

Jesus. Jesus.

Jo laughed unpleasantly. "He hadn't even thought of it. You trust Strode to keep his word, do you? Ah Jack, Jack! You're about as sharp-witted as you are trustworthy. And absolutely *terrific* in a crisis."

I turned my back and walked away without answering. I can't stand sarcastic women.

SIX

RICHARD BRUCE, SUNDAY:

JOANNA WOULDN'T STAY the night; that called for a greater display of trust than either of us was prepared to make, I suppose, although we did drift off to sleep for a bit. The day had been emotionally exhausting for her; it had taken her almost an hour to calm down after learning from Jack's own lips of his inexcusable treachery. I wasn't totally surprised, for the situation we were in was exacerbating all his worst qualities; but his approach seemed clumsy even for him.

What an incompetent Jack McKinstry was. He was born rich, good-looking, and a fool; amazing how often those three attributes went together. Jack had thought no farther ahead than the immediate weekend; get the evidence back and all his problems would be solved. He'd overlooked the simplest, most obvious fact of his predicament—that even if he did get his hands on the statement the helicopter pilot had signed, all Strode had to do was get the man to sign another one.

But recovering the original evidence would buy time, and that was something we desperately needed. Time for me to locate Mrs. Estelle Rankin and pry her out of Strode's grasp. I bore no ill will against the woman; she was doing what she could to survive. It would be a simple enough matter to better Strode's offer, whatever it was. So I would give her that option—cooperate or die. If she showed any reluctance at all, I would say what I always said in these situa-

tions: *Do exactly as I say or you'll never have to make
another decision in your life. All thirty seconds of it.* It
worked most of the time; very few resisted after that. I once
had to dispatch a man with my own hands, instead of delegating the job to someone hired for the purpose. That was
messy; I didn't enjoy it.

As it turned out, I was in a better position than either
Joanna or Jack. Once I destroyed Harry Rankin's letter,
Strode wouldn't be quite so quick to accuse me of murder,
not on the basis of the unsupported testimony of one
woman as to the contents of a single letter written seventeen years ago. Jack's pilot was different. He'd been there,
on the scene; he was an actual eyewitness to what had happened on board that helicopter.

In the same way, Joanna's Texas mercenary was an eyewitness to her one attempt at hiring a killer. That alone was
not evidence that she herself had killed, but it would be
sufficient to create a cloud of suspicion that could prove fatal to someone in the public eye. I didn't think the mercenary would prove an insurmountable obstacle; he was
obviously a man who took money from whoever offered the
most and such men can be dealt with. I offered my help;
Joanna accepted.

She'd unknowingly solved a problem for me, with that
singular admission of guilt she made in the bar yesterday.
I'd been wondering how to stop all the pretense, how to get
it out on the table that we were all capable of killing and
would do so again if sufficiently threatened. Now only Jack
persisted in playing his role of the wrongly accused, but
Joanna and I understood each other. I'd half jokingly taxed
her with using confession as a diversionary tactic, and the
answer she'd given me was just ambiguous enough to allow
me to think whatever I wanted.

In retrospect, I think her admission she'd killed both her parents sprang from a very real sense of imminent defeat and thus was to be trusted as to its accuracy. She saw what was coming and was laying the groundwork for her defense, perhaps even testing it out on Jack and me. She did not whimper and cry and expect someone else to solve her problem for her. That was one of the things that made Joanna Gillespie who she was.

The first time she spoke to me across the dining table on Friday evening, I knew she was a kindred spirit. That sense of self-worth that has nothing to do with vanity—it is so rare to find that quality in a woman that I had long since abandoned any hope of finding a true partner for myself. My wife hadn't had it; none of the women I'd known since her death had had it. But there it was in abundance, in a dark-haired woman sitting across the table from me in A. J. Strode's dining room.

But I'd never heard of her before Friday, when Castleberry introduced her and then Jack McKinstry later sneered at me for not knowing who she was. That same evening, before we got into that fruitless talk session that kept us up most of the night, I'd called one of my assistants in Los Angeles (not a Castleberry type at all) and told him to find out as much as he could about Joanna Gillespie and Jack McKinstry before morning. He already knew who Joanna was; he'd even seen her on television earlier in the year.

When he called back, he'd had enough basic information to give me a handle on each of them. Joanna was clearly the tougher of the two. What with her diabetes and the demands of a difficult career, she had to be tough simply to survive. Jack McKinstry's claiming she was the best violinist in the world had not been an exaggeration, my assistant said, passing along the consensus of the music world; but when he said she was unique, I accused *him* of exaggerating. No so, he said; Joanna Gillespie was one of a kind, in a class of artistry all by herself. She'd even had to make a comeback of sorts; her career had been put on hold during the final illness and death of her parents. But while I was wondering what sword A. J. Strode was holding over her head, it never once occurred to me that she had murdered her father and mother. I couldn't imagine what that must have been like, killing two people that close. What courage it must have taken! I hadn't even known half the crew of the *Burly Girl*.

What an extraordinary woman Joanna was. Her posture was abominable. She didn't bother with make-up. Lovely high cheekbones and golden-brown hair. Her clothes were good, but I suspected she wore them more as a concession to decency than out of any interest in fashion. She was intelligent, and she had to have strong survival skills to be where she was in her profession. Her appearance and her way of walking and talking all broadcast one clear message: *You've got your rules, I've got mine—let's not make an issue of it.* She had that wonderful don't-give-a-damn outlook that comes only from knowing one has a special gift that raises one up over the rest of the world. No matter whatever else happened to her in her life, she would still be Joanna Gillespie, violinist supreme. One of a kind. That uniqueness made her exciting in a way she was all too aware of, and I wasn't the only one attuned to it. Jack had been trying to move in on her all weekend.

Jack McKinstry was more or less what he appeared to be—a privileged, careless man who could turn the charm on or off at will. Jack was the McKinstry who didn't work. Or hadn't worked, according to my assistant, until a close brush with death had changed his attitude some four years back. Jack himself later told us what Strode was accusing him of, and I for one had no difficulty in believing it at all. There was something of the cornered rat about Jack McKinstry, in spite of his glib speech and his carefully cultivated appearance of poise and self-control—*centeredness*, I believe it's called now. He probably had no qualms at all about throwing his friends to the wolves to save himself.

But Jack and Joanna both were amateurs when it came to dealing with the likes of A. J. Strode; I knew as early as Friday night that I was going to have to be the one to come up with a solution for our mutual problem. By Sunday morning I knew I could count on Joanna; she understood the need for drastic action and she had the backbone to go through with it. Jack was the weak link in our chain, but we couldn't do it without him.

We all asked for breakfast trays in our rooms. Then we had to wait a few minutes while Joanna tested her blood sugar. But at last they were both in my room, and we were able to get down to business. Joanna wouldn't even look at Jack; as far as she was concerned, he wasn't there. For his part, Jack affected an air of indifference.

"First of all," I said, "we're going to need a diversion, something to get the guard away from his post long enough for Jack to get in and disable the monitors—and Jack, I asked you to give it some thought. Were you able to come up with something?"

"Do I get some help," he asked lazily, "or am I supposed to do both the diverting *and* the disabling?"

"Of course you'll have help."

"Then it's easy. We just let the monitor show you trying to pick the lock to Strode's bedroom suite." He grinned.

Not bad. It would not only accomplish our mutual goal of getting the guard away from his monitors, but it would also satisfy Jack's private goal of casting me in a less-than-dignified role, in this instance that of failed burglar. "Very

;ood," I said. "We'll use it. How long will you need to dis-
ıble the monitors?"

He shrugged. "Can't tell until I see the wiring. Just keep
'he guard occupied as long as you can."

Joanna was frowning. "This won't give us a whole lot of
ime. They'll be sure to get a repairman out here immedi-
ıtely."

"It's Sunday," Jack reminded her.

"This is New York, not California," she reminded *him*,
ıt last acknowledging his existence.

I said, "The security firm that installed the cameras and
monitors undoubtedly offers around-the-clock service. But
we won't need much time, Joanna, just enough for you and
ne to get back into the house."

She smiled wryly. "Start at the beginning?"

"Right. You both agree there's no way we're going to get
ınto Strode's office vault on our own?" They nodded.
'Well, then, we'll simply have to get someone to open it for
ıs. Castleberry. He can get us into the building and he's
ɔound to know how to open the vault."

"And why, pray tell," Jack drawled, "is Castleberry going to do us such a big favor? Out of the warmness of his
oversized Samaritan heart?"

"What's Castleberry going to be doing today?" I asked
rhetorically. "He's going to be sitting by his telephone
waiting for us to call and tell him which one we've chosen to
sell his House of Glass shares. So that's what we do. We call
and say we've decided, and would he kindly get the hell over
here, please?"

Joanna looked interested, but Jack laughed derisively.
"And which one of us, he asked innocently, did we choose?
It couldn't possibly be Richard Bruce, could it?"

"No. Jack McKinstry. You call the number Strode gave us and tell Castleberry you're the seller. And you also tell him Joanna and I are leaving."

"Why leave, Richard?" she asked.

"Because Castleberry isn't likely to come here if he thinks he has to face all three of us again. He's undoubtedly primed the security guards to let him know the minute any of us walks out carrying a suitcase. So you and I walk, and Jack waits for Castleberry."

"Why Jack?"

"Yeah, why me?"

"Jack has the best line of patter—he can talk rings around someone like Castleberry. Jack, you've got to feign enthusiasm when you talk to him. You're the winner, remember. Tell him we drew straws or played cards to decide, whatever. Convince him it's all settled and that he can safely come here and conclude the business. Can you do that?"

He laughed, lifted one hand and snapped his fingers.

"Then what?" Joanna asked. "You and I come back in through the wine cellar?"

"Yes, but you're getting ahead of yourself. We have to unlock the door from the inside and then wait until Jack disables the security system. We won't be able to get back in until he does, because that rear service gate is electronically controlled."

"How'm I going to do all that if you've already left?" Jack protested. "I need—"

"All right, let's back up," I interrupted. "In sequence, then. The first thing is that Joanna and I pack. Next, you two go to the key cabinet near the kitchen. One of you stands lookout and diverts any passing maid while the other takes the key to the wine cellar. They're all labeled, but it might take a few minutes to find the right one—that's why you'll need a lookout. Once you have the key, I go into

Strode's private wing and pretend to try to pick the lock to the bedroom suite. It was the door to the library that you left unlocked, wasn't it?"

"The library, right," Joanna said.

"So I'll fiddle around with the bedroom lock. The security guard sees me trying to break in and rushes up to stop me. Jack goes in and disconnects the cameras and monitors, and Joanna goes down and unlocks the wine cellar door. Joanna and I leave, separately. Jack calls Castleberry. Joanna, just ride around in a taxi for fifteen or twenty minutes and then meet me by the service gate out back. I have an errand to run."

"What errand?" Jack asked suspiciously.

"I'm going to one of those charming places in Times Square that are open twenty-four hours a day, and I'm going to buy three knives."

"*Knives!*" they both said.

"One for each of us," I nodded, "the biggest, ugliest knives I can find. Granted, that's a trifle melodramatic. But the knives are necessary, I think, to assure Castleberry's cooperation. We're in the intimidation business now, my friends, so we'd better make sure we do it right. Castleberry isn't going to give us any trouble if he's convinced we're all three prepared to stick a knife in him at the slightest provocation."

"Well, all right!" Jack's big grin was back; he liked the idea of a knife.

Joanna was laughing silently. "I'm trying to visualize myself menacing Myron Castleberry with a knife, and I'm afraid it doesn't play. I don't know anything about wielding a knife, Richard."

"I'll show you—there's not much to it. But timing is important here," I cautioned. "I'll be as fast as I can, but the

security repairman is sure to be here before I get back. Jack
make as much work for him as you possibly can."

"No problem."

I do wish people would stop saying *No problem*
"Joanna, when we get back into the house, we'll slip up to
Strode's library and hide there until Castleberry gets here.'

She nodded. "Because the maids will be cleaning in our
rooms. Then we twist Castleberry's arm and force him to
take us to Strode's office? How do we all get out of the
house without either of the security guards seeing us—the
service gate again?"

"No, it won't matter if they see us then. Remember it's
only Castleberry we have to worry about. He has to think
that two of us are gone, but once he's in the house we'll
show ourselves. Jack, he'll probably take you into the con
ference room downstairs to do the paperwork—make sure
you disconnect the sound as well as the visuals. But wher
ever you end up, there's bound to be a phone there. Call us
the minute you two are alone."

"And then we go into our muscle act," Jack said glee
fully. "Ah me, I can hardly wait. Poor Castleberry. You
don't suppose I could get away with cutting off a toe or two
do you?"

"It isn't Castleberry you want to cut," Joanna said
sharply. "Richard, you're trusting several crucial parts of
this plan to Jack. Do you think that's wise?"

"Hey," Jack said.

"I'm sure he can do it," I said with a confidence put on
for the occasion. The last thing I needed was dissension in
the troops.

"That's not the point," she objected. "What's to pre
vent Jack from striking a private deal with Castleberry while
you and I are upstairs in Strode's library waiting for a phone
call that never comes?"

I'd been hoping she wouldn't think of that. I looked at Jack.

He sighed. "Jo, I don't blame you for not trusting me. What I did last night—well, I panicked, okay? Couldn't help myself, honest to god. I just lost control. Didn't that ever happen to you? But you don't have to worry about me. I've had my breakdown. It's behind me now."

Joanna looked unconvinced. I said, "I think Jack understands now that Strode isn't going to honor his part of the bargain. The only way to get hold of that evidence is to take it."

"Hoo boy *yes* I understand," Jack said convincingly. "I know I'm in over my head. I need you two."

Joanna shrugged and accepted it, but without enthusiasm. "When do we start?"

"Now," I said. "First, we pack. Jack, you might want to scout out a place where you can stand and watch for the guard leaving the monitoring room."

"You got it," he said as he left.

Joanna stood looking at me. "You trust him?"

I put my hands on her shoulders and thought about something I'd rather be doing than tricking Myron Castleberry. "I trust his fear. Jack can't cope with Strode and Castleberry by himself—he's not going to take on you and me too. Besides, he's the only one of us who knows anything about electrical wiring."

She gave me a faint smile and went to her room to pack. I was ready in five minutes. We went downstairs together; I carried her suitcase but left mine behind. Then I pretended an interest in the paintings on the wall of that barnlike living room while Joanna and Jack moved off casually in the direction of the kitchen. In a few minutes they were back. Joanna moved a fist slightly away from her side; she had the wine cellar key.

We were ready. I went up to Strode's bedroom and began to poke ineffectually at the lock with a nail file. It didn't take long; in less than a minute I heard feet pounding up the stairs and the guard's voice telling me to get away from that door.

I put on an air of great exasperation. "Mr. Strode put some papers on his desk for me...and then he goes away and leaves the door locked! But as long as you're here, you can unlock it for me."

He refused, none too politely. I offered him money; he declined. I offered him more money; he still declined. He took my arm to lead me away from the door; I grew angry. I shook off his arm and called him a name; he grew angry. I kept this farce going until I saw the little red light in the hall camera die away. I informed the guard that I was leaving this house never to return again. He did not look sorry.

A quick detour by my room to pick up my suitcase and then I stalked out of the house without another word to anybody. The outside guard spoke to me by name in a friendly manner; I brushed by him, radiating as much anger as I could. He'd remember my leaving.

The taxi let me out at one of the camera-cum-junk places in Times Square; I gave the driver a fifty and told him there'd be another just like it if he kept circling until I came out. In the shop I found that the really wicked knives were too cumbersome to be carried in a pocket; they were big as machetes. The others were deadly-looking enough, though. I bought three different kinds—pearl-handled for Joanna, leather for me, and pink plastic for Jack.

The taxi came around about a minute after I left the shop, and a few minutes later we pulled up to where Joanna was sitting on her suitcase not far from Strode's service gate at the back. "Half an hour," she greeted me as the cab drove away. "But the service gate is still out of commission. I tried it."

I carried both suitcases as Joanna pushed back an otherwise electronically controlled series of bolts on the gate. She led the way to the wine cellar door; the guardian camera showed no red-light indicator. And then we were inside. The wine cellar was cool and sparkling clean, with a table and two chairs and four or five big steel racks filled with bottles. I dropped the suitcases and grabbed Joanna; we hung on to each other for a moment, charging ourselves up for the next step.

"We have to be careful," I warned her. "The cameras are still out but we might run into some of the household staff."

"A back way to the private wing?" she suggested, and then vetoed her own suggestion. "No, that's where the staff is most likely to be. We'll have to chance the main stairs. What about the suitcases?"

"Leave them here. Oh... here's your knife."

She tried handling it, first with the blade pointing down, then up. "Which way looks more menacing?"

"Up. Here, hold it this way."

When she felt comfortable with it, we crept up the stairs to the first floor and waited there a moment, listening. When we heard nothing, we made our way to the main staircase and from there to the private wing. We slipped into the library with no trouble. Then there was nothing to do but wait; the next part depended on Jack.

After what seemed an interminable length of time, the phone rang. Jack was pretending to be talking to one of the maids; he called me "dear" and asked me to bring a small case of papers from his room to the conference room. This was it.

Castleberry's face when Joanna and I walked into the conference room was like a bad actor's in a bad horror

movie. Good; if he was starting out scared, that meant less
work for me. He stood up; I pushed him back into his chair.
Joanna was carrying her knife and I took out mine and
showed it to Castleberry. He worked his mouth wordlessly
and then he started to shrink. I don't know how he managed it, but he truly did get smaller as I watched.

"Where's mine?" Jack wanted to know.

I gave him his knife. Castleberry shrank some more.
"Castleberry," I said, "do you understand what's happening here? Do you understand we refuse to accept Strode's
conditions?"

"Pink?" Jack said, looking at his knife. "You got me a
pink knife?"

"Answer me, Castleberry."

He nodded four or five times and stammered, "Wh-what
are you going to do?"

"Well, now," I said, "that depends on you, doesn't it? If
you cooperate, we won't have to do anything to you. But if
you don't..."

Joanna moved around behind Castleberry's chair and laid
the blade of her knife along his cheek. "Oh, Castleberry's
going to cooperate," she purred, "aren't you, Castleberry?
You know what we do to people who don't cooperate."

He was making a *uhn-uhn-uhn* sound, too terrified to
move, his eyes rolled in the direction of Joanna's knife. I
said, "What we want you to do is turn over all the original
evidence you and Strode have gathered against us. That's
all. It's in his office, isn't it?"

"I can't do that!" he squeaked. "Mr. Strode would kill
me!"

"And what do you think we're going to do if you don't?"
I said slowly. "Don't you understand? The only way you're
getting out of this alive is to hand us what we want."

He groaned. Jack was jiggling his knife loosely in his hand and grinning. "I know! Let's take off his shoes and socks."

It was exactly the right thing to say. Castleberry cried out and pulled his feet back under his chair.

"The evidence, Castleberry," Joanna said. "Where is it?"

It took him a couple of tries, but he finally choked out, "In Mr. Strode's vault."

"Can you open it?" I asked.

He nodded, unable to speak. Castleberry was in bad shape; Jack and I got him to his feet, but one look at the man would tell anyone who was interested that something was drastically wrong here. Jack said, "Come on, my man, you've got to do better than this! If anyone even suspects that anything's wrong, you're going to go home without any of your toes tonight. So shape up fast, old buddy, or there'll be no more marathons for you!" He emphasized his points by tapping the blade of his knife on Castleberry's chest; Jack was having a good time.

Castleberry made a supreme effort and managed to make himself appear slightly less terrified; he still didn't look composed, but it would have to do. Joanna led the way; Jack and I followed, one on each side of Castleberry. A repairman was hard at work in the monitor room; Strode's security firm hadn't wasted any time getting there. Both the inside and the outside guards were surprised at the sight of Joanna and me; they'd seen both of us go out but neither of us come back in.

We didn't stop to explain.

CASTLEBERRY HAD DRIVEN his car; we allowed him to chauffeur us to the office. Castleberry's presence got us through the rigmarole with the guards both downstairs and on Strode's floor. The vault we were looking for could be reached only from Strode's private office; it was a room-sized safe, much larger than the one in my office. Castleberry's hands were trembling, but he managed to turn off the various alarms and get the vault door open. Jack was sweating and Joanna was breathing shallowly. I pushed Castleberry into the vault ahead of us and told him to get the evidence.

And there it was. Detectives' reports. Harry Rankin's letter to his wife, Estelle, the envelope it had come in, and the statement Estelle Rankin had signed. And there were her new name and address; she was in Oregon. I slipped that piece of paper into my pocket and said, "Is everyone satisfied?"

"Yes," said Joanna, reading from her own folder.

"It's all here," Jack nodded.

"Then let's have a bonfire." I went out into the office and grabbed the first metal wastebasket I saw. All three folders went in; Jack lit a match and dropped it on the papers. When the flame began to die down, Jack took the basket and went into Strode's private washroom to flush the ashes down the loo, remarking that ashes could be reconstructed.

Castleberry stood in the entrance to the vault watching us. "You can't get away with this," he muttered. "What makes you think you can?" His courage was coming back.

"We've already gotten away with it!" Jack sang gleefully.

I looked over at Joanna and was rewarded with the very first full-hearted smile I'd ever seen from her. She was smiling with her whole body. "Richard, it worked," she said happily. "You got the evidence back for us. You saved us."

I was about to fling both arms around her when Jack stuck out a hand and said, "Put 'er there, Richard, old buddy! I owe you. Anytime you need a favor—*anytime*—all you have to do is say the word." The odd thing about that was I believe he actually meant it.

Castleberry said, "Am I free to go now?"

"Oh no," I said mildly. "For one thing, you're thinking you'll head for the nearest phone to call the police. Kidnapping, robbery, threats of bodily harm, all that. But consider a moment, Castleberry. The police will want to know why it was so important for us to get those three folders. To answer that, you'll have to tell them what was *in* the folders. That means your esteemed employer can be charged with withholding evidence and intent to blackmail. Do you think that will endear you to him?"

He conceded the point. "So what are you going to do with me?"

"Ah, your part in our little charade is not quite finished, Castleberry. You still have another job to do."

"He does?" Jack said, surprised. "What?"

Instead of answering him I turned to Joanna. "Friday night you kept saying we needed to get something on Strode, that that was the only way we'd ever be free of him."

"Yes," she said, beginning to understand.

I smiled and gestured toward the open vault.

"Son of a gun," Jack breathed, and then burst out laughing. "Son of a gun!"

I turned to him. "Jack, you've never seemed to understand that this weekend is...repeatable. Take your own case. The helicopter pilot—Billy is his name? You've destroyed the statement Billy signed, but you haven't destroyed Billy. As long as Strode has him under his thumb, you're not safe. Do you understand *that*?"

His lips tightened; he didn't answer.

"As I see it, you have three options," I went on. "First, you can kill Billy—"

"Kill him? I told you, I didn't have anything to do with that helicopter crash!" Jack said darkly.

"Of course you did!" I snapped. "For god's sake, Jack, stop playing these stupid games. Your second option is to kill Strode."

Castleberry gasped. Jack said, "You're getting carried away, Richard. Kill Strode? You're out of your mind."

He really was the limit. "Will you stop being such a damned hypocrite, Jack! You were the one who first brought up the possibility of killing him—and then you pretended to be horrified when Joanna and I took you seriously. But there's a better way."

"Oh, do tell us," he said dryly. "I can hardly wait."

I took a breath. "It's hard to believe that you and Joanna and I are the only three people Strode's ever put the squeeze on. That vault is probably full of folders like the ones we just burned. All we have to do is help ourselves. If Strode is withholding evidence in other cases and we can prove it, then we've got him. And who knows what else is in there? We have a veritable treasure house at our disposal!"

To the surprise of us all, none other than Myron Castleberry the Fearless suddenly swung into action. He was struggling to close the heavy door of the vault when Jack reached him and jerked him away. "Naughty, naughty!" Jack scolded. "Do you want us to make you stand in the corner for an hour?"

But it was more serious than that. I took out my knife again and went over to Castleberry. Without any warning I nicked his chin, and then held the blade up so he could see the drop of blood gleaming on the tip. "Do you think for one minute," I said, not trying to hide my anger, "do you think that I will let a worthless little flunkey like you stand in my way? Do you think you are that important? You are *nothing*, Castleberry! A means to an end, that's all. You have some slight temporary value at most. You are... disposable. If you wish to come out of this unscathed, you will *do, as, you, are, told.* Is that quite clear? Is it?''

There was an uncomfortable silence that I did nothing to break. Then Castleberry said leadenly, ''I'll do what you say. I'm not going to die for A. J. Strode.''

What a surprise. ''Then start bringing files out of that vault. You know what we're looking for.''

Jack was staring at me with an expression I'd seen before, on the faces of other men. ''I'll...keep an eye on him.'' He went into the vault with Castleberry.

Joanna was watching me closely. ''How very interesting.'' She perched on the corner of Strode's desk and tapped at the side casually with one foot. ''Tell me something. This is what it was all for, wasn't it, Richard?'' she asked in a neutral voice. ''All the plotting, the running around. It was all to get you into A. J. Strode's vault. The destroying of the evidence against us—that was just a way station on the road. It was the *vault* you were after all along.''

There are times when a lie just won't do the trick; this was one of them. ''Do you forgive me?''

A sparkle appeared in her eye. ''You're about to hand me the means of getting A. J. Strode off my back forever and you want to know if I forgive you. Well, yes, Richard. I forgive you.'' She laughed. ''Just don't ever get mad at *me.*''

''Never,'' I promised her.

Jack and Castleberry came out of the vault, each with an armload of folders. ''He says these are the juiciest ones,'' Jack announced, dumping his folders on the desk Joanna was sitting on, Strode's desk.

Once Castleberry accepted the fact that he wasn't going to be able to stop us, he set out to show how helpful he could be. ''Start with this one,'' he said, handing me a folder.

"This man is a money manager who makes a practice of embezzling from his clients' retirement funds. Mr. Strode has been forcing him to invest client money in various enterprises—ones that are of interest to Mr. Strode, of course."

"That's good for seven to ten right there," Jack said gleefully. "Let's divvy these up."

We pulled up chairs around Strode's desk and parceled out the folders among the three of us. We read and asked Castleberry questions, which he answered honestly as far as I could tell. A. J. Strode's reach extended far. In addition to competing businessmen, he also had the goods on a variety of politicians—in Washington as well as New York, all men and women sitting on committees or engaged in special projects that affected Strode's financial holdings in some way.

"Whew!" Jack said at one point. "I'm thinkin' maybe we ought to go into business for ourselves! Blackmailers Incorporated—we'd make a fortune! What do you think?"

"Shut up and read, Jack," Joanna said tonelessly.

We read and made our selections; I kept a list of all the names on the folders we could use against Strode. I was about to bypass the folder of a professional basketball player with ostensible underworld connections when Castleberry stopped me. "I suggest you hold on to that one," he said. "His father is a member of the board of governors of the Federal Reserve System."

Ah. One of the seven men who controlled the nation's credit market. And Strode was using the son to get at the father. "I certainly shall hold on to it. Thank you."

He looked at me slyly. "Perhaps not so worthless after all?"

I thought back; I had indeed called him worthless. "My mistake. You obviously have hidden talents, Castleberry."

That satisfied him; he leaned back in his chair and even smiled a little. The man was a natural-born toady. He should have been thinking of ways to hand my head on a platter to either the police or Strode or both. But instead he was more concerned with convincing me that I was wrong about him, that he was too an important person and a swell fellow to boot.

Joanna was starting to droop a little, so I asked her if she felt all right.

"Yes," she said, "but it's three o'clock and I'm supposed to eat something."

"Oh, good lord! I'm sorry, Joanna, I should have remembered." I looked at my list; it had twenty names on it. "I think we have enough here. Castleberry, will Strode accept a call from you before our nine o'clock deadline?"

He indicated he would. "Mr. Strode said he'd be expecting to hear from me anytime after noon today. He figured that was the earliest you three could . . . reach a decision."

Well, he didn't miss by much.

SO IT WAS ON to the final step. We dragged Castleberry with us when we made a detour to the Port Authority Bus Terminal to divide the folders from Strode's vault among three different lockers; each of us kept one key. Then we bought envelopes and stamps and mailed the keys to ourselves. Next we found a restaurant; we sat around the table eating and planning strategy. Joanna and I wouldn't be going back to Strode's place with the other two because of the risk that Strode might check with the security guard as to who was in the house before he went in. There was a risk in our not going, too, and that was that Jack might not be able to control Castleberry alone. But I made the flunkey understand that if anything went wrong, he would have me to answer to;

Strode wouldn't be able to protect him. He didn't take much convincing.

Castleberry would call Strode and tell him Jack was the winner of the House of Glass sweepstakes (that should surprise him right there) and was at the moment waiting to close the deal. Castleberry said Strode had been staying in a woman's apartment about twenty blocks away, so it shouldn't take him long to get there. Joanna and I would wait across the street until we saw Strode arrive and follow him in. Then we'd put it to him.

Joanna perked up considerably once she had some food in her, and even Castleberry was showing signs of getting into the mood of things; I hoped he wasn't nursing any ideas of coming to work for me. Jack was laughing and making jokes and acting in general like a condemned man who'd received a last-minute reprieve, as indeed he had. As for myself, I felt completely relaxed. In our own ways, we were ready.

It was almost five when Joanna and I took up our positions across the street from Strode's house. We had to stand there for forty-five minutes, looking conspicuous, before Strode finally arrived. He was alone, except for the chauffeur, who drove away once Strode was inside the gate. We crossed the street and made a show of asking the guard if his boss had gotten back yet; he let us in. The inside guard didn't seem particularly surprised to see us; he just said they were all in the conference room.

All. Strode and Castleberry and Jack? The back of my neck began to prickle. Outside the conference room, I said, "Joanna," and stopped her from opening the door.

But it was too late. The door opened from the inside, and there stood A. J. Strode, smiling triumphantly. "Come in, come in. We've been waiting for you. Don't try to run, Jo. There's no place to go."

"I wouldn't think of it," she said coolly and walked in.

I followed, and found myself looking at three men I'd never seen before—big, hefty men, obviously bodyguards and just as obviously armed, if the bulges under their arms were any indication. Castleberry was there, and Jack; the latter was seated at the conference table, the only one in the room not standing. I walked over and stared down at him without speaking.

"Don't look at me, man," he said petulantly. "These goons were already in the house when Castleberry and I got here. What was I supposed to do?"

"They both have knives," Castleberry said quickly. One of the bodyguards collected Joanna's knife and then mine and put them in a drawer of an oak side table, being careful to handle only the blades; I caught a glimpse of Jack's knife already inside, gleaming pinkly. The bodyguard locked the drawer and handed Strode the key.

Castleberry was unhappy. "You promised me you wouldn't see any of them," he said to Strode.

"I thought I wouldn't have to," Strode said. "But I had to anticipate their trying something. I sure as hell never expected them to get into my vault." He turned to me. "My men moved in while you were busy stealing from me. Oh yes, Castleberry's had time to tell me what you were up to. We had a nice long chat on the phone while you were standing across the street waiting."

I turned and pointed to the camera. "I want that removed. And the microphones."

"They're not working," Strode said. "Have you forgotten what your companion-in-crime did to my security system?"

"No, nor have I forgotten seeing a repairman at work in the monitoring room. If you want to talk, you're going to have to get rid of the camera and the microphones."

Strode looked exasperated. "There's a little red light in the camera when—"

"I know about the little red light. I also know it can be disconnected while the camera is still operating."

Strode yielded impatiently, not seeming to care one way or the other. There was a wait while the security guard came in with a half-stepladder and a toolbox and removed the camera from its mount. Then he started unscrewing the light-switch plate.

Jack got up to look. "In there? The mike's in the light switch?"

The guard glanced over his shoulder at Strode, who wasn't paying any attention to them. "It uses the AC lines for both power and transmission," he told Jack. "Transmitters that run on batteries—they have to be replaced almost every day. No good." He took out a microphone-transmitter unit not much bigger than his thumbnail.

"How many of these do you need for a room this size?"

"Just one. That's it."

"You're sure now?"

The guard swore by all that was holy there were no more bugs in the conference room. He gathered up his gear and left.

"Satisfied?" Strode growled when the security guard had left. We sat down around the conference table, all but the three bodyguards. One stood behind Strode, another placed himself behind me, and the third took up a position near the door. "Now let's talk about what happens to people who steal from me," Strode said. "Bruce, do you think you'll just walk away from this?"

"I really don't see how you're going to stop us," I said reasonably. "We do have the folders, after all—I assume Castleberry told you about the lockers and the keys? We can send you to prison for life if we want to. *For life*, Strode.

And that's what we'll do if you ever try to strong-arm any of us again, for any reason whatsoever."

"If I go, I take you with me."

"Understood. And I presume you understand the contrary is true. It's a stand-off, Strode. Neither of us can get the other without incriminating himself."

Strode flicked his eyes toward Jack. "Give me one of them."

"Hey, what?" Jack cried.

"This is between you and me, Bruce," Strode went on, "I can be a powerful ally—we don't have to be at each other's throats. Let me have Jack. Or Jo, I don't care which."

"Richard!" Jack, still protesting.

"Not a chance," I said to Strode. "I couldn't give them to you if I wanted to, and I don't want to. We divided the folders among us. That way no one can turn on the other two."

Joanna spoke for the first time. "Ah—that's why you insisted on three lockers. Smart." I hoped she understood *she* was not the one I didn't trust.

"What do you want?" Strode asked me. "You must want something. Everybody does. Let's do business, Bruce."

I took out the list of names I'd made, the names of the people whose file folders we'd taken, and started to read it aloud. "Harrison Casey. Margaret Kurian. John W. Streiber. Michael—"

"All right, all right!" Strode snarled. "I get the point. Now listen, and listen good. You had your chance, all three of you. This started out as a simple business venture—I wanted to buy somebody's House of Glass shares, and I didn't even care whose. But now it's turned into a goddamn contest to see which of us has the tighter stranglehold on the other. I don't like that. I don't like that at all. So let me tell you what I've done."

"Strode—"

"Just listen. After Castleberry explained what had happened this afternoon, I called my lawyer. I told him I had reason to believe three people named Richard Bruce, Joanna Gillespie, and Jack McKinstry were conspiring to kill me. I said I was *fairly* sure—a loophole, there—I was fairly sure they had killed before and wouldn't hesitate to do so again, especially as they thought I might be in a position to expose them. And then I told him if he didn't hear from me by midnight, he was to call the police and repeat our conversation."

"That's ridiculous," Jack said disgustedly. "Nobody's tried to kill you."

Strode ignored him. "So it's a whole new game now. We can forget about Jo's heartless murder of the two people who gave her life. We can forget about Jack's self-serving destruction of a helicopter full of unsuspecting people. And we can forget about the poor doomed crew of the *Burly Girl*—thirty-seven men who died slowly and horribly because Richard Bruce was having money problems. That's all past history. The charge now is attempted murder, more precisely the attempted murder of me, A. J. Strode. As to proof that I'm not making the whole thing up, in that drawer over there"—he waved a hand at the side table—"are three nasty-looking knifes . . . with your fingerprints on the handles. Got that? *Your fingerprints*. And at midnight, my lawyer calls the police."

Joanna threw me an anguished look. Jack appeared to be in shock. I checked my watch; it said seven-twenty.

Strode leaned back in his chair and grinned wolfishly. "Well, then. What are we going to do?"

PART 3

The Cops

SEVEN

DETECTIVE SERGEANT Marian Larch was negotiating through late-night traffic and practicing looking inscrutable at the same time. Anything that cut short her much-needed personal time was sufficient to raise her Irritation Quotient considerably; but when the interruption was a homicide, then maintaining an image of official cool became something she had to work at. *A bigwig*, the captain had said. *Tread carefully*.

Marian Larch had recently moved into a new apartment; she'd spent the day putting up bookshelves and performing other similar laborious tasks, and she was tired. But man's inhumanity to man rarely paused long enough to accommodate the constabulary's need for home improvement, so Marion was back on the job a few days earlier than she'd planned. Arson and a fatal stabbing, same time, same place, find the connection. All Marian had was a name and address, somebody called A. J. Strode off Park. No parking place, of course. She left the car a block away and jogtrotted back to the mansion marked by police cars and an ambulance and a few uniformed officers there to hold back the crowd of onlookers that for the most part had failed to materialize. People minded their own business in this neighborhood.

Or maybe it was the fact that this was the middle of a Sunday night. Marian showed her badge to the cop at the gate and asked if her partner was there yet. He was. The minute she entered the building, Marian's sinuses began to sting from the acrid bite of lingering smoke. The fire department had come and gone; evidently the blaze had been confined to one small room off the entrance hall. She covered her mouth and nose with her hands and glanced inside. It looked like a monitoring station of some sort.

"Where you been? The guy from the medical examiner's office wanted to take the body but I told him he had to wait for you." The speaker was Ivan Malecki, Marian's partner for the past two years and an impatient sort. "Will you look at this place? Talk about *loaded*."

"I'd better look at the body. Where is it?"

"Upstairs, in a kind of study. Come on." He led the way.

"What have you got so far?"

"Deceased is Andrew Jonathan Strode, wheeler and dealer in the grand old American tradition. Owned a buncha companies, or parts of them. Present at time of death were four servants, three bodyguards, two security guards, three guests, and Strode's executive assistant. The three—"

"Wait a minute. You're saying there were *five guards* in this house and somebody still got to him?"

"Well, one was outside, but there were five, yeah. It was one of the guards who found the body." Ivan started up a wide staircase. "No sign of a break-in. A man's on duty at the front gate, and the back gate is controlled electronically from inside the house. The servants and guards are pretty much out of it, looks like. The three guests all hated Strode, according to Castleberry—that's the executive assistant, Myron Castleberry. Haven't had time to talk to them yet. Castleberry's the only one that's upset by what's happened—the guests were all smiling and having drinks when I looked in on them."

"You think one of those three got past the guards and left a knife in Strode's chest?"

He grinned sourly. "Better'n that. Would you believe *three* knives in his chest?"

Marian stopped short. "Three."

Ivan said nothing more, but opened a door and motioned her inside. The room was a home office or library, and it was crowded with men from the crime lab. In the middle of the floor lay the body of a man about sixty; and as Ivan had said, not one knife but three had been plunged into his chest.

What an incredible sight. It was as if someone were trying to pin him to the floor and wanted to make sure he never got up again. It was a lot harder to stab a man in the heart than people thought; the heart was surrounded by layers of tough protective muscle. But why keep shoving in different knives until one of them struck home? Why not just keep stabbing with the same knife? The bloodstain on the carpet was surprisingly small; Strode must have bled internally.

"Well, Sergeant, glad you decided to join us," said an Oriental man squatting down by the body. "You want to take a quick gander here so I can get going?"

"Hello, Dr. Wu." Marian hunkered down beside him. "Anything other than the obvious?"

"I can't tell you which knife killed him, if that's what you mean. Time of death, approximately one hour ago. Rigor started right after I got here."

Marian examined the handles of the three knives. One was mother-of-pearl inlaid among edgings of some exotic stone Marian couldn't identify; it was a beautiful piece of work. The second knife had a black leather handle, a no-nonsense kind of knife. The handle of the third, curiously, was made of cheap pink plastic. "Prints?"

Dr. Wu shook his head. "Wiped clean."

Marian looked up at Ivan. "Whose knives?"

"The three guests'. One knife each." He folded his arms. "Conspiracy. Gotta be."

"Maybe." She looked back at what remained of A. J. Strode. The body was dressed in peach silk pajamas; the feet were bare. She stood up and pointed to a door other than the one she'd come through. "Where does that lead?"

"To his dressing room," Ivan said. "This is a whole suite of rooms. Evidently he was getting ready for bed when he came in here for something and the killers were waiting for him."

Marian told Dr. Wu he could remove the body. She went into the dressing room and its connecting bath, and then into a bedroom that had more floor space than a lot of small apartments she'd been in. On the other side of the bedroom was another dressing room and connecting bath; they didn't seem to be in use. "Isn't there a Mrs. Strode?" she asked Ivan.

"Don't know yet. Seen enough? Let's go talk to these people. There's a sort of conference room downstairs. If you close the door, you don't smell the smoke."

"What about the fire?" They left the bedroom suite and started back down the stairs.

"Coulda been a distraction. Or it coulda been done to turn off the cameras." Ivan pointed to one mounted high on the wall at the bottom of the stairs. "We need more details."

In the conference room two men were waiting, watched over by a uniformed policeman. The two men were not talking. One sat at the conference table with his head propped up on both hands, looking as if he were trying not to break down. He was in his shirtsleeves, and both the shirt and his face were smudged with soot. The other man was standing by a window. Marian took quick note of his elegant clothes and distinguished bearing; the man fairly reeked importance. Marian liked his looks, even the three or four theatrical gray streaks running through his black hair.

Whoever he was, he was examining the two entering detectives with equal interest.

Marian took the lead. "I'm Sergeant Larch, and this is my partner, Sergeant Malecki. You are . . . ?"

"Richard Bruce," the elegantly dressed one said. "Sergeant, do you have any idea how long you'll be keeping us? I'm a guest here and was on the verge of leaving when everything started to happen—I'd still like to leave. Will it be long?"

"Yes," Marian answered frankly. "This is a homicide investigation, Mr. Bruce."

"This here's Mr. Castleberry," Ivan said, indicating the dejected-looking man at the conference table—who somehow managed to raise his head and nod.

"I understand you can't rush, Sergeant," Richard said with no trace of impatience, "but we were virtually on our way out when it happened and we won't be able to tell you anything."

"'We'? All three of you?"

"I can't speak for McKinstry, but Joanna and I were leaving."

Marian pulled out a notebook and sat down at the table. "Full names, please."

"Joanna Gillespie, Jack McKinstry."

Marian's head jerked up. "Joanna Gillespie? The violinist?"

Ivan looked blank, but Richard Bruce said yes. "If we'd been even five minutes faster, Joanna and I would have been gone by now," Richard went on. "Neither one of us knows what happened. I'd appreciate it if you'd take our statements first so we could be on our way."

Marian stared at him. "Mr. Bruce, surely you realize you're not just a casual bystander. One of those knives buried in Strode's chest belongs to you, doesn't it?"

Castleberry made a strangled sound.

"Sergeant Larch," Richard said, "all three of our knives were locked in that—ah, Officer, would you mind taking a step to your left, please?" The uniformed policeman moved aside to reveal a waist-high side table; the one drawer was open. "Our knives were locked in that side table earlier this evening. Strode had the key. Anyone could have broken it open."

"Including you," said Ivan, going over to take a look. "The wood's splintered and the lock's scratched and bent," Ivan told his partner. "Screwdriver, probably. Marks are too small for a crowbar."

"Do you always take a knife with you when you go visiting?" Marian asked Richard Bruce.

He shook his head. "All three of those knives were purchased just this morning. We had reason to believe we were in some danger here."

"Oh? What reason was that?" Ivan asked.

"It's difficult to explain. This weekend was the culmination of a long period of conflict between Strode on one side and Joanna Gillespie, Jack McKinstry and me on the other. None of us loved him. Things had reached the point where we were uncomfortable being here, in his house. But we had to stay until some stock changed hands...that was the crux of the conflict. So this evening I sold him my stock and was preparing to leave when the fire broke out. And then the bodyguard found that Strode had been murdered."

"During the fire."

"Apparently."

Marian looked at the other man. "Mr. Castleberry? Is that how you see it?"

Strode's executive assistant didn't look well; his face was gray and pinched and his entire body sagged. "I think so. Once the fire broke out, everyone's attention was on the monitoring room. Several of us were trying to put out the blaze before the fire department got here.''

"Who are 'several of us'?''

"The inside security guard and I, and a couple of the bodyguards—maybe all three of them. No one was keeping track of anyone else.''

"Where were you when the fire broke out?''

"In here. I had to call Mr. Strode's lawyer and tell him not to...not to do something. I was checking over the stock sale papers when the fire actually started.''

"Alone?''

"Yes.''

"What about you, Mr. Bruce? Where were you when the fire started?''

"I was in the television room waiting for Joanna. She had to go back to her room to attend to something before we left.''

"Were you alone?''

"Unfortunately. Ah...just a minute, I did ask one of the maids to fetch our suitcases. She might remember seeing me there.''

"Where was Mr. McKinstry?''

"God knows.''

"I think he was in his room,'' Castleberry answered.

"So none of you four were together,'' Ivan commented. "Any one of you could have started that fire and then slipped upstairs during the confusion and killed Strode.''

Castleberry was horrified. "You can't suspect *me* of killing Mr. Strode! You can't think that!''

"Take it easy,'' Ivan said. "We've gotta suspect everybody until we find a reason not to.''

"But that's absurd! *I* was not Mr. Strode's enemy!''

"Well, I was, but I didn't kill him,'' Richard Bruce said. "Look, Sergeant, er...?''

"Malecki."

"Sergeant Malecki, I'll sign anything you want but I really must get Ms Gillespie out of this house." He half grunted, half laughed. "I want to get *myself* out of this house. We've all been under a terrible strain for the last three days, and now this. You can't hold us, you know."

"Can't we?" Ivan grinned. "Here and I thought we could."

Marian said, "We can hold you for twenty-four hours without charging you—that's the law. Now you can spend those twenty-four hours in an interrogation room, or you can spend them here. Here is nicer."

Richard looked at her speculatively. "And when those twenty-four hours are up, you can still take us in and hold us another twenty-four, can't you?" The two detectives looked at him blandly, saying nothing. "I see. Well, if that's the way it is, that's the way it is. I'm going upstairs. It's been a long day." He started out.

"Mr. Bruce," Marian said.

He stopped.

"The pink knife," she asked. "Which one does it belong to?"

His face broke into a sardonic smile. "McKinstry." He went out and closed the door behind him.

Ivan nodded to the policeman in the room. "Make sure he doesn't go anywhere." The officer followed Richard Bruce out.

"They did it, you know," Castleberry said unexpectedly. "One of them or two of them or all three together, but they did it."

Ivan sighed. "You wouldn't happen to have anything in the way of evidence, would you?"

"You'll have to find evidence," the other man said earnestly. "They were the only ones in this house who had reason to want Mr. Strode dead. The rest of us all worked for him, in one capacity or another. But Bruce and McKinstry and Gillespie—they *hated* him."

"Why?"

Castleberry sat up a little straighter in his chair. "Because they couldn't get the better of him! They tried—they tried a lot of things, but they still couldn't get the upper hand. Mr. Strode was stronger than they are, smarter than they are—"

"Deader than they are," Ivan finished impatiently. "Where are the other two—McKinstry and Gillespie?"

"Upstairs, in their rooms. One of the police officers asked them all to wait up there until you got here."

"But Richard Bruce was in here."

"Yes. Mr. Bruce generally does as he pleases."

"Who called the police? And the fire department?"

"I did. One call took care of both."

Marian had a question. "Mr. Castleberry, who inherits?"

"Why...Katie does. Mrs. Strode." Castleberry looked surprised, as if he hadn't gotten around to thinking of that yet. "Yes...Katie will get everything. The will hadn't been changed yet."

"Mr. Strode was thinking of changing his will?"

"Mr. and Mrs. Strode are separated, Sergeant. But it happened only recently. The divorce proceedings hadn't even been started."

"Where is she now?"

"Jamaica. Oh dear—she doesn't know. I'll have to call her."

"Do you want one of us to do that?"

"No, no...I'd better tell her myself. But thank you. I'll need to talk to her anyway. It's time to start thinking about the funeral arrangements, for one thing."

Ivan turned to his partner. "Want to get the necessaries out of the way first?"

"Might as well," Marian said. "Mr. Castleberry, we're going to want to talk to the guards and the servants first off. I think we'll start with the guard who found the body. Do you suppose you could find him for us?"

"Yes, certainly, I'll be, ah, let's see—I'll be in the dining room if you need me." He left, relieved at having been given something to do.

"A bodyguard who discovers bodies instead of guarding them," Ivan yawned. "Do you suppose we could get some coffee? We're gonna be here all night."

"At least," Marian agreed glumly. "There won't be anyone in the kitchen at this hour. Let's wait until we get one of the servants in here and then we can ask."

"Right after the body-discovering bodyguard," Ivan agreed.

THE BODYGUARD HAD the unusual name of Millwalker, and he was on the defensive. A big man who had hitherto done well in the profession of intimidation, he foresaw—probably correctly—that his livelihood would now be threatened by his spectacular failure to preserve the life of A. J. Strode. It took Marian Larch and Ivan Malecki ten minutes to get him to say anything more than some variation of *It wasn't my fault.*

"I did my job," Millwalker was insisting for the sixth or seventh time. "I was where I was supposed to be when I was supposed to be there. I was not negligent."

"Nobody said you were," Ivan answered for the sixth or seventh time, and decided to try a variation of his own. "We haven't had any complaints. Nobody in this house seems to hold you responsible. Ease up, Mr. Millwalker. Don't be so hard on yourself."

Marian covered a smile with her hand.

It worked, to a degree. When Millwalker was convinced the police weren't going to accuse him of anything, he paused in his wallow of self-justification long enough to give them the details they wanted. And in doing so, he provided them with their first indication of why someone might want A. J. Strode to make an early departure from the land of the living.

Millwalker said he personally had taken the three knives away from Richard Bruce, Jack McKinstry, and Joanna Gillespie. On Mr. Strode's instructions, he had touched only the blades and locked the knives away in the side table. He gave the key to Mr. Strode. He stayed in the room with the other two bodyguards while Mr. Strode and his three guests haggled about business.

"Where was Castleberry?" Marian asked.

"He was here too," Millwalker replied, "but he didn't say much. It was Mr. Strode who did all the talking. He wanted some stock the others had, and he told them he'd accuse them of attempted murder if they didn't let him have what he wanted."

Marian and Ivan exchanged a look. "You'd better explain that," the latter said.

Millwalker explained about Strode's phone call to his lawyer and the fingerprints on the knife handles and the midnight deadline. "So they talked it over and decided there wasn't any way out and Mr. Bruce sold his stock to Mr. Strode and that was the end of it."

Marian Larch was getting a bad taste in her mouth. "You mean A. J. Strode blackmailed Richard Bruce into selling his stock?"

Millwalker shrugged. "I guess you could put it that way. From the way it sounded to me, Mr. Strode had tried something like that before but it hadn't worked—just from the things they were saying, I mean.''

"What had he tried before?" Marian asked.

"I couldn't tell exactly. But it was damned obvious he'd been puttin' the squeeze on them and they'd wriggled out. So the fingerprints on the knives—that was his new squeeze.''

"And this one worked," Ivan said, shaking his head. "A real Mr. Nice Guy. So then what happened?''

Then they all dispersed like billiard balls shooting off in all directions after a break. Millwalker and one of the other bodyguards accompanied Strode to his suite. Strode unlocked his bedroom door and waited in the hall with the other guard while Millwalker checked things out.

"Did you look in the library?" Marian asked.

"I sure did. Nobody was in there then.''

"Which was when?''

"A little after eleven. I remember Mr. Strode saying something to Mr. Castleberry about them beating the deadline by an hour.''

"Did you check the door between the library and the hallway?''

Immediately Millwalker was back in his defensive posture. "There wasn't any reason to. When we went in by the library, we didn't check the bedroom door. So why would we bother to—''

"Okay, okay," Marian interrupted. "So you didn't check the hall door to the library. Then what?''

Then Mr. Strode locked the bedroom door behind him and the two guards took up their positions, Millwalker at the head of the stairs and the other man in the wing where the guest bedrooms were located. The third bodyguard was to patrol the house, always on the move. No, Mr. Strode didn't always have such stringent security arrangements; they would be abandoned once these particular guests were out of the house. Mr. Strode didn't trust them.

"With reason," Ivan remarked dryly. "Then the fire broke out?"

Then the fire broke out. At first Millwalker had stayed at the head of the stairs in Strode's wing of the house. But then he could smell smoke and could hear someone yelling for help—Castleberry, he thought. So Millwalker went and pounded on Strode's door and yelled for him to stay inside. Strode had yelled back that he would. Millwalker had gone to help put out the fire in the monitoring room near the front entrance. Who was there? Both security guards, the other two bodyguards, and Castleberry.

But the blaze was a stubborn one; not only was the electrical equipment hissing and sparking and burning but the carpeting and furniture of the room had caught fire as well. The security guard had emptied the fire extinguisher, stopping the worst of it; but electrical fires could be tricky. One of the other bodyguards brought in another extinguisher from the kitchen. They had to take turns using it; the smoke was so bad no one could stay in the burning room for more than a few seconds. But then the fire department arrived and quickly had matters under control. One of the men said the fire had been set deliberately and a fire marshal would be there to investigate in the morning.

Millwalker fell silent; he didn't want to talk about the next part of it. Eventually he said, "I went back up to tell Mr. Strode the fire was out. But when I got to the top of the stairs, I could see the library door was standing open. I thought he'd come out to see about the fire. So I called his name, several times, and then I looked in the library...and there he was. With those three knives in him." He paused. "It was obscene."

Marian asked, "Was Castleberry with you the whole time you were fighting the fire?"

"The whole time. He couldn't have done it—he was still talking to the firefighters when I went back to Mr. Strode's rooms. Why are you asking about Castleberry? You know who did it. Richard Bruce and the other two, McKinstry and the Gillespie woman. They got their knives back and set the fire as a distraction and then went up and killed Mr. Strode. Three against one," he finished in disgust.

"We don't know that yet," Marian said cautiously.

"Well, you'd damned well better know it," Millwalker declared indignantly. "Why else *three* knives?"

"To make us think exactly what you're thinking—that they were all in it together. The use of three knives muddies the waters. The killer wouldn't be foolish enough to use *just* his or her own knife. And he—or she—wouldn't use *just* one of the other's knives to throw suspicion on that person. It's too obvious, for one thing, and for another maybe the murderer didn't know where everybody was at the time."

"What's that got to do with anything?"

"Okay. The pink knife belonged to Jack McKinstry, right? Suppose one of the other two picked that knife to commit the murder with, only to find out later that McKinstry was with somebody else at the time of the killing and therefore had an alibi. By using all three knives, the murderer just increased the odds a little. You see?"

Millwalker shook his head. "They all three did it. Together."

The two police detectives took the bodyguard back over his story and asked a few questions, but he'd told them all he knew. They said he could leave.

"Do you believe all that stuff you were saying?" Ivan asked when Millwalker was gone. "About there only being one killer?"

"Sure do," Marian said. "What better way to confuse the issue than by using weapons everyone can identify as belonging to someone else? Besides, there's a kind of message in using three knives—*I want this man really dead*, something like that."

"Yeah, well, if Millwalker got it straight, they all three had reason for wanting him dead. That Strode must have been a real sonuvabitch. Millwalker's not much of a bodyguard, is he? He doesn't check to see if the library door is locked and he lets himself be lured away from his post. Anyway, Castleberry's out of it, looks like."

"Yes, it has to be one of the three guests."

"*One* of them, she says. God, I can't take this any longer—I've gotta have some coffee."

Marian waited while Ivan went looking for someone to make coffee. Before long he came back grinning and carrying a tray with a coffeepot and cups on it.

"It seems I wasn't the only one dying of caffeine-deprivation," he said. "Danielle was already in the kitchen, brewing the stuff as fast as she could."

"Who's Danielle?"

"The cook. Sixty years old and two hundred pounds and I'm in love with her."

The coffee hit the spot. "I think I'm in love with her too," Marian murmured. "Richard Bruce was the one who let Strode have this stock he coveted so much. Does that make Bruce our number-one suspect or eliminate him?"

Ivan frowned. "Hard to say. If he's the vengeful type, he might go after Strode just to get even. That's stretching it, though. I'm thinking the business between those two was finished."

Marian made a noncommittal noise. "How about the security guard next?"

The security guard came in looking like a skinny Atlas bearing the weight of the world on his shoulders. "*Nothing* has gone right this weekend," he complained. "First Mr. Bruce makes me cover up the cameras and then he and Ms Gillespie come back in the house without me seeing them and the security system goes out and Mr. Strode tells me to take the bug out of the conference room and now *this*. I'm not even supposed to be on duty! One of the regular weekend guys is sick and I'm just filling in for him. I'm supposed to work weeknights."

"Name, please," Marian said.

"Frank O'Connell."

"You say Richard Bruce forced you to cover up the cameras, Mr. O'Connell?"

"The ones in their bedrooms, yes ma'am." O'Connell explained about that and the other things that had made his job less than unadulterated joy that weekend. He backed up Millwalker's statement that Castleberry had been in the monitoring room fighting the fire even before the bodyguard had arrived. The gateman had come in to help. O'Connell was definite that all three bodyguards had been there, making a total of six men trying to stop the fire— three bodyguards, two security guards, and Castleberry. None of the house staff had shown up with buckets of water or whatever; O'Connell said they'd probably all retired for the night and didn't even know there was a fire until it was over.

"Let's back up a little," Marian said. "The fire department is saying arson. How could anyone get into the monitoring room to start the fire? Had you left the room?"

"Yes'm, I'd gone to the bathroom. Sometimes I leave to go check on something—maybe a camera's not working right, or Mr. Strode would have a special job for me to do. I'm not in there *all* the time.''

"How long were you gone?"

"Not more'n a few minutes. Whoever set that fire had to move fast.''

Ivan asked, ''What did you say earlier about removing a bug from this room? Strode found a bug planted in here?''

"No, sir, it was ours. This room was the only room in the house with a microphone in it. Mr. Strode sometimes wanted his business dealings on tape.''

"Why did he want it removed?''

"Beats me. It wasn't even working, because we'd had trouble with the security system earlier and not everything had been fixed yet. And even if it was working, I coulda turned it off from the monitoring center. But no, I had to get my toolbox and a stepladder and go in and take out the mike *and* the camera.''

"Toolbox," Marian said.

"Right," Ivan nodded. "Mr. O'Connell, would you go check your toolbox to see if anything's missing? Where is it?''

O'Connell groaned. "In the room where the fire was. I didn't even think about it! Damn.''

"Let's go look for it," Ivan suggested.

They all went to the burned-out mess that once was the monitoring room. Marian's sinuses shrieked in protest. Ivan was having trouble with the smell, too, but O'Connell didn't seem to notice it. They poked around, mostly using their feet, until O'Connell found his toolbox. The metal was still warm, but not too hot to handle.

"A screwdriver's missing," he said when he'd gotten the box open. "One of those with the reversible tip—regular on one end and Phillips on the other? Dammit, I just bought that screwdriver a month ago.''

"Whew, somebody sure thought ahead," Ivan said, leading the way out of the monitoring room. "Let's get away from this smell."

O'Connell looked at Marian. "What's he mean?"

"He means your missing screwdriver was probably what was used to pry open the drawer where the three knives were locked away. The killer waited until you left to go to the bathroom and then stole your screwdriver before setting the fire."

He worked it out. "So it had to be somebody who saw me bring my toolbox into the conference room—when I removed the camera and the microphone?"

"Right. Unfortunately, that doesn't narrow it down much."

O'Connell hesitated. "Look, this might not mean anything..."

"What? Tell us anyway."

"Well, Mr. McKinstry sure was awful interested in what I was doing. He got up and came over and watched while I took the mike out of the light switch." O'Connell thought about it a moment. "Naw, he was just being curious. I don't think it means anything."

"You never know," Ivan said ambiguously. "Your screwdriver will turn up, Mr. O'Connell. If you find it before we do, don't handle it, okay? Fingerprints."

"Oh, yeah. Okay."

Marian thanked the security guard for his help and told him he could go.

"Speaking of bathrooms," Ivan said.

"Me too."

They found one and took turns. One of the uniformed officers on duty saw Ivan coming out and told them there were four downstairs bathrooms, if they wanted to count the cook's. They thanked him for the information.

Back in the conference room Ivan moved the side table that had held the knives out from the wall, looking for the screwdriver. "I know, I know," he said, although his partner hadn't uttered a word, "there won't be any prints. But we have to check."

"Ivan, I'm usually the one who says that. Getting cautious in your old age?"

"I'm always cautious. And painstaking. And neat."

Marian snorted. "That must be your twin brother."

Ivan moved the side table back into place; no screwdriver. "Castleberry's definitely out. Think we ought to talk to him again before we tackle the three primes?"

"Let's get the rest of these people out of the way first. The gateman and the house staff. Besides, I want to see this woman you're in love with."

"Danielle? She's a doll."

Danielle the cook didn't have anything to tell them; she knew even less than the rest of the house staff, which was little enough. All they'd been told was there'd be three weekend guests during Mr. Strode's absence—

During his absence? both police detectives had interrupted.

Yes, Mr. Strode had been away until this evening. It was clear that something was in the wind; but no one paid any particular attention to that because with Mr. Strode, something was always in the wind. What these three were up to was their own business ... and Mr. Strode's, of course. Mr. McKinstry always left his bathroom in a mess, but other than that there wasn't anything they could tell them about the three guests.

With one exception. The maid that Richard Bruce had asked to fetch his and Joanna Gillespie's suitcases volunteered the opinion that where she had to go to get them was kind of strange. They were in the wine cellar.

What were their suitcases doing in the wine cellar?

She was sure she didn't know. She didn't ask questions. Mr. Strode didn't like it.

And when did Mr. Bruce send her for the bags?

Five after eleven on the nose. She knew because she wanted to go to her room and had been watching the clock.

"So no alibi for Richard Bruce," Marian remarked when the maid had left. "The fire didn't break out for another fifteen or twenty minutes. If he was in the television room at the time, why didn't he come out and help fight the fire?"

"Maybe he didn't want to get his pretty suit dirty," Ivan sniffed. "Well, who's left? The gateman?"

The outside security guard did have one interesting thing to tell them. He said he was surprised to learn Ms Gillespie and Mr. Bruce had come back to the house without his knowing about it. They both had left shortly before noon, carrying their bags, and they sure as hell hadn't come back through his gate. And that gate was the only way in.

The only way?

Except for the electronically controlled service gate in the rear. But why would Mr. Strode's guests use the service gate? He'd have let them in the front way.

When the guard had left, Marian said, "Didn't O'Connell say they had trouble with the security system earlier in the day? Bruce and Gillespie could have slipped in through the service gate when the system was down."

Ivan nodded. "And into the house through the wine cellar? But why?"

"They didn't want to be seen, obviously. But that means they knew ahead of time they'd be able to get in the back way. Do you suppose that 'trouble' with the security system was caused deliberately? Was McKinstry still in the house at the time?"

"We'd better find out." Ivan perched on the edge of the conference table facing his partner. "Marian, you've gotta admit it's looking more and more like conspiracy. Those three were up to something today, you know damn well they were."

"They were up to *something*. It didn't have to be murder. All this was before Strode pulled that little stunt with the knives, remember...and I don't think we've heard anything like the whole story on that, either. But the murder came *after* their 'something' they were up to failed to end their difficulties with Strode. When their plan didn't get them the results they wanted, one of them took matters into his own hands—or hers—and put an end to the problem. Exit A. J. Strode."

Ivan shook his head. "It's conspiracy. I can smell it."

"It's too obvious, Ivan. It's safety in numbers, that's all it is."

"You're crazy."

"And you're pigheaded."

"And you drive too slow."

She stared at him. "What do you mean, I drive too slow?"

"You drive too slow! You gotta keep up with the flow of traffic."

"I do keep up with the flow of traffic. I just don't play musical traffic lanes the way you do."

"That's simply aggressive driving. It's all under control."

Marian made a noise of exasperation. "What the hell are we arguing about driving for? Are we getting tired?"

Ivan looked at his watch. "It's almost three. Yes, we're getting tired."

"Dammit, we haven't even scratched the surface yet! We've got those three upstairs still to question, and you know they're going to lie about everything under the sun. They may not even give us their right names." Her stomach growled. "Sorry. Hungry."

"So am I, but I was too polite to growl about it. I'll go see if Danielle's still up. Don't go away."

"I'm not going anywhere," Marian said tiredly to the closing door, and put her head down on her arms and fell promptly asleep.

IVAN WAS GONE twenty minutes, just long enough for Marian's catnap to do her some good. He came in bearing a plate of rapidly cooling toast, two Granny Smith apples, and a quart of milk. "Danielle's gone to bed. I didn't want to raid their refrigerator without asking, but I didn't think they'd mind if we had some fruit and bread."

"You are a good provider, Ivan," Marian said, pouring milk into their empty coffee cups. The cold toast and the apple were delicious. "Who's actually in charge in this house now? Castleberry doesn't live here."

"Mrs. Strode, I suppose, when she gets back."

"I wonder if she'll live here."

"She'd be a fool not to."

"Hmm. But she'd left here, or was made to leave. And her almost ex-husband was murdered here. The place might have too many bad associations."

"Five bucks she stays."

Marian thought about it. "You're on."

When they'd finished fueling up, Ivan said, "Which one do we start with?"

"Not sure. Do you think Richard Bruce is a sort of spokesman for the group?"

"Because he was waiting here for us? He just wanted to get himself and the violinist out of the house."

"So he was speaking for two at least. Let's save him for the last."

"Okay by me. Any preference?"

"No."

Ivan took out a quarter and flipped it into the air. "Heads, McKinstry. Tails, Gillespie." It came down heads.

But before they could send an officer to summon Jack McKinstry, there was a quick knock and the door opened. Myron Castleberry stood there, in superficially better shape than earlier. He'd cleaned away most of the smudges left by fighting the fire and donned his suit jacket, but his face looked as if it were collapsing in on itself. "Sergeants," he said hoarsely, "I must talk to you. Now, please."

"Of course, Mr. Castleberry, come in." Marian pointed to a chair across the table from her. "Have a seat. What's bothering you?"

But once Castleberry had taken his seat, he seemed unable to speak. He kept clenching and unclenching his fists nervously. *Whatever it is, it must be a beaut*, Marian thought, and glanced at Ivan. Her partner nodded and said, "Were you able to get hold of Mrs. Strode?"

Castleberry took a moment to focus on the question and then said, "Yes, she'll be arriving here tomorrow afternoon. No...I mean this afternoon—it's already Monday, isn't it? She said she'd try to get in today, it all depended on the flight schedule, she didn't have it memorized after all, but she'd see what she could do and take the first flight she could get on and then let me know so I could meet her at the airport—" He broke off, as if suddenly realizing he was babbling. He took a deep breath. "Excuse me. The answer to your question is yes, Sergeant Malecki. Mrs. Strode will be returning here as soon as she can make the arrangements."

"Will she be living here, do you think?"

"Oh yes. Katie put a great deal of herself into this house. I think she was sorrier to lose the house than she was Mr. Strode when they separated."

Ivan held a hand out to his partner. Marian grumblingly fished a five-dollar bill out of her shoulder bag and gave it to him.

Castleberry didn't notice. He'd stopped clenching his fists and now had his hands palm down on the table, steadying himself. "I just can't do it," he muttered. "I can't take that kind of responsibility on myself. It's unfair to ask me to. I can't do it."

Marian waited a moment and said, "What is it you can't do, Mr. Castleberry?"

His head jerked up and he looked her straight in the eye. "I can't keep quiet about what I know. I can't take his money. I'd be living in fear for the rest of my life. And my wife and the kids—what about them? I could be putting them in jeopardy. I just can't do it!"

Marian and Ivan waited.

Castleberry gave a short laugh. "I could be a rich man, do you know that? All I have to do is keep my mouth shut and move to California. Do you know what Richard Bruce was doing in this room when you two first arrived? He was offering me a bribe. He offered me the same salary Mr. Strode was paying me to come work for him, plus the same amount again every year under the table. No taxes. I think he was going to offer something more, but just then the policeman came in and we couldn't talk anymore."

"You've not talked to Bruce since?" Marian asked, more to keep him going than because she thought it was important.

Castleberry shook his head. "I've been avoiding him. It wouldn't be any too easy to talk anyway, what with police all over the place. But I know what he wants. He wants me in California where he can keep an eye on me. He wants me under his thumb." He seemed to be having trouble breathing. "I can't work for a murderer! I can't!"

Marian exchanged a quick look with Ivan. "I think you'd better tell us what you know, Mr. Castleberry. Withholding evidence is itself a crime, you know. If you've got anything at all that links Richard Bruce—"

"Not *this* murder. I don't know which one killed Mr. Strode. I'm talking about the crew of the *Burly Girl*, seventeen years ago. Richard Bruce is responsible for their deaths. This afternoon he burned the evidence—Sunday afternoon, that is. And now he wants me to keep quiet about it, about all of it, for the other two as well."

"Whoa," said Ivan. "What's this *Burly Girl* you're talking about?"

"It's a ship, was a ship, it belonged to Richard Bruce. He sank it for the insurance money and left the crew to drown so they wouldn't talk. He let thirty-seven men die so he could get away with cheating the insurance company! Thirty-seven of them."

The two detectives were stunned. "And he burned some evidence, you say?" Marian asked. "What evidence was that?"

"A letter, an affidavit, private investigators' report. We had something like that on all three of them—"

"All three? You mean Joanna Gillespie and Jack McKinstry as well? What did they have to do with the *Burly Girl*?"

"Nothing, nothing—oh, it's all so complicated. Mr. Strode had something on each of them, you see. Separately. No one of them was connected with the other. As far as Mr. Strode was concerned, they were three separate targets for, uh . . ."

"Blackmail," Marian and Ivan said together.

"Persuasion," Castleberry amended. "But this afternoon, yesterday afternoon, I mean, they got together and forced me to open Mr. Strode's vault. That's what the knives were for, to threaten me with. Richard Bruce even nicked my chin." He thrust his chin out so they could see the small cut. "They burned the evidence, right there in Mr. Strode's office. And then they stole some other papers—"

"Shit!" Ivan exploded. "You mean you had evidence that Richard Bruce killed thirty-seven people—*and now it's gone?*"

"Well, not completely." Castleberry was sweating now. "It's in the computer. All I have to do is print it out."

Both Ivan's and Marian's faces lit up. "In the computer!" the former said. "Then they didn't really solve anything by burning the papers?"

"No. But they don't know that yet."

"There is a God," Ivan grinned.

"Unfortunately, the original of a letter incriminating Richard Bruce is gone—burned. But we did keep copies, of course."

"Of course," Marian agreed straight-faced. "Mr. Castleberry, I think you'd better start at the beginning—the *very* beginning. Tell us everything that happened and tell us in the order in which it happened. One thing followed by another, in sequence. Can you do that?"

"Certainly, that's what I came to do." He paused a moment to get his thoughts in order. Then he took a deep breath and began. "It all started with a company called House of Glass..."

EIGHT

IT WAS DAYBREAK when the two police detectives assigned to investigate A. J. Strode's murder called a temporary halt. Nearly two hours of listening to Myron Castleberry recite the odyssey of A. J. Strode's pursuit of the ever-elusive House of Glass had left all three of them numb. When Castleberry told them Richard Bruce, Joanna Gillespie, and Jack McKinstry were all successful murderers, his two interrogators gazed at him with frank skepticism. Rather than go into detail about what Strode had on them, Castleberry instead recounted their close call with the collapsing crane at Los Angeles harbor and Strode's conviction that Richard Bruce was behind it. When pressed, Castleberry reluctantly admitted their detective had been unable to find any connection between Bruce and the crane operator.

But there were lots of other nasty bits to chew over and spit back out before the case would be closed. The detectives asked for printouts of the evidence Castleberry maintained was stored in the office computer. Ivan Malecki said he needed time to assimilate what he'd heard. Marian Larch said she just needed some sleep. Castleberry left for A. J. Strode's office to get them the evidence they wanted.

"I've got to crash," Marian told her partner, "even if it's only for an hour. Wake me when Castleberry gets back?" She went into the television room and collapsed on the sofa there, leaving Ivan to find his own place to nap.

There'd been a time when Marian could stay up all night and still put in a full day's work the next day. But at thirty-five her staying power was slipping away, along with a few other things she didn't care to think about. Her partner could probably outlast her, if it was ever put to a test; but then Ivan was younger than she was. By almost a full year.

An hour and ten minutes later Ivan woke her with the news it was time to get back to work. "Couple of men from the fire marshal's office are here. And the captain just called, wants to know our progress. He was mad as hell when I told him we hadn't questioned our three primes yet."

Marian winced. "You shouldn't have told him that." She sat up reluctantly; she could have done with another three or four hours.

"Had to—he asked me. He's just grumpy 'cause he didn't get much sleep. Anyway, he's made a statement to the press. He says Strode's murder made the front page of the morning editions."

"Terrific. Any word from Castleberry?"

"Not yet."

"How much of what he told us do you believe, Ivan?"

"Dunno. But why would anyone make up a story like that?"

"No reason that I can think of. I believe Castleberry told us what he thinks is the truth. Maybe some of the details are off, but the basic stuff is probably right on target. It just all seems so incredible."

"Yeah, tell me about it. Let's go talk to these guys about the fire."

The two men from the fire marshal's office were poking through the monitoring room. They'd turned up a charred Energine can in the rubble, and that's what had made them say arson. The cleaning fluid was one hundred percent naphtha, which would do the job very nicely. When questioned, the housekeeper said yes, they always kept a few cans of Energine on hand; there were a couple in the cleaning supplies closet right now. Was a can missing? She had no idea; no one kept *that* close track.

There'd been a change in shifts while Marian and Ivan were grabbing a nap, but the new officers on duty had been well briefed. One of them reported that the screwdriver belonging to O'Connell, the inside security guard, had been found behind a chair near the stairway; evidently someone had just tossed it over the banister. Sorry, no fingerprints. The other thing the officer told them was that Richard Bruce had spent what remained of the night in Joanne Gillespie's room.

Marian grunted. "Nice. He's old enough to be her father."

"Yeah?" Ivan asked. "How old is she? I've never seen her."

"Thirtyish. He's over fifty, wouldn't you say?"

Her partner shrugged. "That's not so much difference. It happens all the time. Nothing wrong with it."

"There's a lot wrong with it," Marian muttered. "I've known a few father-daughter marriages." But that was no time for a discussion of symbolic incest, for just then Myron Castleberry arrived.

The three of them went into the conference room. "I had two copies made of everything, one for each of you," Castleberry said, handing them each three folders. "I thought it would be easier for you that way."

Marian thanked him, getting a quick glimpse of why A. J. Strode had chosen Myron Castleberry as his executive assistant. "Have you thought of anything else you want to tell us?"

"No, I believe I covered everything, except the details of what we learned about Joanna Gillespie and Jack McKinstry. But all that's in the folders. If there's anything that isn't clear, just give me a call. I want to go home and change and then go back to the office, if you have no objection. You can imagine what it's going to be like in there today." He stood up to go. "I almost sent those folders over by messenger. But when the time came, I felt a certain reluctance to let them out of my possession. I'm happy to say they're all yours now."

Marian asked, "Who'll be running Strode's business interests now?"

"That will be up to Mrs. Strode." Castleberry gave them a polite nod and left.

Ivan grinned. "Think he'll get the job?"

"Wouldn't be surprised. He's in a position to know the business better than anyone else."

"Yeah, but can he *run* it, that's the question."

"Oh, Castleberry could probably maintain the status quo, but he's not going to do any empire building. Or empire expanding, I guess it would be." She opened a folder labeled *Gillespie, Joanna*. "Let's see what we've got here."

They both read silently for a while and then looked up at the same time. "Her *parents*?" Ivan asked incredulously.

"That's what it says," Marian replied no less incredulously.

They didn't speak again until both of them had finished reading all three folders. They stared at each other in silence until Marian said, "So? What do you think?"

"I think we've got three killers upstairs, that's what I think! Jesus! All three of them? And Strode was using it to get this House of Glass stock? The man was crazy—he must have been!"

"Money-crazy, at any rate. But those other three…what the hell kind of people are we dealing with here? They do whatever they want and to hell with everybody else? *Don't get in my way or I'll kill you?*"

"Well, Strode was no sweetheart himself," Ivan pointed out. "He ran over people like they weren't even there. He was just the one to bring out that old urge to kill, doncha think?"

"A very killable man," Marian agreed. "Who chose to conduct business with three people eminently qualified to do the job. And now we've got to figure out which one did."

"What does it matter?" Ivan muttered. "They're already murderers, all of them. If we say it's conspiracy—"

"Then we'll be sure to get the right one...and punish the other two for past sins as well? Come on, Ivan, you know we can't do it that way. One set of this evidence will have to go to the captain so he can inform the police where these earlier killings took place. If we can't nail the one who killed Strode, *then* we'll get them all on the earlier charges. But the only murder you and I have to worry about is this one, A. J. Strode's. Let the captain handle the rest of it."

"You know what he'll do, don't you? He'll tell us to put them all under arrest."

"So?"

"So that means we do our investigating in an interrogation room instead of here. Don't you want to keep 'em here at the scene?"

"Sure. But we're not going to have uniformed help much longer. At the end of twenty-four hours they'll all be pulled."

"Yeah, but we've still got today. Just hold off on sending those folders over to the captain until we've had a chance to talk to our three primes. C'mon, Marian, you know damned well once they're locked up we're not gonna get shit out of them."

She sighed. "Okay, in for a penny...we'll hold on to the folders until after we've had a shot at the big three. Which one did we decide on first? McKinstry?"

"Jack McKinstry it is."

"Christ!" Marian suddenly cried. "I just thought of something! The finger pointers. The first mate's widow, the mercenary—"

"Yeah, yeah, what about them?"

"Their names and addresses are all in here. And Bruce and the others read those folders yesterday afternoon."

"Oh, shit. They could have phoned somebody—"

"There's no holding anything back now. We've got to get the captain to get those people some protection. Look, you call him, tell him what's happening, tell him where they're all living. I'll go find one of the uniforms and have him take one set of the folders over right now."

"Right," said Ivan, heading for the phone. "And get Jack McKinstry in here. Fast."

"And get Jack McKinstry in here fast," Marian agreed.

ONE OF THE UNIFORMED officers brought Jack McKinstry to the conference room and then left.

His clothing was rumpled, but Jack came in with a big smile on his face and proceeded to size up the two detectives quickly. "At last—Authority has issued its summons!" he said lightly and sat down at the conference table with them. "I was beginning to think you folks had forgotten about me. Now, what can I do to help you?"

Marian was almost amused by the way he had taken charge, or thought he had. Jack McKinstry was a good-looking man in spite of the shadows under his eyes; he had an easy charm he obviously relied on to get him out of tight spots. Marian found both their male suspects attractive, making for a nice change from the usual run of perps she had to deal with. She introduced herself and her partner. "First of all we want to know your whereabouts between the time your meeting in this room broke up and the time Mr.

Strode's body was discovered. When did the meeting end, exactly?''

"Oh, it must have been close to eleven. We'd been in here for *hours*—god, how I hate this room. Then I went up to my room to finish packing. I didn't intend to spend another night in this house. I was in such a hurry to get out I got careless and dropped the suitcase on my toe. I let out a yell to wake the dead."

"A rough weekend, we hear."

"The roughest."

"How long did you stay in your room?"

"Until I smelled smoke. Then I started downstairs and one of those pet gorillas Strode liked to keep around yelled up at me everything was under control and to go back to my room. So like a good little boy I went back to my room. The next thing I knew everyone was screaming that Strode had been killed and there were police everywhere you looked." He hesitated. "Is it true, about the knives? All three of our knives were used to kill him?"

"It's true."

Jack's grin stretched from ear to ear. "Somebody's got a nice sense of irony."

"Any idea who?"

He pulled his chair closer to hers. "Sergeant, let's skip the games. You know as well as I do that it had to be one of the three of us." He smiled disarmingly. "Now, I *know* I didn't kill him—but you don't. You look at me and all you see is Suspect, with a capital 'S.' But Strode and I had nothing more to do with each other. Once Richard Bruce sold him his House of Glass shares, it was all over. None of us had any further business with Strode."

"Not even the business of the fingerprints on the knives? Strode did have those knives taken away from you, didn't he?"

He raised an eyebrow. "So you know about that, do you? Then you know that's the way Strode was able to force Richard to sell. That's all that was about."

"And you were going to go away and leave a knife with your fingerprints on it in A. J. Strode's possession? Mr. McKinstry, *nobody* would do that."

"What could I do about it? They were locked up, there were guards...sure, somebody broke 'em out during the fire, but I didn't know there was going to be a fire, now did I?"

"Where are the household cleaning supplies kept?" Ivan broke in.

"Why, they're...uh, ah, I don't know—in the back of the house somewhere?"

It didn't work. He knew, and they knew he knew.

While he was still off balance, Marian asked, "Why didn't you just sell your House of Glass shares when Strode first showed you the affidavit the helicopter pilot signed? You could have ended it all right there."

He tried to bluff. "What affidavit?"

Silently Ivan opened a folder and slid the pilot's statement across the table to him. Marian watched as Jack's tanned face slowly turned gray. "It was in A. J. Strode's computer all the time," she said. "Your helicopter and Joanna Gillespie's parents and Richard Bruce's ship. We've got it all."

For a long moment there was no sound, no movement. Then abruptly, violently, Jack McKinstry burst into motion. He jumped up, grabbed his chair, and in one over-sized motion smashed it down on the conference table.

"Hey!" Ivan shouted. He and Marian were out of their seats in a flash.

Jack lifted the broken chair over his head and brought it down on the table again. And again. His white teeth glistened through a rictus grimace; his eyes were slits. Marian grabbed one arm while Ivan made a try for the chair. Jack was strong enough to hold them both off for a few seconds, but then they got what remained of the chair away from him. Marian could feel his body tensed as tightly as a coiled spring; his skin was covered with cold sweat. She held on to his arm and walked him around and around the conference table until gradually he began to calm down.

His breathing was shallow. "I've got to get out of here," he managed to choke out.

They took him outside. The morning sun was shining without enthusiasm, but the air smelled unexpectedly clean. Jack wandered off the back patio on to the drive leading to the service gate, the two police detectives right with him every step. Their suspect didn't go far. Ivan was pointedly looking at his watch when Jack turned to them. "I apologize for that tacky little scene I played in there," he said. "Something just...broke. I don't usually make an ass of myself like that," he finished bitterly.

"Ready to talk to us now, Mr. McKinstry?" Marian asked briskly, hoping to speed him along.

"Sure, why not? You know everything anyway."

"Not quite everything. We know the three of you forced your way into Strode's vault yesterday afternoon—"

"So Castleberry shot off his mouth, did he? Huh. I knew Richard couldn't buy him off."

"—and we know about the power play you tried on A. J. Strode and what his counterplay was. But what we don't know is which of you killed Strode. Or whether all three of you did."

"None of the above, Sergeant. *Two* of us did. You want your killers? Go arrest Richard Bruce and Joanna Gillespie."

"You know that for a fact, do you? That the two of them together killed him?"

"Oh, for god's sake, Sergeant Larch, open your eyes! Those two have cozied up together and...and I don't know how they're going to do it, but they're going to blame Strode's death on me. The two of them have been trying to edge me out all weekend. You know how it is when three people are thrown together. Two always end up siding together against the third. It *always* happens."

Marian waited out the bout of self-pity and said, "Satisfy my curiosity. Why *didn't* you sell to Strode when you had the chance?"

Jack looked straight into her eyes and smiled sadly. "It would have been like leaving a knife with my fingerprints on it in his possession."

Marian thought that over, and nodded.

Ivan was growing impatient. "Look, Mr. McKinstry, we don't have a hell of a lot of time left. You were in your room when the fire broke out, you say. Did you see anything, hear anything?"

"No, Sergeant, I didn't," he sighed. "Nothing more than what I've already told you. I'd love to be able to say I saw Richard Bruce creeping away from the monitoring room with an empty gasoline can in his hand, but the truth is I saw nothing."

"Which means that nobody saw you either," Ivan pointed out.

"Oh, for Christ's sake! I, didn't, *kill him*. Either Richard or Jo set that fire, not me."

"It was cleaning fluid that was used, not gasoline. And you know where the cleaning supplies are stored."

"Hell, we all know. Right next to the wall cabinet where the keys are kept."

Marian exchanged a glance with her partner and said, "You want to tell us about that?"

Jack told them about how they'd borrowed the keys, the ones to Strode's rooms and the one to the wine cellar. He explained how he and Jo Gillespie had searched Strode's bedroom and library and had left the door to the latter unlocked. He explained how Jo and Richard Bruce had pretended to leave the house but then had sneaked back in through the service gate and the wine cellar. He explained how they were able to do that because he, one Jack McKinstry himself, had sabotaged the security system. Any questions?

"So that's how the killer got into the library," Ivan said in a tone of discovery. "Did Richard Bruce know you and Ms Gillespie had left the door unlocked?"

"Damn right he did. He was even *in* the library, later on. He and Jo hid there while I called Castleberry and got him over here. But the plan didn't end there—they just didn't tell me the rest of it."

"You mean the murder?"

"I mean the murder."

Ivan looked doubtful. "And you're convinced Richard Bruce killed Strode and Joanna Gillespie helped him?"

"Or vice versa. Jesus, Sergeant, a woman who'd kill her own mother and father wouldn't have any scruples about getting rid of a man who threatened her! She even admitted it, to Richard and me! Killing her parents, I mean. But they were in on Strode's murder together, I tell you, Jo and Richard. I know they were. They probably took turns shoving knives in him . . . they planned it together and they did it together. And I'm not going to make any cracks about the warmth and wonderfulness of all that togetherness."

"I'm glad," Marian said dryly. "Joanna Gillespie actually admitted killing her parents?"

"She sure as hell did. Saturday afternoon, in some bar where we stopped for a bite to eat."

"I want to talk to Joanna Gillespie while we still have time," Ivan said to his partner.

Marian agreed. "Mr. McKinstry, you know not to try to leave, don't you?"

He shrugged. "I know. How *could* I leave? There's a cop every ten feet." He glanced back at an officer on the patio who'd been following him every place he went. "Besides," he finished tiredly, "I'm not a player anymore. I'm out of it. It's somebody else's game now."

They left him standing in the middle of the service driveway, staring dejectedly down at his shoes.

"I WONDER IF the captain called while we were outside," Marian said as she and Ivan went back in the house.

"Let's not ask," he muttered. "You think McKinstry could be right? Bruce and Gillespie did it together?"

"Sure, it's possible. But that could be sour grapes talking. *Something's* happened to make Jack McKinstry feel left out. But maybe it's nothing more than sex—Joanna Gillespie's preferring Richard Bruce to him, something like that."

"Yeah? What is she, some kind of glamour girl?"

"Far from it. At least I don't think she is. I've never seen her up close. That thing McKinstry said about not being a player anymore—you buy that?"

"Naw, he was just feeling sorry for himself. It won't last."

They stopped in the conference room with its broken chair and marred table only long enough to pick up the remaining set of file folders Castleberry had provided. The nearest police officer told them which was Joanna Gillespie's room, but it would have been easy to find even without directions. In the upstairs hallway two policemen sat in chairs flanking one door. In answer to Marian's question, one officer said yes, both suspects were inside. Marian knocked, and a woman's voice said come in. Marian and Ivan opened the door and entered.

Their two suspects were sitting hip to hip in a bay window seat, their backs to the sun. One of Joanna Gillespie's hands rested lightly and yet possessively on Richard Bruce's thigh—high on his thigh, and toward the inside. She didn't move her hand or change position in any way when the two police detectives came in. The expression on her face—matched exactly by the man sitting next to her—said: *Yes, we are together. What about it?* They hadn't even bothered to smooth out the bed.

Marian, who normally performed the introductions, was momentarily rendered speechless by the intimacy of the scene they'd walked in on. Ivan took care of it and then told Richard Bruce they wanted to talk to Ms Gillespie alone.

Richard slipped an arm around Joanna and gave her shoulder an encouraging squeeze. Then he stood up and walked over to face the detectives. "I called my lawyer in Los Angeles," he said. "Even now he is arranging with a New York firm to represent us—both of us. I don't think we should proceed much farther without legal representation."

"That certainly is your right," Ivan said without expression. "But let me remind you that no charges have been brought, and we haven't detained you as material witnesses."

"Not yet, you haven't," Richard smiled icily. "We intend to cooperate, Sergeant, but there is a limit to how long we'll allow you to inconvenience us. I just wanted to warn you that that limit is fast approaching."

"I gotcha."

Richard glanced back at Joanna Gillespie and left without saying more. Marian found her voice and asked the other woman to account for her whereabouts during the time of the fire and the murder.

She and Richard were planning to leave, Joanna said, when she asked him to wait while she made a quick trip back up to her room. She wanted to test her blood-sugar level; she was a diabetic and needed to run frequent checks. She finished and was leaving her room when she heard shouting and smelled smoke. She saw Jack McKinstry about halfway down the stairs, and one of Strode's bodyguards was yelling at him to go back to his room. She did the same. She waited until Richard came up and told her A. J. Strode had been murdered. That's all she knew.

All the time she was talking, Marian watched her closely. No, Joanna Gillespie was no glamour girl. She didn't need to be. She was one of those people who could never slip quietly into a room; they were always noticed. Marian glanced at Ivan and could see he was puzzled. Ivan liked women who worked hard at making themselves attractive, and Joanna Gillespie obviously didn't fit into that category. He questioned her about the location of the cleaning supplies and the wine cellar; she denied knowledge of both.

"Did Jack McKinstry see you?" Marian asked her. "When he was going down the stairs to see about the fire."

"I don't think so."

"Then he can't confirm your story that you were coming out of your room when you saw him?"

"What do you mean, story? Where else would I have been?"

"You could have been downstairs—you could have seen him from there. Or you could have been upstairs, but heading toward Strode's private wing."

"Don't be absurd. I was exactly where I said I was. I've never been in Strode's private wing. I'm not even sure where it is."

"Oh yes, you know where it is, because you've been there. Twice. The first time with Jack McKinstry when you were searching for some indication as to where Strode might be hiding out. You left the door to the library unlocked, making it easy for the killer to get in later on. The second time was with Richard Bruce. The two of you hid in the library while McKinstry lured Castleberry over here. Oh, you know where the private wing is, all right."

Joanna Gillespie licked dry lips and said one word. "Jack."

"Mr. McKinstry told us part of it, yes, but Mr. Castleberry had already filled us in pretty well. Why don't you stop lying to us, Ms Gillespie? We know about the papers you burned in Strode's office."

Joanna got up from the window seat and moved aimlessly about the room. "Well. I see our secrets are not as secret as I thought. What else do you know?"

Wordlessly Ivan handed her one of the file folders.

She opened the folder and glanced through the contents, not reading everything but just checking to see what was there. She closed her eyes and started rocking back and forth on her feet, saying nothing for a long time. Then she laughed. Sourly, but it was still a laugh. "That bastard." She dropped the folder carelessly, spilling the papers on the floor. "I should have known he'd have one final trick up his sleeve. He just had to have the last word. Even if it was posthumously." She went over to the door, placed her palms against the wooden panels, and braced herself there, her chin pressed down against her chest.

Looking for a way out? Marian wondered. "Ms Gillespie, did you kill A. J. Strode?"

"No," Joanna answered almost carelessly. "But I'll tell you this. Whoever did kill him has my gratitude. I'm glad Strode is dead. Life will be more sane for all of us now. The killer did me a favor, and I don't deny it. I hope he gets away with it." Then, almost to herself: "I didn't think he had the guts."

"Who's that?" Ivan asked, playing dumb. When she didn't answer, he prodded: "Richard Bruce?"

She whirled around from the door. "Of course not! Richard didn't kill him!"

Ivan raised an eyebrow. "Dear me. That leaves only one 'him' around. You must be saying Jack McKinstry killed Strode. Do you have any reason to think he was the one? Or do you just want him to be?"

"Oh, you're very smart, aren't you, Sergeant Malecki?" she snapped. "You come in here and start playing twenty questions with me when you already know the answers. Now you're manipulating me into accusing Jack and making it look as if I'm just trying to protect Richard."

"Excuse me," said Marian, "but I don't think it's my partner who's been doing the manipulating. You oh-so-casually mumbled you didn't think 'he' had the guts to kill Strode—but just loudly enough to make sure we'd hear. Now you're trying to make it appear that my partner tricked you into saying that. It won't do, Ms Gillespie. Jack McKinstry thinks you and Richard Bruce together killed A. J. Strode. I'm beginning to think he might be right."

"Jack McKinstry is a fool!"

"But you're grateful to him, right? Because he did your dirty work for you? Is that what we're supposed to believe?"

"You believe whatever you want. But all three of us wanted Strode dead, and any one of us could have killed him. But whichever one of them found the courage to do it, more power to him."

Marian didn't bother hiding her distaste. "Are you listening to what you're saying? Does human life mean so little to you?"

"A. J. Strode wasn't human. He was a feral beast who preyed on real humans."

"What do you call someone who murders her mother and father?"

Joanna Gillespie smiled coldly. "Ah yes, I was wondering when we'd get to that. Strode used that accusation to hound me too."

"Jack McKinstry says you admitted killing them."

Her mouth dropped open. "He says *what*?"

Marian repeated the accusation. "He says you were all in a bar somewhere when you admitted it to him and Richard Bruce."

Joanna sank down on the side of the bed and shook her head in amazement. "The man's treachery is *endless*," she said wonderingly. "Sergeant Larch, I did not kill my father. I did not kill my mother. I did not tell Jack McKinstry or anyone else that I did. And I most certainly did not kill A. J. Strode."

Just then something of an uproar broke out in the hallway. They could hear Richard Bruce's voice raised in anger and the quieter answering tones of the policemen standing guard. "I demand you let me in there!" he was saying.

Before the other two could stop her, Joanna Gillespie was at the door jerking it open. Richard Bruce came barreling in, shrugging off the two cops who were trying to restrain him. He placed a hand on Joanna's shoulder and said, "They know about the evidence we thought we'd gotten rid of."

"I know. They have copies."

"Don't say another word—not until we have a lawyer."

Ivan asked, "How did you find out about it? We didn't tell you."

"Jack McKinstry," Marian said. "Had to be."

Joanna laughed unpleasantly. "It's always Jack. Richard?"

"Yes, Jack told me," he said tiredly. "Smilin' Jack McKinstry. But this changes everything. What happens next, Sergeant? Sergeants?"

Marian said, "Right now we want you to go back to your own room so we can finish—"

"I don't mean right now. I mean what action do you intend—"

"Take Mr. Bruce back to his room," Marian instructed the two uniformed policemen. "And make sure he stays there. Thank you."

One of the officers placed a hand on Richard Bruce's arm. "Come along. You heard the sergeant."

He jerked his arm away. "I heard her." He turned to Joanna. "Don't say *anything* more. Not a thing." He left the room, followed by the two officers.

As soon as the door was closed, Ivan snapped out a question. "How long does it take to run a blood-sugar test?"

"I think I've just been given good advice," Joanna said tightly. "I'm not going to answer any more of your questions."

"Does that mean you still know something you haven't told us?"

She didn't answer.

Marian stepped over and stood face to face with the other woman. "If he did it, we'll find out. You can't protect him, you know."

"I don't know anything of the sort!" Joanna shot back. "I don't know that he did it, or that you'll find out who did. Are you infallible, Sergeant?"

Marian didn't think that worth answering. "Is McKinstry right? He's convinced the two of you did it together."

Joanna's lip curled. "And we all know how reliable Jack McKinstry is. Sergeant, I'm through talking to you." She went over to the window and stood with her back to them.

Marian and Ivan exchanged a glance and a shrug and temporarily abandoned their interrogation of the world's best-known violinist. They gathered up the papers Joanna had spilled on the floor and left. Out in the hall Ivan said, "Whew. All that stuff about her being grateful to the killer? That's pretty goddam hardhearted. She just doesn't care, does she? And she sure as hell doesn't give away much. She and Richard Bruce, they're two of a kind."

Marian grunted agreement. "They deserve each other. I wonder where McKinstry is?"

One of the police officers in the hallway said Jack McKinstry had gone to Bruce's room shortly before the latter had come storming down the hall demanding to be let in to Joanna Gillespie's room. Then McKinstry had gone into his own room.

Ivan issued instructions. "If either Gillespie or McKinstry tries to leave, stop him. Or her. And don't let 'em talk to each other. Go into their rooms and take out their phones." He knocked on Richard Bruce's door and opened it without waiting for a response.

This room was larger than Joanna Gillespie's, but it had no window seat. Richard Bruce stood in the middle of the floor, his arms folded, waiting for them. He was still wearing yesterday's clothes but managed to look moderately elegant just the same. "I've already told you I'm not going to answer your questions without an attorney present."

On the spur of the moment Marian decided to try something. "Mr. Bruce, we're pretty well satisfied that Joanna Gillespie couldn't have killed A. J. Strode. One of the house staff saw her going into her room right before the fire broke out," she lied. "The maid seems sure of the time and we have no reason to doubt her. There just wouldn't have been time for Ms Gillespie to go back downstairs, get the cleaning fluid from the supplies closet, and get back to the monitoring room before the fire was first spotted. As far as we're concerned, she's in the clear. That leaves you and Mr. McKinstry." Ivan kept a practiced poker face during his partner's fairy tale.

Richard unfolded his arms and took a step toward Marian. "Joanna is no longer under suspicion? Is that the truth?"

"That's right. We've eliminated her as a suspect."

For the first time since Marian and Ivan had met him, Richard Bruce's face lit up in a smile of genuine pleasure. "Thank god," he said quietly. "I can't tell you how relieved I am to hear that."

"Why's that?" Ivan asked in a conversational tone. "Did you kind of think maybe she was the one who got to Strode?"

"Of course not! Don't be ridiculous. But as long as she was suspect, she was in danger. From *you*, Sergeant."

Marian picked out a chair and sat down. "So, Mr. Bruce. Now you no longer have to worry about protecting Ms Gillespie. Now you can let her worry about protecting you."

"You think I killed Strode? You're mistaken. I would have gladly wrung his neck if he'd been here earlier, but as it happens I am thoroughly guiltless in the matter of his murder. A. J. Strode was dispatched without any help from me—not counting moral support, of course."

"*Sheesh!*" Ivan said in disgust. "What is the matter with you people? *Moral* support? For a murderer? You sink a ship full of men and you talk about *moral* support?"

"Encouragement, I should have said," Richard interposed, not at all ruffled by Ivan's outburst. "You already know we all three wanted him dead. Would it do any good to pretend otherwise? And be very careful about the accusations you toss about so casually, Sergeant Malecki. The sinking of the *Burly Girl* was fully investigated at the time and I was cleared. I don't think that jigged-up evidence of Strode's is going to convict me of anything."

"It doesn't look jigged-up to me," Marian said. "And you went to a hell of a lot of trouble to get it back. But that's not our problem. What happens about the crew of the *Burly Girl* is up to the Hawaiian authorities. We're looking for the killer of A. J. Strode, and that's all."

"Then arrest Jack McKinstry," Richard said sharply. "Put an end to this."

"Not just yet," Marian said. "There are still a few holes in your story. For instance, this House of Glass stock. You ended up selling it to Strode. Why weren't you willing to sell earlier, before things got ugly?"

"Things were ugly right from the start, Sergeant Larch. I don't give a damn about House of Glass—I was always willing to sell my stock. What I could not tolerate was the thought of the control of my life passing into the hands of another man. Especially a man like A. J. Strode."

Essentially the same answer as Jack McKinstry's, Marian thought. "McKinstry thinks you and Joanna Gillespie killed Strode together."

A look of disgust crossed his face. "McKinstry doesn't think at all. He's mentally incontinent. Slick as a whistle, sharp as a tack, and original as a cliché—that's Jack. Of course he'd say we did it. Do you think he'd admit killing Strode himself? If you caught him standing over the body with all three knives in his hands, he'd still say, 'It's not my fault' or 'Somebody else did it' or maybe, at worst, 'I couldn't help it.' He'll never accept responsibility for his acts. It's just not in his nature.''

Marian tried a different tack. "Why didn't you help put out the fire in the monitoring room? You were downstairs, by your own account. You had to know something was going on. Yet you stayed away. Why?"

Richard pulled over a chair and sat down facing her. "I didn't help put out the fire because I couldn't," he said simply. "And I couldn't because I was locked in one of the bathrooms at the time."

The two police detectives stared at him.

"I wasn't going to mention this, but now . . . after I asked one of the maids to bring up Joanna's and my suitcases from the wine cellar, I decided to make a quick trip to the bathroom before we left. While I was in there, someone came along and locked it from the outside—to keep me from interfering, I suppose."

Or to give you an alibi, Marian thought. "Wait a minute. How can a bathroom be locked from the *outside*?"

"There's a knob on the outside, the kind that turns an internal bolt. The door can be locked from inside the bathroom, too, with the same sort of arrangement. But there are two separate bolts in the door."

"How'd you get out? Is there a window?"

"Not in that bathroom. I called out and pounded on the door. No one heard me for a while—they were all too busy with the fire, I suppose. Then someone heard me and unlocked the door. I was in the process of thanking him when that overmuscled bodyguard came thundering down the stairs roaring that Strode had been murdered. I was locked in the whole time that fire was burning. So if Strode was killed sometime *during* the fire, then I couldn't possibly have done it.''

No, you couldn't have, Marian thought. *One down.* ''Who let you out?''

Richard leaned forward in his chair and smiled. ''Myron Castleberry.''

There was a moment of silence. Then Marian stirred and asked her partner. ''You have the number?''

''Yeah,'' Ivan said, pulling a notebook out of his pocket. He went to the phone on the bedside table and tapped out a number.

''Mr. Bruce, why didn't you tell us this before? We could have cleared you right away.''

He shook his head. ''Obviously it was the killer who locked me in. As I intimated earlier, I had no burning desire to see the killer brought to what you undoubtedly consider justice.''

''You thought Joanna Gillespie was the murderer.''

''Nonsense! Don't be absurd. It had to be Jack, I knew that. Joanna was upstairs testing her blood sugar and I was locked in the bathroom. Jack was the only one on the loose.''

''So you risked being accused of murder just to protect Jack McKinstry? Are you seriously asking me to believe that?''

''No, of course not. If it looked as if you were going to charge me with Strode's murder, then I would have told you.''

''Even if we hadn't cleared Joanna Gillespie?''

He was saved from answering by Ivan's hanging up the phone. ''Castleberry confirms it. He says he let Mr. Bruce out of one of the downstairs bathrooms only seconds before Millwalker came running down the stairs with the news of Strode's death. He apologizes profusely for not telling us, but it just slipped his mind with all the other things going on."

Richard made a sound of disbelief but refrained from comment.

"Let's go take a look at that bathroom door," Marian said. "You too, Mr. Bruce."

The three of them left Richard's room. In the hallway Ivan reminded the two policemen on duty that the suspects were not to be allowed to talk to each other.

"Is that really necessary, Sergeant?" Richard asked as they started down the stairs. "Since Joanna is cleared and I am cleared—"

"About that," Marian interrupted. "I'm afraid I lied. There was no conveniently passing houseservant to give Joanna Gillespie an alibi. She's still a suspect."

"*What?*" Richard grabbed Marian's arm. "You lied? Joanna hasn't been cleared?"

"You want to let go of my arm?"

"Let go of her arm," Ivan said.

"You were lying? None of it was true?"

"My arm," Marian repeated.

He let go. "What a *rotten* trick! Of all the underhanded, unethical—"

"Hold it!" Marian commanded. "*You're* going to give *me* a lecture about right and wrong? Is that what you're going to do?"

The two locked gazes until Marian thought she saw amusement appear in Richard Bruce's eyes. "Very well, Sergeant Larch," he said. "No lectures."

He led them to the same bathroom they'd both used in the early hours of the day. The door was precisely as he'd described it—two bolts, each controlled from a different side of the door.

"Why would anyone want to lock a bathroom door from the outside?" Marian stepped into the bathroom and closed the door behind her. When she heard Ivan turn the bolt from the outside, she tried the door; it didn't budge. She looked at the hinges; they all fit tightly and she could see no scratches or other indication that the pins had ever been pried out of their sockets. She took a credit card out of her billfold and tried slipping it between the doorjamb and the bolt, but the jamb overlapped the door by a good half inch and the plastic card wouldn't go in. "Okay," she called out.

Ivan unlocked the door. "No go?" A phone rang somewhere nearby.

"No go. Well, Mr. Bruce, it looks as if you're in the clear. You couldn't have been locked in down here and upstairs killing Strode at the same time. You are officially off the hook."

"I am so very grateful," he said with only the lightest trace of sarcasm.

A police officer came up to them. "Sergeants? Telephone. Either of you."

"I'll take it," Ivan said and followed the officer away.

Richard moved in close to Marian. "Sergeant Larch, you must know Jack McKinstry is the one you're looking for. Arrest him. He'll break down and admit everything, and he'll break down rather fast. The man has no backbone at all. Arrest him."

"Can't do that without hard evidence, Mr. Bruce. All he has to do is hold out twenty-four hours and we'd have to let him go."

"He won't hold out twenty-four hours. I can virtually guarantee it. Why put Joanna through all this when you know she's not the killer?"

"But I don't know that. You're the only one around here who seems sure she's innocent. And if you'll excuse my saying so, you're hardly an impartial observer."

"No," he admitted. "But you must not charge her with murder. You *must* not."

Ivan came back. "That was the captain. He wants to know why in the hell we haven't arrested these three people. Time's up, partner."

NINE

WHILE PUFFING UP A FLIGHT of stairs one afternoon a little over a year earlier, Captain Ralph H. Michaels had surprised himself by suffering a coronary. By medical standards, it was a mild one; but by the captain's personal standards, it ran a close second to all-out nuclear war. So he listened when his doctor lectured him about smoking and drinking and overeating. Now, fourteen months and forty-two pounds later, he was proud of his new near-svelte appearance. No one had the heart to tell him he looked better the other way; the baggy skin and the deep creases in his cheeks made him look old enough to be thinking about retirement. Which he wasn't.

He'd turned on the heat in his office, even though the day was mild and pleasant; Captain Michaels claimed he got cold faster now, without all that insulation he used to carry around. He told Marian Larch and Ivan Malecki to sit down and got straight to the point. "Ozzie Rogers and Estelle Rankin have disappeared," he said. "The police in Texas and Oregon can't find them. No one's seen them for a couple of days. Now what do you suppose that means?" he inquired innocently.

Ivan growled. "It means Richard Bruce's men got to them. And no, we can't prove it."

"And Richard Bruce is the one suspect you've cleared in the Strode murder? Have I got that right?"

"He couldn't have done it, Captain," Marian said. "Myron Castleberry let him out of that locked bathroom only a minute or two after Strode was killed. There just wouldn't have been time, even if he had figured out a way to lock himself in. No, he's in the clear. It's one of the other two.''

"Pity," the captain said sarcastically. "He was my pick."

"Mine too," Marian agreed without irony. "He's the most cold-blooded of the lot, but we can't pin this one on him. God, I hope he didn't have those two people killed. The finger pointers. Maybe he's just bought them off.''

"Why would he go after the mercenary?" the captain wanted to know. "The first mate's widow I can under-stand, but Ozzie Rogers is no threat to Richard Bruce. Bruce is just helping out the violinist—why would he want to do that?"

Ivan explained that one, and in his usual inelegant fash-ion. "Richard Bruce and Joanna Gillespie are screwin' each other. They'd never met before Friday, so I guess they're making up for lost time. Bruce must like it a lot because he's doing his damnedest to keep Gillespie out of jail. Any word on McKinstry's helicopter pilot?"

"He's alive and well and in the custody of the Miami po-lice," Michaels said. "When he learned A. J. Strode had been killed, he started talking and hasn't stopped yet. The cops there casually mentioned Jack McKinstry was one of our suspects and let him jump to his own conclusions."

"Which just might be correct," Marian pointed out. "Fifty-fifty chance. If the helicopter pilot is talking, that means at least one of them won't get away with those other murders, and that's something. But we need a little more time to pin down the Strode killing, Captain. Give us at least the rest of today."

"Uniforms come off the site at midnight. That doesn't leave you much time."

"Better'n nothing," Ivan said. "We'll haul 'em all in at midnight, but let us put off charging them until then."

Captain Michaels thought about it. "What can you do here that you can't do here?"

"Maybe get them to talk," Marian said. "Play them off one another. There's no love lost between Jack McKinstry and the other two. A lot of tension there, Captain. If we bring them in now and separate them, the bomb won't go off."

"You guarantee it will if we keep them there?"

"No. But it's a damned good opportunity and I think we ought to take advantage of it."

The captain thought about it some more. "Okay. You got until midnight. But at or before twelve o'clock I expect three arrests. And it would make me very happy, Sergeants, if only two of the three perpetrators are to be held for extra-dition. I want to keep the other one right here, charged with the murder of A. J. Strode. That would make me very happy indeed. Do you think you could possibly manage that?"

"We'll sure as hell try," Ivan assured him earnestly.

"Give it our best shot," Marian agreed.

The two police detectives left, determined to do their best to keep their captain happy.

DIVIDE and ... cross your fingers.

"Show me how you and Richard Bruce got back in the house."

"You know how we got in. Through the wine cellar."

"Show me."

Joanna Gillespie did not heave a big sigh of annoyance but managed to convey the impression that she'd done just that. She led Marian Larch out to the back patio and around to the door that led to the wine cellar.

"Did you lock it after you went in?"

"No."

Marian tried the door; it was still unlocked. Inside was pleasantly cool, just the right temperature for the undoubtedly expensive wines kept there. "Where did you leave the suitcases?"

"There." Joanna pointed.

There were no imprints in the dust on the floor to mark the place because there was no dust on the floor. The entire place was spotless, unlike any other wine cellar Marian had ever seen. A small table was shoved up against the wall with a chair on each side; Marian took one of the two chairs and pointed to the other. "You know Richard Bruce has cleared himself." Not a question.

Joanna Gillespie carefully lowered herself into the other chair. She kept her eyes on Marian. "Yes."

"Did you know he was going to do that? Did he tell you?"

Joanna licked dry lips. "I don't see how that's the police's concern."

"He didn't tell you, did he? Must have been quite a surprise."

She bit. "Look, Sergeant Larch, you know perfectly well Richard thought I was in the clear when he told you about being locked in the bathroom. You lied to him, and now you're trying to make it appear as if he was worrying about saving his own skin all along."

"You mean he wasn't? I thought you all were."

"Well, of course we are!" Joanna snapped. "You know what I mean. What does it matter anyway? Richard *is* in the clear, isn't he?"

"Yes, he is. And then there were two."

Joanna stared at her a long time. "There should be only one. Jack McKinstry."

"Then give me something solid. Something other than your dislike of him. Think back. You must know something you haven't told me."

"I *have* thought back—god, I've been over it and over it. I didn't hear him in his room during the time of the murder. That's all I can think of."

"Would you have heard him? These walls are pretty thick."

"Maybe not," she admitted. "Unless he were making an extraordinary amount of noise."

Marian tried a different tack. "You know, whoever killed Strode must have had it in the back of his mind that he was helping out the other two. He or she. By removing Strode, the killer was removing the near-certainty that Strode would indulge in a little more string-pulling in the future. As long as Strode lived, all three of you were in jeopardy. I don't mean that was the killer's motive—his motive was to save himself. But saving the other two was a kind of bonus."

"But it wasn't! Strode had all his so-called evidence in the computer. Killing Strode didn't get rid of that."

"Ah, but none of you knew about the computer then, did you? The killer *thought* all three of you would be home free once Strode was out of the way. So either you or Jack McKinstry took it on yourself to put an end to it. One of you killed to free all three of you." Marian paused. "All we know for certain is that Richard Bruce didn't kill to save you."

This time Joanna didn't rise to the bait. "You're on the wrong track, Sergeant. There was only one person Jack McKinstry was thinking about when he killed Strode, and that was Jack McKinstry. We got to know Jack pretty quickly this weekend, and he is the most *childishly* selfish adult I've ever met. If it did occur to him he was helping

Richard and me, he probably tried to figure some way to take advantage of it."

Marian thought that was a fair assessment of Jack's character. "But he couldn't take advantage of it, because it didn't work out right. It was bad luck that the murder accomplished just the opposite of what it was supposed to accomplish. Instead of saving everybody, the murder just brought everything to our attention. You know what's going to happen to you, don't you?"

"To me? No, Sergeant Larch, I don't know what's going to happen to me. Why don't you tell me?"

"It's up to the Boston police, of course, but I don't see how they can avoid charging you with the murder of your parents. Personally, I don't think you can even get away with claiming the murders were mercy killings. If I were sitting on a jury and heard testimony that the defendant had tried to hire a mercenary to do her killing for her, I'd think twice before buying the euthanasia story."

"Oh, you've got it all wrong," Joanna said tiredly. "I was thinking of hiring a bodyguard, that's all. Strode bribed Ozzie Rogers to say I wanted him to kill my parents."

"A *body*guard," Marian echoed, pretending to be impressed. "That's very good. Did Richard Bruce suggest that one? You have to have an explanation for consulting Ozzie other than intended matricide and patricide—so why not claim you needed a bodyguard?"

"Richard Bruce suggested nothing! I'm quite capable of thinking up my own..."

"Lies?" Marian suggested politely.

"My own *solutions*. And I decided a bodyguard was not a solution to a problem I was having at that time." Marian looked a question at her. "Someone was sending me threatening letters, Sergeant, but it stopped well over a year ago. There was nothing to it."

"Did you call the police?"

"I did. They weren't any help."

"Where was this?"

"Boston."

Marian made a note of it. "I'll check on it."

"I'm sure you will," Joanna said dryly.

IVAN MALECKI was waiting for her in the conference room. The chair Jack McKinstry smashed had been removed. "Anything?"

"Not really. Joanna Gillespie says she was thinking of getting a bodyguard when she contacted her mercenary. Because of threatening letters. What about you?"

"Nothing. Lots of accusations, but that's all. Mc-Kinstry's on his way to being a basket case."

Marian went over to the phone. It took her longer to charge the long-distance call to the NYPD than it did to find out from the Boston police what she wanted to know.

"*One* letter," Marian told her partner when she'd hung up. "That's all their computer knows about. She definitely told me 'letters'—plural. And she intimated she'd been getting them over a period of time."

Ivan scratched the back of his neck. "She coulda just reported the first one," he said, "and when the police didn't do anything she didn't bother with the rest."

"Possible," Marian agreed reluctantly. "But Joanna Gillespie strikes me as a person who wouldn't let something like that ride. I'm surprised she didn't rush right out and buy a gun."

"Maybe she did."

"But she didn't go looking for Ozzie Rogers immediately—there's a time gap. I think she got one letter, reported it, and now is using that as her excuse for consulting a mercenary."

"None of which brings us any closer to finding out what happened here Sunday night," Ivan said. "You're doing the Boston police's work for them, Marian. Let it go."

"I know, you're right. Damn, but she's hard to pin down! So what do we do now—switch?"

"Might as well. Watch out for McKinstry—he might blow up in your face. I didn't tell him about the helicopter pilot. If you can get him calmed down enough to listen, you can throw that at him."

"He's that rattled."

"Was. He was starting to run out of steam there toward the end. See what he does first."

WHAT JACK MCKINSTRY DID first was make a pass at her.

He started out by asking Marian if she ever went to California. He told her about the big house in Malibu and assured her she would be welcome anytime she cared to visit. Then he moved in close, placed both hands on her shoulders, gazed deeply into her eyes, and expressed the sincere desire that they would see each other once "all this" was over.

For a seasoned playboy, it was an extraordinarily clumsy approach, Marian thought. Ivan must be right; Jack McKinstry was cracking up. Marian was a plain woman, and she knew it. Some plain women could slather on the makeup and affect outrageous hair and clothing styles and become TV personalities or rock stars. Marian Larch was not one of them. She decided to try diplomacy and told Jack she never mixed business and pleasure.

"Oh, come on, now, Sergeant...by the way, what's your first name?"

"You got it right. Sergeant."

He sighed theatrically. "You are a stickler for the proprieties, aren't you? I can't believe you're this formal all the time. You've got a male partner, after all—I'll bet you loosen up once in a while. Am I right?''

That was absolutely the wrong thing to say. "I hate to burst your balloon," Marian said, "but contrary to popular opinion it is possible for a man and a woman to work together without jumping into the sack together. What I do and with whom I do it is none of your business. So back off."

Jack immediately turned contrite, almost convincingly so. "Oh hey, gee, I didn't mean to insult you. Christ, I meant just the opposite! Two left feet, that's me." He squeezed her shoulders in what was probably meant to be an intimate gesture. "I want to get to know you, Sergeant Ms Larch whatever your first name is, and we're in such a peculiar relationship here, cop and suspect, that I don't know how to go about it. Help me. Stop playing mystery woman. Let me come into your life."

She put an end to it by telling Jack that his helicopter pilot was in custody in Florida and was talking his fool head off.

Jack's face collapsed. His hands dropped off Marian's shoulders and he stood there staring at her like a lost child. "That's it, then," he said in a tight voice. "You'll believe him, and Strode's lies, and whatever Joanna and Richard tell you. I don't have a chance. You're going to pin it all on me, the helicopter crash and Strode's murder and anything else you can think of. It's all decided, isn't it? I take the fall."

"You'll have to answer to the French authorities for the helicopter crash, yes," Marian said, "but I'm not arresting you for the murder of A. J. Strode just yet."

"Yet," he echoed glumly.

"Maybe not at all. Let's go over it again."

They were in the dining room, Marian had found him in
the kitchen jollying Danielle into fixing him something special to eat. One of the maids laid another place for Marian,
who was surprised to find out how hungry she was. Jack
told Marian his story again—where he was, what he did. It
came out the same as last time.

Marian got up and walked around the dining table,
thinking. "Tell me what you did while you were in your
room."

"I was packing."

"I know, but take it one step at a time. Tell me everything."

"Whoo." He thought. "Well, first I went into the bathroom to get my shaving gear and like that. No toothbrush,
the house staff puts out a new one every day with fresh
towels. I'd already packed most of my clothes—I didn't
bring a whole lot, it was only for a weekend. Then I started
looking through drawers to make sure I had everything."

"Pajamas?"

"Don't wear 'em. Oh yeah—I found a pair of shoes under the bed. Then I closed the suitcase and picked it up, and
it slipped and fell on my toe. I was hopping around holding
my foot when I smelled smoke."

Something clicked. "Wait a minute," Marian said. "That
business about dropping your suitcase on your toe—you
mentioned that before."

"Yeah, so?"

"The first time we talked to you. You said you dropped
your suitcase and let out a yell..."

"To wake the dead, right. So?"

"Did you really yell, or are you just telling a good story?"

"I yelled, lady. That hurt. Do you want to see the bruise
on my toe?"

"No, thank you. But I do want you to yell again. Not now," she added hastily as Jack took a deep breath, "and not here. Let's go upstairs."

"You want to cue me in? What's so important about my yelling?"

"Later." She led the way out of the dining room and told the uniformed officer who was watching Jack to find her partner and send him up to Mr. McKinstry's room. Upstairs, one policeman was down at Richard Bruce's end of the hall; Joanna Gillespie was downstairs somewhere with Ivan Malecki. They went into Jack's room. The villainous suitcase was on the floor by the bed.

"Where were you standing when you dropped the suitcase?" Marian asked.

"Uh...about here." He took a position near the door.

A minute later Ivan knocked at the door. "You got something?" The cop Marian had sent after him peered over his shoulder.

"Maybe. I want you to go across into Joanna Gillespie's room. Close the door and stand as far away from it as you can. Then tell me if you hear anything."

Ivan raised an eyebrow but did as she asked. At Marian's nod, Jack let out a yell that should indeed have sufficed to raise the dead.

Ivan came back and said, "I could hear him hollering. Is that what you meant?"

"Yep. Now go into her bathroom and close the door. See if you can hear from there."

Jack repeated his performance, and Ivan said that he could still hear him. "Why, Marian? What's it mean?"

She took a breath. "About the same time A. J. Strode was being stabbed, Jack dropped a suitcase on his foot and made a lot of noise about it. Joanna Gillespie told me she couldn't hear Jack in his room during the time of the murder."

When he realized what that meant, Jack McKinstry let
out a third yell, but this time it was a cry of triumph. "She
couldn't hear me because *she* wasn't in *her* room! Ha! Aha!
I *told* you she did it! Sergeant Malecki, didn't I just tell you
that? Not more than an hour ago, I said she did it! Joanna
Gillespie killed A. J. Strode, not me! And now you've got
her!"

"Hold it, hold it," Ivan cautioned. "It's just his word
against hers," he said to his partner.

Marian shook her head. "Jack didn't know she'd told me
she didn't hear anything. He'd have had no reason to make
up the story."

Jack was seated on the end of the bed taking off his shoe
and sock as fast as he could. He stuck a bare foot up in the
air. "Behold—my bruise! My beautiful, colorful, alibi-
providing bruise! Could anyone acquire a bruise like that
without yelling? What a bruise! Did you ever see such a
bruise? A wonderful bruise!"

Marian and Ivan were examining Jack's wonderful bruise
when Richard Bruce burst into the room. "*What* is going on
here? I could hear Jack yelling down at the end of the hall!"

Jack let out a whoop and flopped backward on the bed.
He lay there laughing, waving his bruised foot in the air.
"Oh Richard, Richard! What perfect timing! Evidence,
dear Sergeants Malecki and Larch, that a good healthy yell
can be clearly heard on this floor—*by anyone who's around
to hear it*. Ask the cops in the hall. I'll bet you thirty pieces
of silver they heard it too."

"Of course they heard it!" Richard snarled. "We all did.
I repeat, what is going on here?"

Jack sat up. "What is going on here, Richard, my friend,
is that your inamorata has tripped herself up. Given herself
away. Sunk her own ship. Joanna blew it, Richard. She blew

it bad. And not even you can make it right again. Isn't that a sad story?''

Richard turned to Marian. "What is he babbling about?''

Marian almost hated to tell him. "It looks as if Jack's cleared—of Strode's murder, at least. No hard evidence, but enough indication to satisfy me.'' She looked at her partner; Ivan nodded *yes*.

"What do you mean, 'indication'?'' Richard asked in his most sarcastic manner. "Since when is an *indication* sufficient to charge someone with murder? What has this accomplished liar been telling you? You should have learned by now you can't believe anything he says!''

"Oh, pardon me all to pieces, O Truthful One,'' Jack answered in kind. "And forgive my speaking up in the presence of such personification of moral rectitude as thyself, but I must point our, Your Virtueship, sir, that you ain't gonna pin this one on me. Fuckin' right you're not. It was your fiddling dolly that stuck it to Strode, not me. And they know it.'' He jerked his head in the direction of Marian.

Richard raised an eyebrow. "My, my—aren't you the brave one all of a sudden. You think you've found a way to weasel out? That's what you do best, Jack—weaseling. Weaseling and undercutting. Hiding behind lies. Blaming someone else for your own inadequacies.'' His voice was cold and unforgiving. "You disgusting little chicken-prick—you're just about the most *useless* human being I've ever met. Utterly worthless.''

Jack jumped up off the bed, his face red and angry. "Jesus, you really do think you're God, don't you? Looking down your nose at everybody else, so goddamned pleased with yourself! You've been lording it over me ever since you got Jo in bed, but what did you get? You got a murderer who was quite willing to let *you* be suspected of her crime.

Both of us. She doesn't care who gets hurt. You're an ostrich, Richard! You can't see what's right under your nose!''

Richard looked at him wonderingly. "You really are hopeless, aren't you? Jack, if I have to see you, or listen to you, even one minute longer, I am going to commit a criminal act, right here in the presence of the police!''

Jack laughed nastily. "That wouldn't be your first mistake. It could be your last.''

The two of them kept at it. Ivan looked as if he were enjoying the brouhaha, but Marian turned tiredly away from them all and stared down through the window at the street. Why did they do it? It didn't matter whether it was one-on-one-upmanship like now, or ganging up and calling it football, or really ganging up and waging war; it was still all the same game. *I'm bigger and badder than you.* She felt the beginnings of depression.

Eventually Ivan stepped in and stopped them when it looked as if they were ready to start swinging. Marian's depression deepened, and it had nothing to do with the two angry men ready to tear each other's throats out. Every time she and Ivan started getting close to nailing a killer, Marian felt a heaviness come over her that wouldn't go away until several days after the job was finished. All the disillusionment garnered in an adult life of dealing with those who considered themselves above the law seemed to peak at that moment when she had to face another human being and say: *You are a murderer. Your humanity has failed you, and we are less because of you.*

Once Ivan was safely between Richard and Jack, the latter became even more belligerent, throwing threats of physical mayhem at Richard Bruce over Ivan's shoulder. Ivan wasn't having any of that. He spun Jack around and pulled his wrists together to slap the cuffs on him. "You're under arrest. You have the right to remain silent—''

"Aw, hey, man, don't go spoiling it! You got your murderer. What do you care what happened in France four years ago?"

"You have the right to an attorney. If you can't afford one—"

"I can afford one, I can afford one! You're not really going to send me back to France, are you? All because of that stupid Billy shooting his mouth off—"

"Everything you say will be taken down and used against you in a court of law. Any questions? You're Mirandized, buddy. Put your shoe on. Let's go."

"Ah, *Christ!*" Jack wailed. "Sergeant? Sergeant Larch? Can he do this?"

"He certainly can."

"And you're just going to stand there and let him haul me away?" He pulled on his sock and shoe. "Because of some stupid helicopter that malfunctioned four years ago?"

"It wasn't the helicopter that malfunctioned, Jack," she said without expression. "Your best chance now is to tell the truth, all of it. If you know how." In rapid succession his face showed disappointment, self-pity, anger, and then some new cunning—all in the space of half a minute. *A grasshopper mind,* Marian thought.

Ivan waved a hand toward Richard Bruce. "Marian?"

She nodded. "I'll take care of him."

Jack broke away from Ivan long enough to lurch over to her. "Marian," he said smugly. "Your name is Marian." He grinned toothily at her and let Ivan lead him away.

"Childish to the last," Richard Bruce murmured as the door closed behind them. He leaned against the wall and folded his arms. "Well...*Marian*? My turn?"

"Your turn."

He listened to her read him his rights without interrupting. Then he asked, "What's going to happen to Joanna?"

"If we can find enough evidence to convince the DA's office to indict, she'll be charged with A. J. Strode's murder and tried here in New York. If we can't, she'll be extradited to Boston and tried there for murdering her parents."

"So you've got her either way, is that right? It doesn't really matter whether you can prove she killed Strode or not."

"Oh, it matters. It matters a lot. You knew all along she killed him, didn't you? You were angry just now, when you found out Jack had been cleared. But you weren't surprised. You knew, didn't you?"

He smiled sadly, didn't answer. "Sergeant—don't look too hard for your evidence. Let her take her chances in Boston."

That caught her off stride. "Now why should I do that?"

"Because if ever there was a man who deserved killing, it was A. J. Strode. In Boston, she can plead mercy killing and possibly get off with a light sentence."

"You know she killed Strode...*and you don't care*. It doesn't matter in the least to you! I don't understand you people, I don't understand you at all!"

"No, I don't suppose you do," he said distantly. "But your career won't suffer if you fail to charge Joanna with Strode's murder. After all, you and your partner will have brought in three big bad criminals that are wanted elsewhere. That'll be quite a feather in your cap. You don't need to name Strode's murderer too."

"It seems to me you ought to be worrying about yourself instead of Joanna Gillespie. You *are* going to be tried for the murder of thirty-seven men, you know. You can't possibly be taking that as casually as you appear to be."

He waved a hand dismissively. "There's one vital piece of proof missing from the police's case against me. The rest of it is hearsay and second-hand evidence."

The letter, Marian thought; *the first mate's last letter to his wife*. Was this the way it was going to end? One to be arrested for Strode's murder, one for past crimes, and one to get off scot-free?

"Of the three of us," Richard went on, "I'm the one most likely to walk away. In fact, I intend to do just that. No, it's Joanna I'm concerned about. Sergeant Larch, I'm not so foolish as to try to bribe a police detective. But I will tell you that if you decide you want to improve the quality of your life, I am the means by which you can accomplish that wholly understandable goal. And you can accomplish it both painlessly and permanently. All that's required of you is that you let Joanna go to Boston."

"And that's not a bribery attempt. Uh-huh."

He smiled sadly. "All I'm asking is that you think about it. Think of what you want the most, and then think of how little you have to do to get it. Just look the other way, Sergeant Marian. That's all you have to do."

What a seductive offer, Marian thought. But then the man himself was seductive. He had the hypnotic appeal of a man used to succeeding, used to getting what he set out to get; she could understand Joanna Gillespie's attraction to him. But fortunately for truth and justice and the American way, Sergeant Marian Larch was not a very seducible woman. "Forget it," she said. "She'll go to Boston only if the DA here fails to charge her with Strode's murder. And I'll tell you now, I'm going to do everything I can to make sure that doesn't happen."

Richard Bruce's expression didn't change. "Just think about it," he urged.

She took out her handcuffs. "Hands behind your back."

Then his expression did change. "Oh, really, Sergeant! That's not necessary. I'm offering no resistance."

"Hands behind your back," Marian repeated mechanically. He made a sound of annoyance but clasped his hands behind his back.

She'd just finished cuffing him when Ivan Malecki walked back in. "McKinstry wants his suitcase." He picked it up.

"Ah yes—I'll want mine too," Richard Bruce said. "It's still down in the television room. The black one."

"I'll get it," Marian said.

"I just called in and left word for the captain," Ivan told her. "Desk sergeant says this guy's lawyer's there, his and Gillespie's."

"About time," Richard muttered.

"Ivan?" Marian stepped out into the hall and motioned to Richard to stay inside.

Ivan followed. "You're not thinking of arresting her on the basis of not being there to hear Jack McKinstry yell, are you? The captain would have us both transferred to Juvenile. She could claim you misunderstood her or she just forgot about hearing him."

"I know. But when she sees Richard Bruce in handcuffs, she's bound to be thrown off balance a little and that would be a good time to go at her again. So..."

"So you want me to take both Bruce and McKinstry in and get the paperwork started, right? Okay. I wasn't getting anywhere with her anyway. I'll get back as fast as I can."

"Thanks, Ivan. I'll go get his suitcase." She turned Richard Bruce over to the one police officer left in the hallway and hurried down the stairs.

Joanna Gillespie was standing at the foot of the stairs, a police officer not far away. She looked anxious for the first time since Marian had met her. "What is it?" she asked. "What's happening?"

"We've just arrested Richard Bruce," Marian told her. "Jack McKinstry is also under arrest."

She didn't care about McKinstry. "What are you charging him with? You've arrested him for what?"

"For what he did to the *Burly Girl* and the thirty-seven men on board. We've made no arrest yet for the murder of A. J. Strode."

Joanna looked past Marian up the stairs. Richard and Ivan and the uniformed officer were coming down.

Richard stopped when he reached Joanna. There was no public display of affection between the two, but they looked at each other in a way that shut everyone else out. "Don't talk to them anymore," Richard said softly. "We have legal representation now. Don't even tell them your name until you've had a chance to talk to the lawyer. Don't say a word, Joanna."

She nodded, not saying a word.

"Don't worry," he tried to reassure her. "It will be all right."

"No it won't," Ivan couldn't resist saying. "Come on—let's go." He and the officer took Richard Bruce out to where Jack McKinstry was waiting in a police car.

Marian went on to the television room. A black suitcase and a blue one were sitting there hip to hip, the same way Joanna Gillespie and Richard Bruce had been sitting on the window seat. She picked up the black suitcase and started out—but then stopped.

Joanna Gillespie was claiming she'd been in her room checking her blood-sugar level when A. J. Strode was murdered. But her suitcase had been right here in the television room at the time. What kind of equipment did a diabetic need for blood testing? Was it small enough to carry in a purse? *Would* she carry it around in a purse?

Marian put down Richard Bruce's suitcase and laid the blue one on its side. The suitcase was locked, but the keys were on the chain that held the luggage tag. Locked personal property at the scene of a crime; she ought to have a search warrant to be on the safe side. Marian hesitated but then opened the suitcase and started gently feeling among Joanna Gillespie's clothing, taking care not to disturb anything. Underwear, a bulky sweater, a nightgown.

And there it was. *Home Blood-Glucose Monitoring Kit*, the label said. Right there, in a suitcase that had not left the television room since shortly before A. J. Strode was murdered.

Marian sat on her heels for a few moments, thinking about that. Then she replaced everything the way she found it and ran back up the stairs to Joanna Gillespie's room. She checked the bathroom and all the drawers in the bedroom; no second kit. Back downstairs again, she took Richard Bruce's suitcase out to the police car parked in front of the house. Richard and Jack McKinstry were handcuffed in the back, and Ivan Malecki was sitting in the passenger seat in front. Marian handed the suitcase to the police officer who would be driving and watched him stow it in the trunk. She made some remark about the tight parking space and wondered if he had room to get out.

"No problem," the officer said. "I'll just nudge that car in front of me a little and make room."

"I really would prefer you found some other solution," Marian said sweetly. "That's my car."

"Ah. In that case, I'll nudge the car parked behind me."

"Good thinking." She gestured to Ivan to get out of the car.

"What took you so long?" he complained, following her out of earshot of the police car's two unwilling passengers.

Marian's depression had settled on her shoulders like a yoke. "Tell the captain we could do with a search-and-seizure—for Joanna Gillespie's locked suitcase."

"We're looking for what?"

"Her kit for checking her blood-sugar level."

It took him about two seconds to catch on. He whistled appreciatively. "If it was downstairs all the time—wait a sec. What if she's got two kits?"

Marian felt herself sagging. "I checked her room. Nothing."

"The captain's gonna want to know if you have reason to believe it's in that suitcase."

Marian looked him straight in the eye. "I have reason. In fact, I'm *convinced* it's in there."

Ivan winked at her. "Right. Okay, I'll take care of it. Goddam, that'll do it, won't it? Haw. *Hours* before our deadline! The captain is going to love us." Ivan was elated, just the opposite of Marian. "Have you got another pair of cuffs? Good. Hey, you're really drooping, kid. Buck up. We're almost home."

She smiled at him wanly and went back into the house. Ivan climbed into the police car.

Richard Bruce had noticed Marian's depression. "Is something wrong with Sergeant Larch?" he asked curiously.

"Marian? Naw, she always gets like that when we're closing in on a killer," Ivan answered. "Real down in the dumps. It never lasts more'n a couple of days."

"I hope it lasts *twenty years*," Jack McKinstry said through clenched teeth.

Ivan sighed and told the driver they were ready to go.

MARIAN DREW ASIDE the police officer watching Joanna Gillespie and instructed him to go into the television room and guard a blue suitcase he'd find there. No one was to come near it until Ivan Malecki got back with a search warrant. She told him he could watch television if he liked, so long as he sat with his feet on the suitcase.

Then after a moment's thought Marian took Joanna outside to the patio. Something was needed to break down the pattern of resistance the violinist had established; maybe a change of setting would help. Besides, A. J. Strode's house was beginning to make Marian feel claustrophobic. The day had a pleasant mid-afternoon look to it, with a light breeze stirring. She picked out chairs for them that allowed her to sit with her back to the sun. Joanna slumped indifferently in her chair, squinting a little at the light in her eyes.

"Have you guessed what's happened?" Marian asked her. "We've arrested Richard Bruce and Jack McKinstry for past crimes, but not you. You, we're saving for something else."

Joanna said nothing, didn't even look at her.

"Now, you know *we* know you did it," Marian said in her most reasonable tone of voice. "You're the one who killed A. J. Strode, and you did it without any help from Richard. He has a lot to answer for, but not Strode's murder. That's on your shoulders, Joanna. Yours alone."

Joanna turned her head and looked at her coldly, still not speaking, heeding Richard's admonition to maintain absolute silence.

"You'll talk eventually, you know," Marian went on. "If your lawyer's any good, he'll advise you to cooperate. You're under arrest—the charge is homicide." Marian read her her rights. "Any questions?"

Joanna wouldn't give her the satisfaction of a reply.

But Marian wasn't ready to settle for no response. "When you do talk, I'm going to want to know more about that meeting Sunday night...when Strode showed up for the first time. It was that meeting that pushed you into an act of murder. What happened—did Strode overreach himself? He finally went too far, didn't he? Did you foresee a lifetime of being at the beck and call of a man you despised? And did you see the same thing for Richard? Must have seemed intolerable.''

Joanna slumped down farther in her chair.

Marian tried to visualize what had happened. "While you were supposed to be up in your room testing your blood sugar, you were actually downstairs breaking out the knives and starting the fire. You had to be heading toward the stairs when you saw Richard going into the bathroom. On the spur of the moment you turned the lock, quite effectively providing him with an alibi. You do know how to think on your feet, don't you? But by locking Richard in, you were cutting the list of suspects down to two. You must have been pretty sure we'd fix on Jack.''

The other woman would neither confirm nor deny it. She waved away a fly that had come buzzing in too close and stared at Marian insolently.

"Why did you think we wouldn't settle on you?'' Marian persisted. "Because musicians are sensitive people who never resort to violence? Because you're a woman?'' She paused. "Or because Jack McKinstry makes such a good patsy?''

Joanna's eyes narrowed, and she broke her silence at last. "You're making all this up, you know. It's a piece of fiction.''

Ah, she speaks, Marian thought with satisfaction. "Maybe you had a different reason for locking Richard in. Richard was the one person in the house likely to go looking for you, wasn't he? With him locked safely away, you could take your time. Was that it?''

With insulting slowness, as if speaking to a retarded person, Joanna said, "I did not lock Richard in the bathroom. Nor did I kill Strode. Are you listening?"

Marian was listening, but not buying. "By the time you'd locked Richard in, the fire had taken hold. You barely made it up the stairs and were on your way to Strode's private wing when Jack burst out of his room yelling that he smelled smoke. You saw him get halfway down the stairs before one of the bodyguards shooed him back up. You went on to Strode's wing—the cameras were out of commission by then. Then you let yourself in to Strode's library. Strode was in the bedroom-dressing room part of the suite." Marian paused. "How'm I doing so far?"

A look of disgust passed over Joanna's face.

"I wonder how you got Strode to go into the library. If you made a noise, he wouldn't have gone in to investigate by himself—not with you three in the house. Maybe he just remembered the guard hadn't checked the door to the library and went in to see to it. But for whatever reason, he did go in...and you caught him by surprise. You drove a knife into his chest before he knew what was happening. He must have fallen to the floor then, but that wasn't enough for you. What did you do, kneel down on the floor beside him? Was he already dead or only dying? You used the second knife on him, and then the third. If you'd had more than three knives, you'd have used them too. More than anything in the world, you wanted to make sure A. J. Strode never got up again."

Joanna shifted position uneasily.

Marian leaned toward her. "How did it feel, killing a man? Correction—how did it feel killing *that* man? What did it feel like, Joanna?"

Joanna's expression was one of revulsion. "What a ghoulish thing to ask."

Marian leaned back; time to crack through that perfect shell. "You'd have done better to stay in your room and test your blood sugar the way you said you were doing. Although that would have been a mite difficult, seeing as how your kit was downstairs in your suitcase all the time."

Joanna didn't react immediately. Then as she understood that her story had just been blown to pieces, a flash of panic showed on her face. She disguised it quickly, but not quickly enough. Marian saw.

"Right now my partner is getting a search-and-seizure warrant," Marian said. "If that kit is in your suitcase—and I feel damned sure it is—well, there goes your alibi, right down the toilet. Is the kit in your suitcase, Joanna?"

The other woman's breath was coming in short, shallow gasps; her eyes were darting back and forth. She made a move to get up.

"Don't bother," Marian told her, waving her back. "I've got a cop sitting in the television room with his size-eighteen feet planted on that suitcase. You don't have a chance in hell of getting to it."

Joanna collapsed back into her chair without making a sound, her face carefully blank. Both hands gripped the arms of her chair, the only solid things within her grasp.

Marian watched her closely. "Do you have a second kit with you? There's none in your room. What about your purse—do you carry a testing kit around with you? Joanna, show me a second kit in your purse and I'll withdraw the homicide charge right now. Where did you leave your purse? Come on, let's go look for it." Marian stood up, waited.

Joanna didn't move, avoiding the police detective's eye. Then her head slowly began to droop forward.

"Huh. I thought so." Marian walked around behind Joanna's chair. "But maybe I got part of it wrong," she said to the back of the violinist's head. "Maybe Richard Bruce *was* in on it with you after all. Maybe the two of you planned it so that you'd lock Richard in somewhere. In fact Richard could have planned the whole thing, couldn't he? Is that what happened?''

Joanna twisted in her chair and looked up at Marian. ''Richard,'' she said carefully, ''is innocent.'' Still admitting nothing.

Marian nodded, thinking that was as close to a confession as she'd ever get out of Joanna Gillespie. ''I believe you. Richard has plenty of dirt on his hands, you all three have—but this dirty job is yours alone. And you're going to pay for it... alone.''

Joanna's shoulders began to heave; it had finally sunk in on her that she wasn't going to walk away from this one. Her whole body shook soundlessly as she went through some unreadable process of acceptance and adjustment.

Marian waited until Joanna was still again. She put her hands on her hips, considering. ''You three—you're really something, you know? You're all three attractive people, you're all well-to-do, you all have your special gifts... even Jack, in his own way. But you—yours is the greatest gift of all. And what's going to happen to it? It's going to go to waste, that's what's going to happen to it. Allowed to atrophy in prison. You're going to *lose* it, Joanna! And all because you developed the nasty habit of killing people who get in your way.''

Joanna Gillespie looked at her with unconcealed contempt. ''I'll never lose it, not ever. What do you know about losing a natural gift? Did you ever have one to lose?''

Marian sighed in exasperation. ''Well, I don't think we'll wait for my partner to get back with the warrant. I'm going to take you in now. As soon as we open the suitcase and find what we're looking for, we'll book you. Then you can talk to your lawyer. Come on, Joanna. It's time.''

The other woman got heavily to her feet, and then did what was for her an unusual thing; she raised her head and straightened her shoulders. The casual, slouchy look was gone; she was holding herself erect, almost proudly.

Marian couldn't stand it. "Look, I've got to make one more try—there's something that's bugging the hell out of me. Would you have gone so far as to kill Strode if you hadn't met Richard Bruce? If you and Jack McKinstry had been the only guests here this weekend, would A. J. Strode still be alive? Joanna, *did you kill for a man?*"

Joanna Gillespie stared at her for a long moment—and then burst out laughing. It was loud laughter, almost raucous. "A crime of passion? Oh, that's wonderful." She laughed again. "Is that a legal defense in this country? I'll have to ask my lawyer about that one." The laughter faded, and Joanna's face turned grim. "Now I'm tired of this, Sergeant. If you're going to take me in, do it now."

Well, it was an answer, Marian thought, shuddering at the other woman's callousness. She told Joanna to hold her wrists together in front of her and put on the handcuffs. They went inside and passed through the dining room where Joanna picked up her purse, the one that did not contain an extra testing kit; she made no move to open it. On their way out, Marian told the guard at the gate they wouldn't be coming back.

Marian was getting out her keys to unlock the car when a cream-colored limousine pulled up parallel to the space left by the police car Ivan and the others had driven away in. The rear door opened and Myron Castleberry got out; he held the door for another passenger in the car—a tall, attractive woman in her mid-forties, beautifully dressed. *That must be Katie*, Marian speculated. *Come to claim her inheritance.*

Castleberry caught sight of her and Joanna Gillespie and steered the woman over toward them. But before he could perform any introductions he spotted the handcuffs and his mouth fell open. He had to swallow before he could speak. "You?" he finally said to Joanna. "It was you?"

Joanna stared off into space.

"Surprised, Mr. Castleberry?" Marian asked without curiosity.

"Yes!" he blurted out. "I thought it was, umm." He clamped his mouth shut.

Richard Bruce, Marian supplied mentally. "You can relax now. It's over."

Castleberry shook his head wonderingly. "Ah, excuse me...Katie, this is Sergeant Larch. And, umm, Joanna Gillespie. Mrs. Strode."

"I'm sorry for what's happened here, Mrs. Strode," Marian said. "I know this is a terrible time for you. But we won't be bothering you. There's a policeman in your television room guarding a suitcase, but as soon as my partner gets here with a search warrant they'll both be gone."

"Thank you Sergeant, that's very considerate." Her words were for Marian but her eyes never left Joanna. She stepped in closer, examining the violinist's face as if trying to memorize it. "*You* are the one who killed my husband?"

Joanna held her head higher, didn't answer.

"Thank you," whispered Katie Strode.

She turned and went through the gate toward the house. Castleberry shot an appalled glance at Marian and hastily followed.

The hint of a smile played around Joanna Gillespie's mouth. Marian shoved her roughly into the car and drove away.

The long weekend at the House of Strode was over.

HOUSTON IN THE REARVIEW MIRROR

First Time In Paperback

A MILT KOVAK MYSTERY

SUSAN ROGERS COOPER

Milt Kovak doesn't believe for an instant that his sister shot her cheating husband and then tried to kill herself. And when the country sheriff goes after the bad guys in the big city, not one, but three attempts on his life prove him absolutely right....

"Chief Deputy Milt Kovak is a competent, low-key, really nice guy devoid of heroics and committed to getting to the truth."
—*Washington Post Book*

THIS
BLESSED
PLOT

M.R.D. MEEK
A LENNOX KEMP MYSTERY

Rich and poor. Lennox Kemp knew they all had their peculiarities. On the other side of the tracks—although disguised behind fine crystal and patrician smiles—were the Courtenays.

Twins Vivian and Venetia were rich, reckless and probably quite ruthless. They needed Kemp to oversee the legalities of the rather bizarre plans for their massive inheritance....

"M.R.D. Meek moves ever closer to the charmed company of Ruth Rendell and P. D. James."

—*Detroit News*

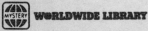

BARBARA PAUL
IN-Laws
and Outlaws

Gillian Clifford, once a Decker in-law, returns to the family fold to comfort Raymond's widow, Connie. Clearly, the family is worried. Who hates the Deckers enough to kill them?

And as the truth behind the murder becomes shockingly clear, Gillian realizes that once a Decker, always a Decker—a position she's discovering can be most precarious indeed.

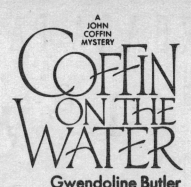